*Lisa,
We must never turn technology against God's will for a moral and ordered society.*

*H L Wegley
2 Pet 3:3*

Virtuality

H. L. Wegley

Romantic Suspense

This book or parts thereof may not be reproduced in any form, stored in a retrieval system, or transmitted in any form by any means without prior written permission of the author, except as provided by United States of America copyright law.

Publisher's Note: This is a work of fiction, set in a real location. Any reference to historical figures, places, or events, whether fictional or actual, is a fictional representation. Names, characters, and incidents are the product of the author's imagination or are used fictitiously, and any resemblance to actual persons, living or dead, or to events is entirely coincidental.

Cover Design: Samantha Fury
http://www.furycoverdesign.com/

Copyright © 2018 H.L. Wegley

All rights reserved.

ISBN-13: 978-1-732763630
ISBN-10: 1732763631

Also available in eBook publication

OTHER BOOKS BY H. L. WEGLEY

Against All Enemies Series
1 Voice in the Wilderness
2 Voice of Freedom
3 Chasing Freedom

Pure Genius Series
1 Hide and Seek
2 On the Pineapple Express
3 Moon over Maalaea Bay
4 Triple Threat

Witness Protection Series
1 No Safe Place
2 No True Justice
3 No Turning Back

DEDICATION

This book is dedicated to the Christ-sharing, culture-shaping ministries that seek to protect American individuals, American families, and American society against the many destructive forces at work in our nation. I have listed only a few of these organizations, because providing a comprehensive list would be impractical. But, I am referring to organizations like Focus on the Family, Chuck Colson's ministries—including Breakpoint and Colson Center—and Ravi Zacharias International Ministries. We are grateful for your faithfulness in the work that you do for us and for Him.

As this book, *Virtuality*, attempts to do, these organizations remind us of God's timeless truths, while alerting us to threats coming from new technology, new legislation, government policy, judicial rulings, and cultural trends.

CONTENTS

OTHER BOOKS BY H. L. WEGLEY iii
DEDICATION iv
CONTENTS v
ACKNOWLEDGMENTS vii
Chapter 1 1
Chapter 2 12
Chapter 3 27
Chapter 4 31
Chapter 5 41
Chapter 6 51
Chapter 7 57
Chapter 8 68
Chapter 9 75
Chapter 10 79
Chapter 11 94
Chapter 12 107
Chapter 13 111
Chapter 14 126
Chapter 15 134
Chapter 16 139
Chapter 17 143
Chapter 18 150
Chapter 19 158
Chapter 20 166
Chapter 21 179
Chapter 22 184
Chapter 23 199
Chapter 24 219
Chapter 25 227

Chapter 26	240
Chapter 27	248
Chapter 28	266
Chapter 29	279
Chapter 30	282
Chapter 31	290
Epilogue	298
Author's Notes	305

ACKNOWLEDGMENTS

Once again, I want to thank my wife, Babe, for being willing to listen to me read her this story twice, even though she didn't like the story after the first draft. It evidently got better, because she stopped complaining.

Thank you, Samantha Fury, for taking a landscape-oriented image and revamping it for use in a portrait-oriented book cover. And thanks for designing another wonderful cover.

Thanks to my niece, Vicki, an experienced climber, who taught me a little about biners and quickdraws—which I learned had nothing to do with an old West shootout. She sanity checked my climbing scenes and cringed when I tried to take my hero, a novice climber, up a rock face, solo, without enough rope.

Thank you, Gail Ostheller, for proofing the manuscript with eyes that are much sharper than mine.

Thanks to my sister-in-law, Duke, who read the second draft to see if I'd brightened a potentially dark story so that it could be enjoyed by women readers who prefer clean, flinch-free fiction.

Thanks to Del Tackett, tour guide for Focus on the Family's Truth Project. His lectures gave me perspective on who man is, and where his self-awareness lies, as I wrote about the interaction of the brain and the immaterial self that lies at the core of our existence.

Finally, I thank my Lord for words and wits enough to write another story.

I am praying, Father, that you will not take my disciples out of the world but that you will protect them from the evil one.
John 17:15 (paraphrased)

Chapter 1

July 3, 11:30 p.m. Snoqualmie, Washington

Vince van Gordon glared at Patrick, the geek Vince had threatened to beat into submission. He pointed at the phone on Patrick's desk. "Jess is in danger and it's all your fault. Call LACO, now!"

Behind Vince, a thump came from the office door.

He whirled toward the door.

It swung open.

A slender form leaped into the room.

Jess. How had she gotten away from—

"Vince, I took out Larry. But Curly and Moe have assault rifles." Jess's strong, slender arms gripped Vince's shoulders. "We've got to get out of here."

The Three Stooges? What was she talking about? Jess had somehow escaped her kidnappers, but—

"Now, Vince. They're going to kill us."

Vince gripped her shoulders and studied her eyes. Jess was the brightest person he had ever known, seldom wrong about anything. But the wild look in her eyes—had the kidnappers drugged her? "Are you okay, Jess? Did they hurt you?"

"I'm okay. But not for long, unless we leave." She grabbed his hand and pulled him from Virtuality's office toward the building's main entrance.

Vince glanced back as he left the room.

Patrick Michaels had disappeared.

They could deal with Patrick later.

After the events of this day, the thugs Jess mentioned probably wouldn't have capture on their minds. As she had indicated, capture had turned to kill.

Vince cracked the main entrance door and peered into the near darkness outside.

The city of Snoqualmie had not fully developed this property. Instead of bright city streetlights, only one weak light and a crescent moon threatened to expose them in the midnight darkness.

"Do you see anyone?" Jess's head pressed against his shoulder.

The corner of the building lay to Vince's left. The shadows covering the near end of the parking lot might give them cover to reach the corner. Beyond it, the forest began, offering more hiding places.

"No. I don't see them." If the gunmen who had chased Jess weren't near, maybe they could get to his car and—

Her hand gripped his and squeezed. "Don't even think about getting in your car. We'd never make it out of the parking lot. Curly and Moe are looking for me in the trees on the other side of the lot."

"Then we'll go around the corner and into the trees." He tugged on her hand.

Jess leaped beside him.

They ran around the corner of the building. Now the building would give them cover from any shooter in the parking area.

With hands clasped, Vince and Jess sprinted to the trees, slowing as they entered the darkness of the forest canopy.

He glanced back before tree branches cut off visibility to the parking lot.

Two gunmen scurried toward Vince's entry point into the forest.

"Keep going, Jess. They saw us."

The two men slowed and crept forward, ten yards apart, holding what looked like automatic rifles.

"Where's the third guy?"

"I told you, Vince. I flattened Larry's nose."

"You kicked him?"

"Yes."

"But that wouldn't keep—"

"He's a wimp. You can forget about him for now."

"Jess, these aren't the Three Stooges. You need to tell me who these guys really are."

"I'm not sure. But, from the way they talk, I think they're from New York."

Cracking of twigs sounded behind them.

Vince took the lead. "Hurry. They're forcing us toward the road."

"That's not good."

"But it's not necessarily bad, unless they spot us crossing the highway. Let's beat them to it." He grabbed her hand and pulled.

"But on the other side of the highway is—"

"I know, Jess. The Snoqualmie River. Let's hope these goons—"

"No. Stooges. The Three Stooges. If you saw them you'd understand."

"If these guys are The Three Stooges, why didn't you just tell Larry to pick two?"

"Not funny, Vince."

"That's right. Even when we were kids, watching them on TV, you never did think they were funny." Vince slowed to a walk in the shadow-shrouded forest. "I hope these guys aren't familiar with this area."

The staccato belching of an automatic rifle sounded.

Vince dropped to his knees and pulled Jess down with him.

A branch above their heads dropped to the ground, filling the night air with the pungent odor of evergreen sap.

"Go, go, go!" Jess sprang forward, jerking Vince with her.

Vince sprinted by her and pulled Jess toward the highway.

She let him take the lead.

If he could break visual contact with their pursuers, maybe they could cross the highway unseen.

When they emerged from the trees, Vince led Jess onto the highway.

As they crossed the white centerline, fifty yards up the road, two shadowy figures emerged.

"Jump the ditch and go into the bushes."

As they jumped the ditch lining the road, another burst of fire chewed up vegetation to their right.

Vince and Jess landed beyond the ditch and ran pell-mell through bushes and small trees.

"They know we crossed the highway, Vince."

"Yeah. I know."

"And the river is—"

"I know. But we'll be safe after we cross the river."

"You've lost it, van Gordon. That water is swift. It's coming straight from glaciers in the mountains. And you know what's two-hundred yards downstream?"

Vince pushed branches aside and stepped from the trees onto a dirt road. "Snoqualmie Falls. That's why I said cross the river and we'll be safe."

"And that's why I said you're crazy."

"But there's a safety line just above the falls." He pulled Jess toward the river, now only twenty yards ahead. "We'll swim as hard as we can, then grab the safety line, when we drift into it, and—"

"Drift? Don't you mean when we get clotheslined by it?"

"We'll grab the line and pull ourselves along it to the other side. They can't follow us."

Jess stopped. "Just grab it? What if the current's too strong and we miss it?"

Above the sound of rushing water, a deep rumble came like distant thunder.

He tugged on her hand to get her moving toward the water. "If we miss it ... then, I guess we've got nothing to worry about."

"Right. Nothing to worry about because we cross another river, the Jordan. I'm not ready for the Promised Land, yet." She lowered her voice. "Because you and I—"

"Save it for later." If there was a later for them. Regardless, Vince didn't have time for distractions. And despite their danger, with her hand curled around his, Jess, the incredible girl he'd known since they were both five, was a big distraction.

The sound of rushing water grew louder.

Something grabbed Vince's t-shirt and pulled. A thorn ripped into his left forearm. "Blackberries. Be careful."

They skirted a blackberry bush.

The dark water of the river lay only a few steps in front of them. They needed to be in that water swimming, right now.

This night in early July was warm. Probably still in the upper sixties, though it was after midnight. But their ambient temperature would soon drop ... thirty degrees.

Jess stopped and tried to pull him away from the river.

Vince overpowered her and pulled her with him. "Look at me, Jessica Jamison. We can do this. If you'll swim upstream of me, I will take you to that rope. I can keep you safe."

She stared at him without replying.

Crunching of leaves and twigs sounded upstream, barely audible above the sound of rushing water.

"Sounds like they're looking for us upriver," Vince said.

"Of course," Jess blew out a blast of air. "Because they don't think we're crazy ... not yet anyway."

"But we're crazy like a fox."

"Don't you mean like a drowned rat?" She gasped when Vince pulled her into the icy water. "Vincent van Gordon, I'm going to cut off your ear myself."

"Just cut the van Gogh stuff and swim hard. Don't hold back anything." Vince positioned his body downstream of hers, but the overpowering current already swept him downstream at a rate he hadn't anticipated.

Something else Vince hadn't anticipated—twenty yards out, hardly a third of the way across, Jess's arms slowed.

He dog paddled a few strokes and watched her.

After she raised an arm, it fell limp into the water. Though Jess could break boards with her legs, her fit and trim one-hundred-fifteen-pound body worked against her in the chilling water.

At two-hundred twenty, with about five pounds of insulation he could stand to lose, Vince fared much better. But how long would that last?

Over the past twenty seconds, the current had grown even stronger, propelling them downstream. They approached the dim lights of the Salish Lodge.

Jess was strong for her slender build, much stronger than most women, but her swimming power appeared gone. Hypothermia claimed several lives each year in the Snoqualmie and Vince and Jess now suffered from its insidious effects.

Vince's injured left hand didn't mind the frigid water. It had gone numb, ending the merciless throbbing, a consequence of his near fall from the rock face twelve hours earlier. He glanced at Jess, splashing in the water upstream from him.

Her stroke had degenerated further. She looked like someone taking their first swimming lesson.

Vince grabbed the back of her tank top and tried to tow her through the water. But forfeiting a swimming arm, and the increased drag of Jess's body, slowed their progress.

How far were they? Halfway? Maybe. But they'd already used up more than half the distance to the falls. Not good.

Drowned rat seemed to be winning out over crazy like a fox. Vince was a fool to endanger Jess like this.

A dark object appeared downstream on the surface of the water. The safety line.

They hit it hard, before Vince had time to react.

He threw his free arm upward. It went over the line and jerked him to a stop.

But the current ripped Jess from his grip, pulling her under.

He stabbed the dark water with his free hand, grabbing for anything.

Her hand reached out of the water, but it slipped under the safety rope.

Vince ducked under the line. Gripping it with his sore left hand, he clamped his right onto Jess's hand as it sped along the surface of the water.

In a fierce tug-of-war with the current, Vince hung onto Jess for life, for love, for anything and everything he'd ever wanted from life on planet Earth. He would let go of the rope before he would give up his grip on Jess. Dying with her ... Vince would take that over the alternative.

While the constant pull of the current drained his remaining arm strength, Vince inched Jess's body upstream toward the rope.

Her head popped up. Jess's free hand snagged the neck of his shirt and stretched it three or four sizes.

With his last bit of strength, Vince worked their bodies under the rope to the upstream side.

After Jess surfaced beside him, they planted their chests against the line.

Arms draped over the rope, Vince heaved deep breaths. Repaying his oxygen debt or going bankrupt? Too close to call.

The encroaching numbness claimed his toes and half of his feet. But the water seemed to have lost much of its biting chill. That probably was not a good thing. Hypothermia's deadly grip had tightened on Vince van Gordon's body, and they were hardly halfway across the river.

Now, a deep rumble resonated in his chest, reminding Vince of the importance of the safety line. He leaned close to Jess. "Make sure you've got a good grip on the rope. We'll go hand over hand. If you get tired, put your arms over the rope and rest."

"The water is sucking out all my energy. I've never felt anything like this. I—I'm not sure I can make it."

"We can do this. Only twenty yards to go. Less than that to shallow water." He had fudged a little on the distance, but Jess needed encouragement, because—

Gunshots.

Columns of water exploded into the air around them.

The flashes of light had come from a spot on the shore even with Vince and Jess.

Despite the near darkness, gunmen with automatic weapons could easily spray them with bullets from this distance. Even a flesh wound would be fatal, given the current and the water temperature.

The thought of Jess taking a bullet—he couldn't let that happen.

More gunfire.

They had only one option.

Vince hooked an arm around Jess's waist and, before she could protest, pulled her beneath the frigid water.

Under the water, Vince kicked hard for the shore and pawed the water with his free hand.

They bobbed up several yards downstream of the safety line.

Upstream, a flashlight beam probed the river along the line. Hopefully, the gunman believed he and Jess would never let go of the rope and risk the falls. Otherwise, the shooting would start again.

Vince put his mouth against Jess's ear as they glided downstream. "Swim hard. Give it everything you've got. I'll stay below you."

She pulled loose from his grip. Her legs kicked, and her hands pawed at the water. Jess had some strength left. The deep roar, increasing in volume, should give her a shot of adrenaline.

The current surged, propelling them at an alarming rate. The rumble of hundreds of tons of water, exploding at the end of a three-hundred-foot fall, drowned all other sounds.

Above them, shadowy forms of trees blocked much of the night sky. They were almost to the far side of the river—almost safe or almost dead?

Over the last four or five strokes, Vince's arms had turned to lead. His kick had lost its power.

Jess's arms still moved, but there was no strength in her strokes.

Something had to change, or they weren't going to make it.

Her body bumped into his.

"Jess, you found the strength to break six boards. I need you to find it again, now."

The thought of water shooting them out into a mist-filled void, then dropping them the length of a football field to be pounded to death by an entire river hitting them at hundred miles-per-hour, sent a strong dose of adrenaline through Vince.

Jess was nearly spent. He grabbed a handful of her tank top with one hand. He kicked furiously and pulled on the water with his other hand.

Jess kicked too. Not strong kicks, but she hadn't given up.

Correction. Jess had gone limp now. Her slender, fat-free body had succumbed.

What if it all came down to going over the falls? He would wrap his body around Jess, and pray that his body would, somehow, protect hers when they landed three-hundred feet below.

Vince kicked and pawed at the water, while his mind analyzed their chances of surviving the falls. As a kid he'd jumped into water fifty feet up on an old railroad bridge. He'd found that a person could enter one or two degrees off from vertical, arms extended upward, with no serious repercussions. But leaving an elbow slightly bent, instead of holding his arm straight up, had almost dislocated Vince's shoulder. Forgetting to point his toes had split the bottom of his foot open when it slapped the water. But falling three-hundred feet in a deluge, while flailing for balance, would be much worse. It would split—he couldn't let his thoughts go there.

Vince's legs weakened further and sank deeper into the water. He kicked, trying to raise them to a horizontal plane.

Pain shot through his right foot.

He had kicked bottom. But the line of dark, shadowy rocks marking the top of the falls lay less than ten yards away.

Vince needed to anchor to the bottom, now.

The undulating current sent him under into a nearly silent world. Vince bounced off the bottom and bobbed back up, managing to keep his hold on Jess.

When he surfaced, the sound of the falls pounded his eardrums like a thunderclap.

He jammed his shoes onto the rocky river bottom to stop his movement toward the falls. Vince tried to stand while gripping Jess.

Though the water was only three-feet deep, the current's relentless pull on his body overpowered him. It ripped at his legs and hips.

Vince's feet slid along the river bottom as the torrent shoved him downstream. He pushed his shoes deeper into the rocks and gravel. If he lifted a foot to try stepping toward shore, in an instant, the current would sweep him away.

He buried his fingers more deeply into the fabric of Jess's tank top and burrowed his feet more deeply into the river bottom.

Jess's body in the water was the biggest problem, the greatest drag pulling him downstream. But his cold, spent arms couldn't lift her out of the water.

Vince slid several more inches downstream.

The dim light from the lodge across the river revealed their location. Ten feet in front of him, the entire Snoqualmie River plunged into a black void that roared its fury at them.

And the ferocious current continued to push him inexorably toward the blackness.

Vince squeezed on Jess's tank top with all the strength he had left and pulled. But what he had left was like Vince van Gordon, the man ... simply not enough.

He had failed Jess. He had failed to fulfill his promise to his brother, Paul, to protect Virtuality and its dangerous technology. Vince's only consolation ... it would be his last unhappy ending, either written in his second-rate novels or lived out in Vince's second-rate life.

I'm so sorry, Paul ... I love you, Jess.

Chapter 2

Three and a half days earlier

Murdering her is my best solution.

And Vince van Gordon knew exactly how he would kill her. He put his pen to the page of his spiral notebook and—

"Blast it!"

The opening drum roll of the Washington State University Fight Song blared from Vince's cell and echoed through his Denver townhouse.

Maybe the Cougars were going to go, fight, win, but his alma mater's song had blown away all his carefully crafted words. It had done so precisely when he'd formulated his plan to kill off the fiendish antagonist. Murdering her wouldn't guarantee a happy ending to the story. Vince hadn't decided how to pull that off yet. But at least justice would be served. Wouldn't that satisfy his readers?

Bright sunshine streaming in through his study window on this late June morning lit the large retro clock on the wall. 7:30 a.m. This was his most productive writing time. Who would be calling at this hour?

Maybe he wouldn't answer.

As the fight song started the second verse, Vince sighed, pulled his cell from the pocket of his cargo shorts, and swiped a finger across the touchpad, praying this was not his agent, Jamie. If it was, he could forget this scene for at least an hour.

On second thought, maybe he should forget the scene anyway. It was a lame ending to a mediocre story. One more in a long line of lame endings. Such was life. But readers didn't want real life, they wanted incredible adventures.

He sighed again, in resignation, and answered the call.

"Vince, this is Jess." Her voice came soft and low, as it had since she was just a girl.

Vince nearly choked on the breath he sucked in.

Jess had been Vince's best friend for the first seventeen years of his life. But he hadn't talked to her for nearly seven years. Why was she calling now? To finish the discussion he had left hanging years ago?

"Vince, are you still there?"

"Yeah. Sorry. You just, uh, surprised me. But it's good to hear from you."

Her heavy sigh blew across the receiver, creating static in Vince's ear. "I wish it wasn't—I mean ... I've got some bad news. It's Paul."

Had his cancer returned? Vince's brother had fought cancer twice and won. Surely, he could do it again, especially with all the new advances since Paul went into remission two and a half years ago.

"What happened, Jess? Is it his cancer?" If so, why wasn't Paul calling him instead of their next-door-neighbor, Jess?

"Yes. His cancer's back. I'm at the hospital. Paul asked me to call you, because he's too weak to make calls. It doesn't look good this time."

Paul couldn't be dying. He conquered all obstacles, without exception. Besides, Paul was the best man Vince knew—a model big brother, a model Christian. People like Paul didn't die at thirty-one ... or did they?

"Jess, is my brother dying?"

"It came back with a vengeance this time. Paul didn't tell anyone until he realized he couldn't fight it off. I think he was still holding out hope for another miracle. But he called me day before yesterday and told me his condition.

He asked me to do some things for him and to call you. But listen, Paul needs you, Vince. He needs to talk with you. He said it was important. Please, will you come home?" Her voice broke on the last word.

Jess never cried. Well, almost never. But if she were losing Paul ... "I'll catch a plane first thing in the morning."

"Okay ..." Jess paused. "But while you're out here, we need to talk. Promise me you'll do that, Vince. This is important too."

What could Jess want from him? She'd made her choice. She wanted Paul. The only surprising thing was that Vince had never received an engagement or wedding announcement. Maybe Paul hadn't wanted to saddle her with the uncertainty of his cancer.

Jess's end had gone silent.

"Jess, are you still there?"

"I'm here."

"I promise ... and tell Paul I'm coming and that I'm praying for ..." What does a person say they're praying for to a brother who is dying?

"I'll tell Paul. Got to go. The doctor's making his rounds and he just came in. I need to hear what he has to say. See you tomorrow. Goodbye, Vince."

Three minutes ago, the only thing Vince had worried about was the ending of his novel. Now, he was going to lose the brother he loved, a great man who had left a large shadow and a big set of shoes. Vince could never fill them.

He had always lived in Paul's shadow—at school, at church, in the community, everywhere but on the football field. None of that had ever bothered Vince until he lost Jess. When that happened, the shadow had turned to total darkness.

When Jess's heart turned to romance for the first time, it had turned to Paul, not Vince. He had never understood that. Vince and Jess had been closer than any two friends he'd ever known. Despite Jess's introversion, they had shared everything. And yet, Vince *had* been surprised. Devastated.

Jess had still wanted her best friend, but playing that role grew increasingly painful. Vince had begun pulling away from Jess sometime in their junior year of high school and, eventually, left Seattle to attend college across the state at WSU. He had walked away from a full-ride, football scholarship at UW to become a walk-on at Washington State.

Since he left for college, he'd never returned to Seattle to live. He'd never had a talk with Jess, and he had never brought any kind of closure to their relationship. He'd wanted to tell her how he felt about her and about living life in Paul's shadow, but that would've hurt her too much. And, after he shared those most intimate feelings, hearing her rejection would've killed Vince. It had been easier simply to go.

She'd never given him that dear John speech to let him down easy. Is that what Jess wanted to talk about? With Paul dying, it was a little late for speeches. And what did Paul want to tell Vince? That raised worries of a different sort.

Hopefully, Paul wouldn't give Vince the reins of Virtuality Incorporated. Paul had made the business a success. But Vince knew nothing about the IT industry. Maybe that's what Jess wanted to talk about. She was beyond brilliant and had an MS in Computer Science. Did Paul want the two of them to run Virtuality, together? It wouldn't work.

No obstacle had ever stopped his big brother. Cancer hadn't. Lack of money to start his business hadn't. He'd found a Christian partner, Patrick Michaels. They pooled their resources and launched the fastest growing high-tech company in the Puget Sound area. Why did Paul have to die now?

It seemed that God had big plans for Paul, until this unhappy ending interfered. It sounded like a Vince van Gordon novel, full of excitement and intrigue until the end, then emptiness.

No. Not a novel. It sounded like Vince van Gordon's life.

His vision blurred. Vince swiped at his eyes.

The drum roll for the WSU fight song came from the vibrating cell he still held in his hand. He answered, praying it wasn't Jess with more bad news.

"This is Jamie, Vince."

Great! This time it was his agent. "Jamie, I'm getting ready for a trip to Seattle. I just learned that my brother is dying."

The other end of the call went silent.

After several seconds, Jamie's sigh blew into her phone producing a static-like sound. "Sorry to hear about your brother. I'll be praying for you and your family."

"Paul and I are all that's left of our family. This is going to put my writing on hold until I see what I need to do in Seattle."

"I know this isn't the best time to bring this up, but it's important."

He started to interrupt her, but Jamie continued. "I read your draft and ... you have to make some changes to the story."

He'd just told her his brother was dying. Didn't she get it? "What do you mean?"

"Alright. Straight to the chase. Have you ever been in love, Vince?"

What kind of question was that?

"Yes." Why had he said that? He still was, but he wasn't going to tell Jamie that.

"It didn't end well, did it?"

"Jamie, will you just get to the point?"

"You're from Seattle and you're going back to see your brother. Will you see her there too?"

"I appreciate your concern, but you are my agent, not my counselor."

"That's not quite correct. According to our contract, I'm your professional counselor. And, as such, I'm advising you to make a happy ending of some sort for yourself, if you want to be able to write one. A wise person once said an author can't tell a better story than they've lived. And it seems that Vincent van Gordon has some things he needs to live."

He didn't reply to her remark. What could he say? Happy ever after wasn't in the cards for Vince van Gordon. Not this side of heaven.

"Vince, you write with so much passion, until you reach the end of your story. Then poof, it's all gone. I can't sell it. Nobody will buy a story with an ending like that."

Maybe real life did seep into a writer's stories. But what could Vince do with his? He would make sure the readers saw that justice was served. But how many readers would that satisfy? Not enough.

Jamie was right. He'd written a lame ending.

"Is she married?"

"No." He blew out his exasperation.

"Well, that's a positive development. Listen, you have enormous potential as a writer. Change the ending."

"I'll rewrite it as soon as I get a chance."

"Not the story, Vince. The real-life ending. That's what you need to change. Make it happy. If you don't, I'm not sure you can make it as an author." Jamie sighed into the phone again. "So sorry about your brother. I'll be praying for both of you. We'll talk again after this is all over. Goodbye, Vince."

She ended the call.

A real-life happily ever after? Only in fairy tales and Hallmark movies. And those weren't the kinds of stories Vince wrote.

Vince's cell vibrated in his hand, playing the WSU fight song.

Not again.

He looked at the incoming call displayed on the screen. It was the same 206 number Jess had used. He answered, praying he wasn't already too late.

"It's Jess again. The doctor just finished his rounds. Paul is weakening rapidly. His doctor says we don't have much time." Jess paused. "You've got to come now, Vince."

She had known how to give Vince commands since they were five, and she had just delivered the most forceful one he could ever recall.

"Which hospital?"

"Virginia Mason. Please hurry."

"Be there in about six hours. I need to talk to him too. Tell him I'm coming. Ask him to wait for me, Jess."

"I will. Bye, Vince."

In a few hours, he would be looking into her face. What would he see in those pale blue eyes? How could he ever— he didn't have time for that now.

Vince hit the speed dial number for Alaska Airlines.

"This is Vincent van Gordon. I need to make an emergency travel reservation on your next available flight from Denver to Seattle. Whatever you've got. I can be at the gate in forty-five minutes."

"We have a single seat in first class on flight 747, departing at 10:45 a.m. arriving at 12:30 p.m."

"Nothing earlier than that?"

"Uh ... no, sir. Not until late afternoon."

"I'll take it."

Vince gave the agent his frequent flyer and credit card information and got his confirmation number. He called a cab to take him to the airport, then he opened his call log and added Jess's number to his contact list, where it should have already been, and returned Jess's call.

"Hello, Vince."

She had recognized his number. How long had Jess had him in her contacts? "Jess, I'll be arriving on Alaska flight 747. It should arrive at the gate at 12:30 p.m. I won't check any bags, so—"

"Don't rent a car at Sea-Tac. We're running out of time. I'll be at Alaska's passenger pick-up at 12:35. See you then."

"Yeah. See you then, Jess."

Vince would soon have to face Jess, the woman he loved, but who, at most, only wanted her close friend back. Then he would talk with his dying brother. Which would be harder? Truthfully, he didn't know.

He'd barely gotten his max-sized, carry-on bag packed and his laptop placed in its case when the taxi pulled up in front of his townhouse.

A minute later, Vince shoved his laptop and carry-on into the cab and slid in behind them. "Airport, please. Alaska Airlines."

In a few minutes, the departure area came into view.

The cab stopped at the curb.

Mentally dizzy from the mix of thoughts swirling through his mind, Vince paid the driver, then carried his bags through the double-wide, glass doors leading to Denver Airport's Alaska ticket counter, doors leading him back to the genesis of unhappy endings.

Vince checked himself in and slipped into his airport autopilot mode. When he reached his gate, he hardly remembered clearing security.

He took a seat and waited for his flight's boarding call.

After he sat, the happy beginning that had held so much promise for a young boy came rushing at him, exhilarating to recall, but unrecoverable. A time more than sixteen years ago, when a young girl's eyes danced only for Vince van Gordon.

Jess had just had her birthday, though her parents seemed to ignore that special day. Jess had caught up with Vince. They were both nine-years-old. And, as he frequently did, Vince would try to stump her incredible mind with a new riddle. Jimmy Grant—the neighborhood bully who wasn't invited—stood with Jess and Vince on the van Gordon's front lawn.

"Here's the riddle, Jess. Bet you can't solve it." Vince grinned.

Jess rolled her eyes and huffed a blast of air. "Whatever."

Jimmy grunted out his bad-boy laugh. "So van Gordon's gonna stump Jamison. This I've got to see."

"Okay," Vince began. "There was a young man who wanted to marry a farmer's daughter, but the farmer said he had to solve a riddle first. If he did, he could marry the beautiful daughter."

"Why don't you just cut to the math, Vince. That's where you're going, isn't it?" Jess blew out another breath.

Bored? That wouldn't last long. This was a doozy of a riddle. He would have Jess sweating in another minute. Vince gave her his best attempt at an evil grin.

She stuck out her tongue.

"You need to listen, Jess. It gets complicated." He paused.

She put her hands on her hips and stared him down.

Okay. She asked for it. "The farmer tells the young man to go out to his orchard. He will pass three gates on the way out. In the orchard, he has to pick enough apples to feed the horses inside each gate. At the first gate, he must leave half the apples he picked and half an apple more. At the second gate, he must leave half the remaining apples and half an apple more. At the third gate, he must leave—"

"I know, half the remaining apples and half an apple more."

"Uh, yeah. And then he has to have one apple left to give the farmer."

"And then he has to marry the farmer's ugly daughter." Jimmy laughed again and whipped out his pocket knife. "Half an apple? No problem."

"No. We're not done yet. Jess, he can't cut any apples."

"What?" Jimmy's voice rose half an octave.

"Can't cut any apples," Jess said softly. "Let's see ... three, five, seven, nine ... eleven ... thirteen." She paused. "Fifteen apples. That's it. He picks fifteen and has one left to give the farmer and then marries the beautiful, warrior princess ... I mean the farmer's daughter."

"Yeah. But, Jess, how did—"

"It's pretty simple. Since he can't cut any apples, he starts with an odd number and always has to remove an even number, so he'll have an odd number left and won't have to cut an apple the next time. I just had to count up to the first odd number that worked ... fifteen."

"I should have known," Jimmy said. "She's a geeky nerd. She's not the beautiful farmer's daughter. Maybe she's one of his pigs."

Vince took a step toward Jimmy, but Jess had already planted the toe of her shoe on Jimmy's shin, sending him hopping on one foot, howling and spitting out words Vince and Jess didn't allow into their vocabularies.

"You're gonna see what that feels like on your nerdy nose." Jimmy turned toward Jess with his arms ready to throw punches.

Vince cut him off. "Don't touch her, James!" Vince taunted him with the formal name Jimmy despised.

"Okay, first, you get it van Gordon. Then she does." Jimmy balled his fists, but his posture was all wrong for boxing.

Vince planted his right foot in front of Jimmy and threw a straight punch, as his father taught him, with the power coming from his body, through his shoulder and out through his arm.

The blow caught the bully in the center of his face, sending him flat on his back on the lawn. He climbed back to his feet with blood streaming from both nostrils. He bellowed out something that sounded like profanity, then lunged at Vince.

The air exploded from Jimmy's mouth when Vince's body punch hit Jimmy's belly. He fell back onto his rear on the grass, sucking hard but obviously getting no air.

Vince had hit his target, Jimmy's solar plexus. The fight was over.

"Jimmy, if you ever even look cross-eyed at Jess or do anything to her that I don't like, somebody will have to carry you away when I'm through with you." Vince stepped beside Jimmy, hovering over him. "Remember, I warned you."

Jess grabbed Vince's arm and pulled him away from Jimmy, who still sat on the grass, making noises that sounded like a frog croaking.

Jess and Vince watched to make sure Jimmy wasn't going to croak.

He made it to his feet after a few moments. But he puked all over the van Gordon's lawn, before he ran toward his house with his nose still dripping blood.

Jess hadn't let go of Vince's arm. She slid her hand down to clasp his. The look she gave him with those light blue eyes grew soft and warm. "Vince, you can't keep doing that to every boy who does something you don't like. By the time we're in the sixth grade, we won't have enough guys left for a football team." She squeezed his hand and her eyes morphed to that dancing, happy look.

He'd learned when Jess said one thing and did another, you trusted what she did more than what she said. And she had just taken his hand for the first time that Vince could remember. Her hand, curled around his, sent a strange, new, warm feeling through Vince's heart. "Not every boy, Jess. Only the ones who try to hurt you."

From that time on, he and Jess had taken on the world. With Jess's brains and his brawn, accompanied by some choice words from Vince's oversized vocabulary, the world had always lost, until someone came along, unexpectedly, a few years later. It was someone whom Vince would never punch, someone he loved too much to punch, someone else who made Jess's eyes dance with that happy look. And Vince would never ask a girl like Jess to settle for less than she deserved.

When it became clear she wanted Paul, Vince had bowed out of the competition. He couldn't and wouldn't compete with his big brother, especially over a woman who preferred Paul.

That was the beginning of unhappy endings. Correction. It was the start of one long one that had lasted for seven years.

Maybe Jamie was right. But there was no way to fix it. Jess wanted Paul, and his death would only make that worse. Now Jess wouldn't get the man she wanted, and Vince would never make Jess settle for less, someone like him, a man who always came up short.

Vince gasped. What time was it?

He looked up at the gate. The final four or five passengers in what had been a long line were showing their boarding passes to the agent at the gate. He jumped up to join them.

What kind of look would he see in Jess's eyes when he arrived at Sea-Tac? With Paul dying, it wouldn't be that dancing, happy look. Besides, when he left seven years ago, any possibility of that had already evaporated.

* * *

A four-lane traffic jam lay in front of Vince when he walked out through Sea-Tac's double doors to the passenger pickup area. The mass of vehicles stretched as far as he could see to his left and his right. He hadn't asked Jess what kind of car she would be driving.

Movement in the third lane from the curb caught his attention. Jess stood beside her car. Their gazes locked, and twelve years of childhood memories rushed at him bringing a choking sensation. That tall, slender girl he had known most of his life would stand out in any crowd.

Vince stifled the impulse to run to her, wrap her up in his arms, and do what he shouldn't do.

Jess reached the curb and stopped ten feet away. She smiled. "Vincent van Gordon, I see that you still have both your ears."

The van Gogh insults. For some reason, she was still playing that game. Jessica Jamison lent itself well to some *pun*-ishment too. "And Jesse James must have dodged Robert Ford."

The smile faded, and Jess's long, slender legs closed the distance between them in two quick strides.

Before he could react, she had pulled him into a bear hug and nearly squeezed the breath out of him. "Not Jesse. It's Jess, Vince. Always has been, always will be." Her voice broke. Jess pulled an arm free, leaned back and swiped at two streams of tears on her cheeks.

He took in her face, close up. Light blue eyes, framed by gentle waves of long, dark hair. Tear-streaked cheeks, runny nose and all, Jess's beauty was still breathtaking. That proverbial, girl-next-door kind that can't be manufactured medically or painted on by a beautician. And Jess seldom painted on anything. But what was even more rare than makeup was to see tears on her cheeks.

Vince slipped his hands behind her shoulders, ready to pull her back into that close embrace, but he stopped when she looked up.

Jess's eyes widened. "Vince, why are you looking at me like that?"

"Because I—"

"Do not park your vehicle except to load or unload passengers!"

Vince lurched away from the noise blasting from an airport security vehicle that had targeted Jess's car.

The spell, or whatever it was they had both experienced, had been broken.

Jess turned toward her car. "We need to hurry. Just one bag and a laptop? Is that all you've got?"

"Yeah."

They scurried between vehicles to Jess's car.

He opened the back door and slid his bags into the back seat. "I travel light these days."

"So I noticed. And Seattle doesn't seem to be on your itinerary much ... these days."

That was true. But Jess knew why, didn't she?

Jess's drive to Virginia Mason Hospital was only marginally less harrowing than Vince's taxi ride through Kuala Lumpur in Malaysia on his recent book research trip. Her driving speed and aggressive maneuvers certainly minimized conversation. Maybe that was a good thing, because Vince needed to focus on Paul, not all the relational baggage he and Jess had to deal with.

Vince glanced at his watch. Seventeen minutes from the time they pulled away from the Sea-Tac terminal, Jess pulled into a spot in the 9th Avenue parking garage at Virginia Mason. It had to be a record for Seattle, especially approaching from the south in the early afternoon.

He opened the door and slid out.

Jess rushed to the trunk and opened it. "Put your stuff in here. It'll be out of sight."

Vince grabbed his bags and set them in the trunk.

She slammed it, took his hand and tugged. "We need to hurry. The Critical Care Unit is across campus on the ninth floor."

As they entered the CCU, Vince steeled himself for what was coming. He'd seen his brother near death once before, but this time was different. Paul's death was certain, and Vince had no time to make up for lost time. No time for anything but parting words.

For the first time in months, he prayed, begging God for the right words to say to his big brother.

Following behind a legend like Paul—with all of Paul's accolades, and with Paul overshadowing Vince—would have split up most sibling relationships. But none of that had mattered until Vince lost Jess. Then it all mattered. But that wasn't something he could say to the brother he loved. Certainly not now.

Vince would never try to steal Paul's glory or his girl, even if Vince loved her more than life. And that was something he had demonstrated to himself the day he left Seattle for good.

But, dude, maybe you left Seattle for bad. What are you gonna demonstrate this time?

Chapter 3

I was proud to be the wife of a Hollywood movie producer. But, now, I'm ashamed of you, Trenton Del Valle. I want no part of this, nor will I allow our kids to be around a man who produces pornography.

Emily's words still stung after eight years. Trent's wife had taken his two boys and disappeared. But now, Trent sat in the throne room of the Hollywood offices of Mature Media Incorporated (MMI) where, as CEO, he commanded a seven-figure income. He would soon show her that she might have become another Melinda Gates if she hadn't gotten involved with those Jesus freaks.

Trent drummed his fingers on the imposing wooden desk that dwarfed everything else in his elegant corner office. He had big plans for a big game, and it was kickoff time.

He picked up his cell and pressed the voice search icon. "Virginia Mason Hospital, Seattle, Washington."

"Here you are, Virginia Mason in Seattle."

Trent spotted the phone number in the query results and pressed the call icon beside it, then waited.

"Virginia Mason Medical Center, how may I direct your call?"

"I'm calling to find out how my friend, Paul van Gordon, is doing."

"One minute, please ... Mr. van Gordon is in our CCU. Only immediate family may visit."

"Sorry to hear that, but thanks for the information, ma'am." Trent ended the call.

Paul van Gordon wouldn't be around much longer. Whether Vince van Gordon realized it or not, he would soon catch the ball on the goal line. Then came the run back.

Trent hit Lorenzo Russo's number in his contacts.

"Russo, here. What you want, Trent?"

"Lorenzo, Tony Manetti said you might have some people in the Big Apple, or maybe across the river, who can help me with a little job. I'm willing to pay top dollar for three or four of the right men."

"Yeah, I can probly help. What you need done?" Russo's New York City speech murdered the king's English, but the man was sharp, efficient, good for his word, and nobody pushed Lorenzo Russo around. He was the kind of man Trent could rely on to handle sensitive matters while keeping them confidential.

"I need surveillance and some high-tech spying."

"You talkin' about some hackin'?"

"Yes. And, if I give the word, maybe a little muscle. Nothing more than intimidation. Hopefully, nobody gets hurt and nobody calls the cops."

"My friend, Frankie, has some people who can do all that. When you need them?"

"In about twenty-four hours," Trent said.

"That's pretty quick. Where?"

"Near Seattle."

"That's pretty far. You gotta take whoever's available."

"I figured that would be the case. Call me when it's all lined up, and I'll send the advance."

"I'll get right on it." Russo ended the call.

With Russo on it, this shouldn't take long. Trent placed his cell on the desk and scanned the information and list of instructions he'd printed out for the men he planned to hire.

Before he finished reviewing the list, his cell rang, playing *New York, New York*.

"Hello, Lorenzo."

"Del Valle, the advance will be fifty Gs. You got three guys, so it'll cost you three thousand a day to cover expenses. But if you need, you know, more than you asked for, it's gonna go way up. In that case, we gotta renegotiate, dependin' on specifics."

"I understand. I'll transfer the advance as soon as we're done here. Same account number as before?"

"Yeah. Same one. Once we get it, we're all set. Sal Romano will contact you when he arrives in Seattle with his two team members. Mention my name and he'll start takin' orders from you."

"Thanks, Lorenzo."

If Trent's sources of information were reliable, the only potential hitch was Paul's little brother, Vince. If he didn't interfere, the cost shouldn't go up. But Vince van Gordon was supposed to be a big, tough guy, a loose cannon with a big mouth and a big vocabulary. And some people who knew him said he had a bad temper. He was also way out of his league when it came to running Virtuality, a company Trent had had his eye on for the past four months. Hopefully, Vince wouldn't be inclined to take the helm and would simply sell the company.

Regardless, Vince would soon catch the kickoff at the goal line. Then came the run back.

But Vince had no blockers. At this point, he wouldn't realize he needed any. Maybe a hard hit would make him fumble the ball.

Trent would see how well the special-team guys performed, the hard hitters he'd just hired. That performance would determine if Trent needed only surveillance or some strong muscle. Hopefully, he wouldn't need anything more than that. However, if someone had to die to make Trent's dream a reality, he would come up with the cash to make it happen, regardless of the cost.

But that would make things so messy.

Chapter 4

When Vince entered Paul's room in the CCU, his brother's eyes were focused on the entryway like his gaze had been locked on it for hours, waiting. The determination in those eyes crushed Vince's heart like a two-ton weight on his chest.

Paul had willed death to wait. He had held on just for Vince.

Paul reached out a hand through the railing. Before Vince could take it, the arm dropped, dangling off the side of the bed.

Vince's vision blurred with unshed tears when he took his brother's hand, the hand that had shown Vince how to throw a football and scoop up hot grounders on the baseball field.

Paul's visible muscles flexed, taxed to their limit simply by trying to make his chest rise one more time.

"Vince, you came." He forced the words out from a body that had few words left in it. Though death was approaching, Paul's voice remained calm, unlike the room with its beeping equipment, flashing lights, and a nurse hurrying in and out.

"Yeah. I came ... I love you, big brother."

"A weak smile flickered across Paul's dry cracked lips. "Guess it's time for the real Paul van Gordon to leave."

"Tell Mom and Dad that I can't wait to see them up there."

"I will, but you need to wait a while. There are people here who need you. I'm going home to a place prepared for me. It's my time." Paul stopped and drew several short breaths. "My brain will shut down. But, Vince, I don't exist in my brain. It's only an interface ... to the real me."

Theology? Psychology? "Paul, what do you mean?"

"You don't need to understand now. Just remember what I said. Soon, you'll see it for yourself. Got to hurry. Listen ... everything I'm leaving behind is yours. And, Vince ... don't sell the company." His voice crescendoed. "Don't sell it to Patrick or anyone else. You need to run Virtuality. Promise me you will."

Why would Paul, genius and entrepreneur, want Vince to run a high-tech company? "I ..."

"Promise me, Vince." Paul's gaze grew fierce.

"I—I promise." But how could he fulfill such a promise? Regardless, he had to try.

"And be careful. Someone has been spying on Virtuality. There could be danger. Danger for you and for Jess. About Jess—listen to her. Trust her. She can ... help."

Paul coughed. His breathing turned to wheezing. "Jess ... needs you, Vince. And ... you need ... her ... so ..." Paul's eyelids fluttered. He drew a ragged breath. His eyes closed.

As the breath drained from Paul's lungs, life drained from his body.

The monitor confirmed it, flat lining with a piercing tone, an electronic wail. The death note.

Jess ran into the room and stopped, studying Paul's motionless body.

Three women in scrubs scurried into the room after Jess. They stopped near Paul's bed, checked him, but then appeared to be in no hurry.

One looked at the clock and wrote on the clipboard she'd taken from the foot of the bed. The other two disassembled the monstrosity of tubes, bags of solutions, and electronic devices.

Jess turned from Paul's lifeless body and pulled Vince outside to the nearby CCU waiting room. Once again, she faced him and circled Vince's neck with her arms. "He's home now, Vince. No more cancer. No more chemo. But did he talk to you?"

Though she had just observed Paul's lifeless body, there were no tears in Jess's eyes. And the concern Vince saw there seemed reserved for him.

The confusing signals from the only woman he had ever loved messed with his thinking. Her reaction swirled in his mind, mixing with thoughts about losing his brother and about Vince being the last living member of his immediate family. Then the mental activity stopped.

Over the next few moments, Vince's eyes dried. The emotions that had assaulted him at first sight of Paul fled, replaced by ... nothing.

What was wrong with him? His brother had just died, yet Vince couldn't feel anything. But that wasn't entirely true. Beyond the numbness, a terrifying emptiness waited to swallow him.

Paul was right. Vince needed Jess. Life without her would become a void that devoured him. His life would become that terrifying emptiness.

"Vince, are you okay?" Jess's hand clamped onto his arm.

"Yeah. I'm okay."

Jess's squinting eyes and frown said she wasn't buying it.

"Paul talked to me, Jess."

Her frown faded. "Thank God, we made it in time."

Good. She'd accepted his change of subject. "Don't thank Him, yet. I'm still trying to make sense of what Paul said. He said you could help."

"Yes. I ..." Jess met his gaze, studied his eyes, and her eyes flooded. She still held his arm and used it to pull Vince closer, then pressed her head against his neck and cried softly.

Vince curled an arm around her and brushed the tears from her cheek. She seldom cried, but when she did—well, she wouldn't be able to help for a while.

Questions about the danger Paul mentioned could wait until later. He wrapped her up in his arms, thankful he had Jess to see him through the events of the next few days.

Jess clung to him, her body shaking with each sob. A broken heart was the only thing that had ever made her cry. Not even a broken arm had been able to do that.

Had Paul's death done all the breaking? Jess's reactions seemed to say it was something about Vince that brought her to tears. But that was probably his wishful thinking. And, right now, he couldn't afford to bet any of his depleted emotional capital on that longshot.

She must be crying over Paul. Vince couldn't blame Jess for loving Paul. Everybody loved Paul. But Jess, the girl next door, had been Vince's closest friend since they were five years old. They had grown up together, shared their secrets, and he had always assumed—no, he had presumed. And when life and love didn't go as planned, Vince had left.

Paul got the girl and Vince hadn't opposed Paul. That never happened in the van Gordon household.

But Jess had lost too. And her arms still clung to Vince, hanging on to her dearest childhood friend, the nearest thing to Paul she had left, Paul's little brother, standing in Paul's shadow.

* * *

Did Vince realize why she was crying? For seven years, she had prayed Vince would come home. When he did, it was for Paul, not for her. And, now, Vince had lost Paul. Whether Vince knew it or not, he needed her right now. Maybe if she supported him through this time of grieving, he would see that Jess Jamison loved him.

But, could Vince ever give his love to someone like her, someone her own father didn't even love? As kids, Vince had given her his heart. Then something changed.

Jess was what Meyers and Briggs called an INTJ, the research scientist personality type, always analyzing and predicting. But she hadn't predicted that Vince would leave. And none of her analysis had told her why. Her best guess, she wasn't good enough for a man like Vince. Not that he was perfect. But he was perfect for her. Vince's strengths were her weaknesses and vice versa. They made a perfect team. Invincible.

Standing in the CCU waiting room, Jess took a deep breath and relaxed in Vince's arms. Her arms still held Vince, pressing his body against hers in a more intimate embrace than she would ever give to a friend. Vince should have realized that, but he was distracted, still trying to come to grips with the loss of his brother.

As awful as it sounded, Jess had taken advantage of the situation, but she didn't feel guilty about it. How could she after sharing twelve years of her life with him, starting when they were in kindergarten? She had always thought they were meant to be together—well, almost always. There was that foolish, teenage crush on Paul. But Paul had outgrown her and Vince. And, once again, it was Vince and Jess against the world.

Now, Paul had outgrown them again, graduating to his eternal home. She had expected this for a few days. But Vince, only for a few hours. And Paul's death had accomplished something neither his life nor Jess's wishes had been able to do. It had brought Vince home where he belonged. If only he could see that ...

She needed to untangle herself from Vince before her wrap-around hug made him uncomfortable.

Jess tiptoed and kissed his cheek. "Thanks, Vince."

When they locked gazes, Vince's eyes held an expression she seldom saw there, confusion.

Vince gripped her shoulders, held her at arms' length, and studied her the way he had done since they were seven or eight. It was his way of determining if she was okay. He drew her close again, gave her a hug, and kissed her forehead. "No. Thank *you*, Jess. It's good to be home. Especially now."

The impulse came to tilt her head up and do something she would probably regret. Since she couldn't do that, she needed to say something to get beyond the awkward closeness. "Did he tell you about the business and about the project?"

She took a step back, and Vince's arms released her.

The look of confusion returned to his eyes. "He told me a few things. But what's so dangerous? Is it the technology, the project, or something to do with his partner, Patrick?"

Jess sighed sharply, still struggling a bit to regain her composure. She had a reputation to live up to. The ice girl. The girl who never cried. But, since Vince had arrived, she had cried more than in the past seven years. Correction. More than in the past six years, ten months, and two days.

"Danger? The technology, the project, or Patrick? Maybe all of the above. But this isn't the time for that discussion. Later, Vince."

"You're right. We've got a funeral to plan."

We? Vince had included her like she was family. He had done that as a kid. The van Gordons had been more like family to her than her own. But not in one way. Jess could never view Vince as a brother.

"No. Paul took care of all the arrangements for his memorial service a couple of days ago, before he grew too weak to talk on the phone."

"Why didn't he call me then?" Vince's eyes welled.

Paul hadn't meant to hurt his brother. But Vince seemed to think otherwise.

"I think he still held out hope for a miracle. He could communicate and think rationally until he went to sleep last night. This morning was a different story. He didn't get a chance to let you know there wasn't going to be any miracle. No remission this time."

"I guess the third time's not the ..." His voice trailed off.

Jess shook her head.

"Then we'll meet with Patrick tomorrow and he can answer my questions."

She laid a hand on his shoulder. "You and I need to talk first."

Vince nodded slowly, digesting her meaning. "Okay. But all this has left me feeling exhausted. How about I pick you up tomorrow morning for coffee? Well, I'll pick you up if you'll drop me off at a car rental."

"Coffee sounds good." She stuck a hand in the pocket of her denim shorts and pulled out the key ring Paul had given her. "No need to rent a car. Here are the keys to Paul's car and his house. He said to tell you to do anything you want, make any changes you want, because they're yours and that he's got a better home now."

"That sounds like Paul." Vince turned his head away and wiped his eyes.

"I have to return my friend's car that I borrowed today. But—"

"You don't have a car? Seriously?"

"Vince, I have a motorcycle."

He raised his eyebrows, but didn't say anything, though it was obvious he wanted to.

"My bike's in the shop for some repairs. But you don't have to pick me up. My apartment's only a few blocks from Starbucks."

"Then Fairwood Starbucks it is."

"What time?"

"Seven o'clock?"

She gave him a weak smile. "That's right. You're the early riser."

"Come on, Jess. You got up early a lot of times."

"Whenever I had a good reason."

"Am I a good enough reason?"

He was reason enough to stay up all night if that's what Vince wanted. But she wasn't sure how he would respond to that. And she wasn't sure how much of this bit of shared intimacy was due to feelings about Paul's death, rather than Vince's feelings for her.

And why did Vince's actions seem to convey more than mere friendship? Wishful thinking?

When she didn't reply, Vince's gaze dropped to the floor. "Maybe I'm not—"

"Vince, you should know you're always a good enough reason … for almost anything."

"Anything? Someday, I might hold you to that."

Jess drew a sharp breath.

"Or maybe you should forget I said that." Vince looked away, staring out a window, toward Denver.

"No." Her hand went back to his shoulder. "I should file it away for safekeeping."

Safe? Just being near Vince was no longer safe for her heart. And with the mysterious events in Patrick's lab and at Virtuality, the rest of Jessica Jamison may not be safe either. But being safe was highly overrated.

The adage about it being better to be safe than sorry wasn't true. A person could be safe and still be sorry.

Safe but sorry and living with regret. Jess vowed from this day forward she would never do that again. But, if she risked exposing her true feelings, how would he react? Leave again?

"A penny for your thoughts."

Vince's voice pulled her back from her questions into the reality of their situation. "Vince, I told you—"

"I know what you told me seven years ago. A poor, starving writer couldn't afford to—"

"That's not what I said."

Vince didn't reply.

"You can't buy my thoughts for a penny. But you'd be surprised what coffee can buy."

Vince gave her a weak smile. "Whatever you want tomorrow morning, it's on me." The smile morphed to a grin, and he touched a finger to the tip of her nose, something he did as a kid to annoy her.

But this time it didn't. In fact, right now, Vince could touch her face any way he wanted, provided he didn't do some silly, little-boy thing like trying to poke his finger in her—" Vince, stop it. That is so gross. Besides, you're the one with the nose issues."

"You think I need a nose job?"

"I never said you need a nose job. But it wouldn't hurt to consider it, unless you were, say, an Aardvark." She'd done it again. They weren't in high school. And she'd gotten over all that, hadn't she?

But why couldn't she act like a mature woman around Vince van Gordon? Maybe their truncated relationship left them stuck at seventeen, two hurting kids doomed to remain teenagers until they could heal each other's heart.

What if they couldn't? Would Jess continue flying down freeways on her motorcycle, climbing rocks as she had been doing, climbing increasingly difficult rock faces until she reached the limits of her ability to—had she actually been doing that?

That Jess had allowed herself even to think such a thought frightened her. But a broken heart was a frightening thing. It made rational people do irrational things.

She looked up at Vince and opened her mouth to speak.

I need you to rescue me, Vince. Like you used to do.

But other words came out. "I need to take you home, Vince. We're both tired."

Vince nodded, then stared at the floor, clenching and unclenching his fists. He'd done that since he was six or seven if something was bothering him.

Jess reached out and lifted his chin until their eyes met. "What is it?"

"Jess, has anyone been spying on Paul, on you, or on Virtuality?"

"Why are you asking me that?"

"I was just thinking about something Paul said."

"He's *your* brother, but I guess you can't ask him what he meant."

"But you would know, because you were his—" Vince stopped.

"His what?"

Vince didn't reply.

What was he insinuating? "Say it, Vince. I was his what?"

"Nothing."

"You got that right. *Nothing.* And that's all you understand, isn't it?" His eyes said he wasn't going to tell her what he'd been thinking.

Vince had stopped working his fists and, now, his eyes had confusion written all over them.

"Look. I worked for Paul for about three months, but I don't know anything about any spying, alright?" But she did know it was time to take clueless Vince home while he still had his ears. Because Jess had words on the tip of her tongue sharp enough to cut both his ears off.

Chapter 5

What a mess!

Jess's sheets looked like some giant had tried to eat them like spaghetti, rolling them around his fork. A night that was hot by Seattle standards had only contributed to a small part of her restlessness.

Her alarm! She had forgotten to set it. The blue letters on her alarm clock said 6:35 a.m. Jess had only twenty-five minutes to get ready and, since her motorcycle was in the shop, walk the four blocks to Starbucks to meet a man who considered being late a mortal sin.

She had not planned this day to start on such a disastrous note, especially after her sharp words before they left the hospital. After a sixty-second shower, Jess scampered to her closet, praying this wasn't a harbinger of how things would go today between Vince and her.

The forecast high for the day, displayed on her digital alarm, read ninety-two degrees. Jess threw on a pair of skorts that she had never worn because they looked so much like a skirt, a mini-skirt. One look in the full-length mirror on her closet door told her a skirt that short wouldn't be decent. As shorts, they were decent, and the sweltering day would make them acceptable. But, what if Vince thought—

Girl, get a grip. You're trying way too hard to get that man's attention.

Jess choked the annoying voice coming from her left cerebral hemisphere until it shut up.

At 6:56, she locked the door of her apartment and jogged down the sidewalk toward the coffee shop. As her jog sped to a loping run, her angst over being late morphed to angst over the subjects they would discuss over coffee, the danger Vince had mentioned and the highly inflammatory subject of *them*.

Jess burst through the doorway of Starbucks at 7:00 a.m. Though she'd tried not to, she'd broken a sweat, not enough to be smelly, but still ...

Vince sat at a table near the wall on the opposite side of the shop. When his eyes focused on her bare legs, his lips formed the little O that boys used for whistling.

Great. Vince's brother had just died. There were ominous things happening with the business. And what was Jessica Jamison doing?

Trying to appeal to a man's baser proclivities.

Jess muted the irritating voice inside, painted a smile on her lips, and approached Vince.

He stood, finally looking up from her legs, which were visible from midthigh down. "Jess, you're—"

"Late. I know. Sorry, Vince." She sat and scooted her legs further than necessary under the wooden table, well outside of anyone's view of—wonderful! Now there were several other sets of male eyes gawking at her.

"Late? That wasn't what I—"

"It sure is hot this morning. These skorts were the only cool thing I had to wear. Have you ordered yet?" Did he get it? It wasn't a mini-skirt. It was a pair of shorts.

Vince sat and leaned back in his chair with a confused look in his eyes again.

What was wrong with him? Big, confident Vince never used to look confused.

All movement in the coffee shop seemed to have stopped. A quick scan of the room told her why, and it raised a question. How could she discuss critical issues with Vince while every guy over the age of twelve was gawking at her hot, sweating body?

Hot. How could she have even thought that word under the circumstances?

A big, warm hand came to rest on hers. "I hope it's okay, Jess ... I already ordered for both of us. Let's see, you always drank a triple, grande mocha, extra hot."

Please, please, please. I hope he didn't.

"But that was seven years ago. You look so—uh, I mean it's hot, so I ordered you an iced, triple-grande, nonfat, vanilla latte."

"Thanks, Vince." After she broke into a sweat in her run down here, she didn't need three shots of hot espresso poured into her. And, at twenty-five, almost twenty-six, mochas took a lot more exercise to burn off than at seventeen.

"Our order's up. I'll get it." Vince left the table.

Jess took a deep breath and sighed, long and loud, letting her lips vibrate.

A three-year-old boy with a moo-stache on his upper lip eyed her from the next table. "Dat's cool. Could ya show me how ya do dat?"

She gave him some semblance of a smile. "Sure. You just act like an idiot until you're embarrassed, then sigh really hard to make it all go away."

The boy frowned for a moment, then raised the vanilla steamer to his mouth, adding to his moo-stache.

Vince set her cup on the table and took his seat. "You sure stirred things up in here when—"

"Don't we have something more important to discuss than ..." Than what? She wasn't going to say it, though Vince's eyes said he clearly knew it. Sliding into those skorts was a stupid, juvenile thing to do.

But wasn't juvenile right where she and Vince were picking up their teenage relationship, the one that had ended more than seven years ago with the equivalent of a one-sided, no-fault, teenage divorce?

Something had hurt Vince and he had left, but he'd never explained why.

Now, his eyes shifted to a look she knew well from the times that trouble had come their way.

"Vince, I think it's time for you to tell me what Paul said. And then I've got a story you need to hear."

* * *

Vince couldn't remember Paul's exact words, but what he had communicated pushed Vince to high alert, DEFCON 3, maybe DEFCON 2. Jess needed to hear it too, since she might also be in danger.

He looked across the table at the beautiful woman with glowing cheeks, the one who had caught everyone's eye when she came in dressed like, and looking like, a supermodel.

Jess had embarrassed herself. Her clothes were out of character and her lips appeared to have a touch of lipstick, something she seldom used. Her pink cheeks would have been a cute reaction, but nothing about Jessica Jamison could be called cute. She was a stunning beauty and—

"Come on. It was just yesterday afternoon. You couldn't have already forgotten what he told you."

Her normally soft, alto voice had hardened. It ended Vince's musings, drawing his focus back to Jess's pale blue eyes.

"Jess, I—" How had he ever left her? Jess was his childhood soulmate, beautiful inside and out. And Vince van Gordon was a fool. He should have gone head-to-head with Paul for this woman. And for not doing so, maybe he *should* cut off an ear.

Yeah, dude. Starting right below it ... right on your jugular.

Jess's dark eyebrows nearly touched. "I don't like suspense, unless it's in a book or a movie. Are you going to tell me, or—"

"I'm sorry." He blew out a breath and tried to organize his thoughts. "Some of this sounds crazy, and I'm not sure what it means."

"Just tell me, unless Paul told you not to." Her gaze dropped to the tabletop.

"No. He didn't say that." Vince paused. "He said it was time for him to go home, then something about not existing in his brain—that a brain is only an interface to the real person."

"That's what Paul believed about the nature of human beings, a sort of dualism, body and spirit. He thought that God created us with a real self that existed in the spirit, apart from the physical body. He said it was a biblical view. But I'm not sure why Paul mentioned it while he was dying, unless it has something to do with the nature of his work."

"You worked with him. Wouldn't you know that?"

Jess's frown and the questioning look in her eyes surprised him.

"I only worked for Paul for three months. Then a day here and there to squash bugs in the software. And even then, I didn't have much interaction with him. Vince, I don't think you understand how it was with ..." She paused and shook her head. "Besides, I don't have a security clearance. I can tell you about that later. But surely Paul told you more."

Little interaction with Paul? They certainly didn't sound like a couple. Had distancing himself from Jess been Paul's way of handling his illness, or did it reflect Jess's lack of feelings for Paul?

Regardless, what Jess had revealed opened the door a crack for Vince to come back into her life. But he had been mistaken about Jess once before, and he wouldn't put himself through that agony again.

"Yeah, he told me more. He told me that everything he left behind was mine. Then he made me promise not to sell the company, not to Patrick nor anyone else. I don't know anything about Paul's software business. The truth is, I don't know anything about software, except that I want it to run right when I'm using it on my laptop. Why would he want me to keep the business? Any ideas?"

"Maybe. But what else did Paul say?"

"It got a little spooky at that point. I think Paul suddenly realized life was leaving his body and ..." Vince swallowed hard. "He hurried, trying to tell me about somebody spying on him and about some kind of danger that threatened me and possibly you, Jess."

"Me? That is spooky."

"Got any idea what he was referring to?"

"It would only be speculation. And it's rather far-fetched. What else did he say?"

"He didn't have any time left. He ..." Vince's throat constricted, choking off his words.

"No. He didn't have much time." Jess laid her hand on his. "We made it here with hardly two minutes to spare."

"He was hanging on for me, Jess. I think Paul would've refused to die until we got there."

"You're probably right." She rubbed Vince's hand.

He took hers gently, allowing Jess to opt out.

She didn't.

Hopefully, she wouldn't prod further. He didn't know how to approach the sensitive issue of Vince and Jess's broken relationship, an issue that seemed to be on Paul's mind only seconds before he died. His last thoughts on earth were about Vince and Jess. What had Paul been doing? Giving Jess to Vince?

Jess studied his eyes and squeezed his hand. "He told you more, didn't he?"

Vince opened his mouth to speak. Nothing came out but a dry hack.

Jess waited, watching him.

What if he was wrong about Paul's reference to Jess? What if Vince had misunderstood? His heart picked up its tempo to allegro, and the coffee shop suddenly felt like a sauna.

Just say it, dude. Jess needs to hear it.

Vince cleared his throat and broke eye contact with her. "Paul said ... you could help me and ..."

"And?"

"And that I should help you, because ... you needed me." There. He had said it. Well, half of it. Vince lifted his gaze back to Jess's face.

Her lower lip quivered, and her eyes welled, nearly overflowing.

Jess pulled her hand free, looked away, and wiped her eyes. "I guess it's my turn now."

Her short, pained reaction would be the only feedback Vince got, for now. That was Jess, an INTJ, a personality type rare in the feminine world, a brilliant combination of logic and intuition. People like her were loyal to a fault and, generally, not inclined to show a lot of emotion, except to the close friends they acquired, friends that could usually be counted using a person's thumbs.

Evidently, Vince still owned one of her thumbs.

"I don't have a security clearance, so I've never been inside Virtuality's lab. I've used their configuration management tool to push software to the lab from a server in the office, but that's as close as I've gotten to the lab and the work being done there."

"But you knew what your software did. That had to tell you something about the project."

"It told me that Paul's sophisticated algorithms, which I coded from his specs, were used for lossless compression of human nerve impulse data—analog data, digitized and compressed after being recorded from human nerves located in various parts of the body, while that body performed certain activities about which I can only speculate."

This was more than weird. "What are we talking about here, Jess? Making androids or something?"

"No. Paul's company, Virtuality Incorporated, is making highly realistic simulations of certain kinds of human activity while people interact with their environment. The specific application was classified Top Secret, so I never knew how the technology would be used by the military. I assumed it was for combat training."

Sometime during her explanation, Jess had taken his hand.

Vince looked at their clasped hands and almost lost his train of thought. "Why combat training?"

"Paul and Patrick had contracted with a military organization that oversees advanced Army combat training. I think the goal was to give our soldiers a leg up on the enemy by preparing them for warfare using highly realistic combat simulations. The simulations are created using virtual reality amped up by stimulating the human body with recorded nerve impulses."

"Stimulating the human body? You mean they can actually play the nerve data back into—"

"Yes ... well, I think they can. You know, like a CD player, where digitized music is converted back to analog and played through a stereo system."

"But the stereo system we're talking about here is the human body. So what are they creating? A virtual Frankenstein?"

"I told you what I think, Vince. I don't know for sure. And there's still a lot of magic that would have to occur to mimic a real combat situation using nerve data, virtual reality, and millions of lines of application code to make it all work together in some meaningful way."

Jess kneaded his hand and her eyes took on that calculating look Vince had learned to recognize as a kid. "You know, you can tell the brain lies through the nerves for only so long. The human brain will discover the truth and start compensating for the lies ... unless something stimulates the brain, directly?"

Direct brain stimulation? "That's science fiction. Forget the virtual Frankenstein. That's one step closer to a real monster." It was too much for Vince to wrap his mind around, let alone think of an application that might endanger Jess and him.

"Vince, did you know that Patrick was a medical student for a while and has a biology degree? After that, he got his MS in computer science, like me."

Like Jess? No matter how bright Patrick was, he was not like Jess. As far back as Vince could remember, Jess could outthink anyone she was pitted against. To the best of his knowledge, she had never lost a chess game. "My head is spinning just trying to put this in a meaningful context, something like a novel plot."

Jess smiled warmly at him. "That's a great idea. Pretend this technology is driving a technothriller that you're writing. What might the plot look like? You know, something that would make it dangerous."

Vince leaned back in his chair rubbing his chin. "That technology might help soldiers kill more effectively, but I don't think that's the kind of danger Paul was talking about. And the spying he mentioned—maybe that was because of the project's classification. Classified projects often become targets for espionage."

Paul's eyes had looked intense, maybe even frightened as he spoke about the danger. But with Paul that close to death, Vince shouldn't read too much into Paul's expression.

"I agree," Jess said. "But he could have meant something that would endanger Americans—kids, families, maybe something criminals would use. But we shouldn't rule out foreign spies. After all, this project is Top Secret."

"And Paul never mentioned being in danger, himself?"

Jess shook her head. "If the danger was physical, I'm guessing it arose after he got really sick."

"If that's true, Paul was worried about more than the technology and its application. Something must've happened recently that changed everything, something that factored danger into the equation. I think it's time for us to have a talk with Patrick."

Jess took a sip of her coffee then set her cup on the table. "You know, he may not let you in his office. If he does, he'll stonewall you with security issues. You don't have a clearance so, just like he did with me, he'll say that he's not authorized to—"

"Not if I ask the right questions. When we talk to Patrick, wanna play good cop, bad cop with me?"

She laughed. "I wouldn't be any help. I can't act. You should know that."

"Then I guess I'll just have to play Columbo."

Chapter 6

Time for the coach to reveal his game plan.
Trent shoved open the conference room door.
The other six members of the MMI board sat around the large table engaged in conversation as they waited for their tardy chairman.
The murmuring in the room stopped when Trent stepped into the room.
He scanned their faces and wondered who would be left at the end of the day. One does not make the sweeping changes required to turn a struggling corporation into a powerful global enterprise without ruffling a few feathers and putting uncooperative heads on the chopping block.
Trent strode to the head of the long table, flipped on the display device and slipped the USB drive holding his PowerPoint presentation into the USB port.
When the big monitor on the wall flashed the opening visual, the faces of the other six tilted up to the screen.
Say goodbye to old MMI.
We're moving to Vegas!
Trent waited while they read it and then surveyed their faces for initial reactions.
Marco Acosta's intelligent, inquisitive brown eyes focused on Trent. "What are you up to, Del Valle? Hope you're not gonna upset our applecart."
"I'm not going to upset it, Marco. But the cart's too small. If you'll all bear with me for a few moments, I'll show you a much bigger cart filled with a thousand times more apples."

He paused to let them ruminate on his words. The buzz in the room started again and grew louder by the second.

"I said, if you'll please bear with me."

Trent waited until all attention returned to him. "Here is the current, sorry state of our industry, gentlemen ... and Ms. Gray."

Regina Gray, the aging porn star, turned business executive, gave him her patented smile. "I can handle a move to Vegas ... if there's profit in it."

"There's a tax break in it, for sure, Regina. The profit—I'll get to that in a moment. First, can anyone tell me why the adult movie business is floundering?"

"That's easy. Not enough sales and too much competition." Jack Dalton leaned forward on his elbows and gave Trent a blank stare.

"Yes. And that's because people don't want to pay for the same old content they've always gotten, when somebody on the Internet will give it to them for nothing. Well, nothing but exposure to some annoying advertising. That's all we're making money on with our websites ... the advertising. And we have to beat the bushes for it, because not every business is comfortable with placing ads on our X-rated web sites. The net effect, our profit margin is thinner than a Slim Jim, but it's not unlocking any doors for us."

Trent forwarded to the next visual. "Look at the numbers. Thirty-seven percent of worldwide Internet traffic is pornography, but we aren't making diddly from it. To top it all off, some of the social media sites are secretly horning in on what little is left of our business."

Trent paused to let them digest the first round of information. "And, meanwhile, what are our competitors doing?"

Regina slipped into her amateurish British accent. "Like Playboy, they're turning respectable."

"Exactly. And, though it's ten percent of their revenue, some of the big hotel chains are dropping adult videos, while the state of California passes laws that make it more difficult to shoot our movies," Trent said.

"Are you trying to tell us were going broke, Trenton?" Al Compton's bushy eyebrows pinched together.

"It doesn't have to play out that way, Al. Not if we do two things." Trent moved to the next image in his presentation. "First, we appear to go respectable too. We change our name when we move." He pointed to the name and new logo on the screen. "MMI becomes Custom Adventures Incorporated. You'll understand the name if you'll bear with me."

"Trent, just what does 'go respectable' mean? I'm not sure we know how to do that." Regina gave him a palms-up shrug. But her crooked smile said she was on board. And she made a good ally. Regina was sharp and boardroom wise.

But everyone needed to hear the answer to her question, because appearing respectable would soon become their life and their lifeline for the foreseeable future. "It means we climb in bed with all the tech companies. We attend their trade shows, schmooze with their CEOs and with their senior technical staff. We make them feel comfortable with our presence. They see that we're ordinary folks, just like them. Then we give them some business. Contracts to build sophisticated apps for streaming our content to handheld devices—cell phones, pads, tablets."

Trent changed to the next visual in his presentation. "Second, we slowly leave the video world and enter the brave new world of next-generation, virtual reality. And, just as we have for the last twenty years, the adult entertainment industry will drive the technology with our investments. We've got to make sure we're at the leading—no, the bleeding edge of personal entertainment technology. I'm talking fully interactive VR, where the customer becomes a character in his own story, his own fantasy world, a world so real you can't tell the virtual from reality. If we're first to market with these next-generation VR products, we will be wealthy beyond our wildest dreams."

Tony's eyes had lit up on the words, wildest dreams. "Have you done the math, Del Valle? What does the market for VR look like?"

Trent focused on Tony. "If we're first in, the rewards are staggering. Twenty billion dollars in year one. That matches the annual U.S. video game sales. Eighty billion in year two. And, if this technology delivers like I believe it will, we could become the first trillion-dollar-a-year business not far down the road."

The murmuring started again. He had baited the hook and Trent would let them swim for a while, then see which board members bit.

Tony Manetti waved his index finger. "I get your point. But what I don't get is how we're gonna get this bleeding edge technology?"

Trent drew a deep breath and blew it out in slow, dramatic fashion. "I was wondering who would be first to ask that question. To make it in our industry, to rise above the competition, you need actionable intelligence. You see, I've got a longtime friend in the Pentagon, one who does contract administration and who is—how shall I put this—hooked on our products and doesn't want anyone to know it. He has a Top-Secret clearance, one of those compartmentalized kinds, that he doesn't want to lose, because that would end his career."

Trent had a half-dozen carefully selected, porn-addicted informants who would do his bidding, within reasonable limits. But that was information best kept to himself. "This DOD employee is overseeing a contract dealing with the very technology we need. Tony, you asked how we get the technology. Well, here's how it works. The basic technology gets developed for the DOD at the government's expense. With very little investment, we take it commercial with our products, using our relationship with the video games giant, LACO."

Dick Cunningham folded his arms and rocked in his executive-style chair. "How can we be sure this comes off without a hitch? There are a lot of moving parts in your plan. A lot could go wrong."

"Point taken. And that's why I called Lorenzo Russo in New York. He's providing us with surveillance—high-tech spies—and a little muscle, in case anyone needs a little persuading. Persuading shouldn't be hard to do, because this is a win-win. There's plenty of profit here for everyone involved and nobody is stepping on anyone else's turf."

Cunningham's eyes said he wasn't happy. However, he did unfold his arms and he stopped rocking. "So who's prime on this DOD contract, you know, the people developing our technology for us but don't know it yet?"

Trent locked gazes with each pair of eyes, sequentially. "Don't discuss this outside of this room. Got that?"

Heads nodded around the table. Each person's assent was visible to everyone in the room. That, alone, was enough to hold them accountable, because violations of trust brought extremely unpleasant consequences at MMI. Disagreement was acceptable, but once a decision was made, mutiny was a mortal sin.

"The prime contractor is a high-tech startup in the Northwest, run by a couple of geniuses who are years ahead of the competition," Trent sat and folded his hands on the table. "One of the two partners has already committed to LACO's vision for the future of virtual reality. The uncommitted partner is in a hospital, dying. That opens some interesting possibilities. The company's called Virtuality Incorporated."

Trent scanned the room. A couple of shrugs, but no head shaking. "As I mentioned, LACO has an in with one of Virtuality's partners and we have one with LACO. I'm drafting a document formalizing our agreement with LACO. You will all have the opportunity to review it before we sign. For now, that's all I'm going to say about the contractor and LACO." He paused. "Are we ready to vote on our new virtual reality venture?"

When they voted, ten minutes later, Trent's proposal won in a *virtual* landslide.

Chapter 7

Confrontational, volatile, intense, fiery, explosive.

Jess had tried to describe the upcoming meeting with Patrick in three words. But three words had become five as she considered Vince's temper. He hadn't been exposed to Patrick's stonewalling tactics. That was about to change.

Vince should be leaving Paul's house in Fairwood, on his way to pick her up for the meeting with Patrick in Snoqualmie. As Jess dressed, events from yesterday replayed, creating something like the delightful aroma near the Cinnabon shop at the mall.

After their discussion at the coffee shop, they had walked the Soos Creek Trail together. Their three-mile walk on the paved trail, lined with lush vegetation, the air filled with the songs of birds and the sun warm on their bare arms and legs, had enticed Jess like the aroma of fresh-baked cinnamon rolls.

Before either had realized it, they were walking through the wetlands hand-in-hand as if the clock had been turned back eight or nine years to a time when Vince and Jess were closer than any two friends she had ever known. But, before they returned to Vince's car, cinnamon rolls had turned to a coiled, hissing serpent. If only she hadn't asked him that question about their senior year of high school.

For several years, their relationship had been heart-to-heart, soul-to-soul with nothing in between. There were no secrets. Jess had assumed it would always be that way. But presumption was probably the greatest breaker of human hearts. Relational expectations became emotional time bombs that exploded into heart-shattering breakups.

Were there ever second chances? Maybe not after one person blows everything to bits. And that person was Vince, not her, wasn't it? Or could Jessica Jamison be so flawed that no good man would want her?

Jess tried to shake off that depressing thought as she slid into her cut-off jeans. She pulled on a tank top and threw a lightweight cotton blouse over it. After pulling on her favorite running shoes, she sauntered into the living room.

There would be no makeup today and no making a spectacle of herself by what she wore.

Outside the living room window of her apartment, Vince's car rolled to a stop.

Jess painted on a smiling face, pulled her locked door closed and prayed for Cinnabon.

Vince stood at the curb, waiting for her with the passenger door open.

As she approached, Jess held her breath and tried to read the expression on his face.

He gave her a crooked smile. "Much better. I know this person."

She blew out her relief. "The frumpy female next-door is back, looking like something the cat dragged—"

"I'm sorry, Jess. Please forgive me for yesterday."

Maybe the Cinnabon prayer had helped. But she had no words for this turn of events.

"No matter what you're wearing, or not wearing, you're beautiful."

"Not wearing? I'm not sure how to take that, Mr. van Gordon."

"I was talking about the make-up."

Vince's brother had just died, and they had serious business matters to discuss with Patrick, but the relational issues between her and Vince were the elephant in the room, dominating everything. They got as far as flirtatious banter, but neither of them seemed willing to go further, to address the giant pachyderm.

What if it trumpeted and charged? That would happen sooner or later. If Vince and Jess didn't voluntarily approach the subject, it would approach them.

Jess slid into the passenger seat with pictures of a charging elephant playing through her mind.

Vince circled the car and took the driver's seat.

Since they hadn't resolved the spat from yesterday, Jess needed something, even a temporary resolution, to avoid being trampled to death by a rogue elephant.

Girl, why don't you just ask Vince for what you really want?

It was worth a try, if she could find the right words. Jess looked up into his eyes. "Vince, can we just start over again? Please?"

"Okay. You go back to your door and come out again, and I'll—"

"No. I mean roll the clock back thirteen years to when we were twelve. You know, to when we were the closest friends ever, and try to go forward from there? The rest never happened. Okay?" It was what Jess wanted, but it sounded crazy and a bit juvenile when she put it into words.

Vince hit the ignition, started the car, then swiveled in his seat to face her. He took his time as his gaze followed a path from her shoes on the floorboard up to her face.

In an instant, her cheeks grew hot. Probably hot pink. She raised a hand to block Vince's view of her face.

"Okay. We start over from twelve. But, Jess ... I'm not looking at a twelve-year-old girl, and there's no way I can pretend that I am."

Great. He had noticed her red face. She reached for the air conditioner control and turned it on full blast.

Vince laid a hand on her shoulder. "See what I mean?"

The air conditioner wasn't helping. Neither was Vince's hand on her shoulder. "We're meeting with Patrick in about forty-five minutes, Columbo. Shouldn't you be planning all those clever questions?"

* * *

The awkward moment had passed. They had set their relational clock back more than a decade. And Vince decided to give Jess some mental space to settle into their new normal while he drove toward Virtuality's lab.

The Virtuality Incorporated offices and laboratory lay about twenty-five miles east of Seattle on the edge of Snoqualmie. The city had been trying to develop the old mill site since Weyerhaeuser moved out more than ten years earlier. The western edge of the property bordered Mill Pond Road which ran along the snow-fed waters of the Snoqualmie River.

Vince swam in the Snoqualmie River as a kid, when he went to a Christian camp near Carnation. Even in August, the temperature of the treacherous water reached only about forty degrees, cold enough to claim several lives each year.

Thirty minutes later, Vince drove his car slowly through the site. Most of the buildings on the property appeared vacant. He pulled into a parking spot near what looked like the entrance to Virtuality's office.

He and Jess got out and Vince offered her his arm.

Jess took it, and they walked toward the main entrance.

Hopefully, the meeting with Patrick would go as smoothly as business transacted between two friendly partners. That's how it had started between Paul and Patrick, supposedly two committed Christians. But Vince had only vague clues about how it had ended, and Paul's clues worried Vince.

The main door opened before they reached it.

Patrick stood several inches shorter than Vince remembered. Patrick shook Vince's hand, but ignored Jess. The short man had gained a few pounds and, apparently, lost his manners.

Jess seemed to take Patrick's rudeness in stride, but Vince had to bite his tongue to stop remarks he would probably regret.

Vince and Jess took seats at Patrick's desk and the conversation began.

Five minutes into their discussion, Patrick was still trying to control the direction and content of the conversation and his tone ... condescending. "Vince, you're an author. You write words, not code, and I don't think you have much interest in software development."

Painting Vince into a corner using Patrick's choice of color—that wasn't going to happen. "Actually, Paul piqued my interest. Virtuality's products could be the wave of the future."

"But there's always risk when you start a new business venture. You can make a lot or lose your shirt." Patrick tugged on the collar of his polo shirt in melodramatic fashion.

Vince chuckled. "Sort of like writing and self-publishing a novel. It's like a box of chocolates. You never—"

"Let me come to the point." Patrick clasped his hands on the desk. "I can remove all risk to you. I'm willing to purchase your share in Virtuality for a fair market value. Our lawyer says, at this stage of development, and with the Army contract partly completed, the company is valued at a little under eight million dollars. That includes our equipment, software ... all our assets. I'm prepared to write you a check for four million dollars. Invest it wisely and you're set for life."

"What about the human assets?"

"Paul's dead. All we have is his intellectual property contained in specifications."

"Specifications that Jess coded."

Patrick pointed a thumb at Jess. "But she's not part of Virtuality. Any of my programmers could have coded Paul's algorithms, using his specs."

Jess had taken everything Patrick dished out in silence, so far. But now her feet shuffled under her chair like she was dancing the Bop to one of those old '50s songs. She wouldn't remain quiet much longer.

And Patrick Michaels was looking more like that bully, Jimmy Grant, with each condescending look and verbal jab he gave Jess.

"Dude ..." Vince reached over the desk and poked an index finger into Patrick's chest. "... I think you need a reality check."

Patrick flinched and leaned back in his chair.

Jess was probably one of a small handful of people on the planet who could have understood and correctly implemented Paul's work. Patrick must realize that. But did Patrick realize how close he was to getting his nose flattened? At the moment, knowing how much Jess disliked Vince's bad temper was the only thing saving Patrick.

Vince looked across the desk and studied the short man's face.

Eyes darting, beads of sweat on his upper lip—Patrick knew something was about to happen. He certainly didn't have the composure of a good poker player.

Vince hadn't had an opportunity to examine Virtuality's books. He'd only glanced at a bank statement he found at Paul's house that indicated the company's available cash was far less than four million dollars. This was the perfect time to bluff.

Vince glared at Patrick. "I have it on good authority that Virtuality only has about a million dollars in the bank. A check for four million—where's that coming from?"

A shadow flickered across Patrick's face and the knuckles of his clasped hands turned white. "Uh, it's from ... investors, venture capitalists."

Jess scooted her chair toward the table. "If you bring in venture capitalists, you'll end up with less than the forty-nine percent of the company you now own. Why would you want to do that?"

She was one step ahead of Vince. He wanted to give her a smile and thumbs up but opted for silence and the opportunity to watch Patrick stew in Jess's insinuation. She had either called him a liar or implied he was stupid. Either way it seemed to fit.

Patrick cleared his throat and opened his mouth.

Jess cut him off. "Maybe you've found a creative way to acquire the venture capital, one that doesn't force you to give up controlling interest."

"Something like that." Patrick's bushy eyebrows pinched closed. "But, Jessica, I didn't invite you to this meeting. Vince is a big boy. He can handle his own interests without a wom—uh, without your help"

Compared to Jess's intelligence, Patrick was Forrest Gump minus his box of chocolates and his platitudes. And Vince had heard enough from this guy. He balled his fists and stood, ready to get in Patrick's face.

Jess's hand clamped on his wrist and tugged. She wore her enigmatic smile, a look that had meant trouble for Jess's adversaries since she was eight years old. And, as he'd just reminded himself, she was smarter than Patrick.

Vince sat, challenging Patrick to a staring contest.

The short man must have felt the daggers coming from Vince. Patrick rolled his chair back from his desk, eyes darting between Vince and Jess.

Maybe a little intimidation went a long way with this guy. In that case ...

"Here's how it is. I'm not selling, Patrick. I retain controlling interest in Virtuality. That's my best and final offer. And I don't want to hear yours."

Patrick clutched the front of his polo shirt tight enough to pop off the buttons. "You're going to regret this, Vince. You've made a bad decision, a very bad decision." His attempt at a fierce expression looked more like a pouting child's face.

Vince stood and gave Jess his hand.

She took it, stood beside him and nodded toward Patrick.

"Come on, Jess. I think his meeting's over."

* * *

Jess hurried out the door of Patrick's office, hoping Vince would follow her, not turn around and beat the stuffing out of the stuffed polo shirt. She shot a glance at Paul's car that Vince had driven this morning.

A tall skinny man in work coveralls, like janitors and mechanics wore, walked away across the large, mostly vacant parking lot. He headed toward a building on the far side.

Vince nudged her toward the car. "Let's get out of here, Jess, before I lose patience with that stuffed polo shirt."

Stuffed polo shirt. Jess smiled as she opened the passenger door. Vince and Jess had always thought alike about people and important issues, except one. At that thought, she stopped smiling.

Vince slid in and started the engine. It idled roughly then sputtered and died. He restarted it and pulled out of the parking spot, headed toward the highway.

"Jess, do you know where I can get my hands on a copy of the partnership agreement between Paul and Patrick?"

"Paul probably kept a copy of the contract in the safe at his house. Why? Are you thinking, like me, that Patrick would do just about anything to gain control of Virtuality?"

"He would never have offered me four million dollars, at this juncture, unless he knew he could make a fortune. Someone must be guaranteeing his success. Someone like the people Paul feared would abuse the technology. And maybe that's the danger Paul referred to. But how would that endanger you?"

Vince turned onto Highway 202 and headed toward North Bend.

"I don't know if it could endanger me, but Paul did give me zero-point-nine percent of the company. It was part of his payment for coding his algorithms. But that still left him in control." She paused and mentally shoved the decimal point seven places to the right, then rounded up. "If Virtuality turns out to be a billion-dollar business, that would give me a cool ten million. I could retire and write novels."

"Jesse James an author? That'll be the day."

Vince went silent as he drove. Probably cooling off after nearly losing his temper. He didn't speak again until they had exited from I-90 onto Highway 18, a highway that bypassed Seattle far to the east.

Highway 18 climbed part of Tiger Mountain then descended through the foothills of the Cascades to the Puget Sound Basin, rejoining I-5 fifteen miles south of Seattle. It was the shortest route to both Fairwood and Jess's apartment in Kent.

Near Tiger Summit, Vince glanced her way. "I don't think Paul meant financial danger. If that were the case, he wouldn't have looked so frightened."

"Frightened? Even facing death, that doesn't sound like Paul."

"Jess, Paul knew where he was going after he died. He must have been afraid of something happening to us."

"Your brother was seldom wrong. If we could track the four million dollars to its source, we would probably find the source of the danger."

As they topped Tiger Summit and began their descent, Vince eyes widened, and he jammed on the brakes.

But the car kept going.

Jess watched Vince's foot, but couldn't feel the brakes engaging.

Instead, the engine revved and the car accelerated.

Vince shoved the gear shift lever into neutral.

"What are you doing, Vince?"

The engine wound up until it roared.

"Anything I can think of. Hang on."

The roar turned to a high-pitched whine.

A muffled pop sounded.

Now the engine sounded like an old lawnmower.

The noise stopped.

The car slowed, but Vince fought the steering wheel like it had a life of its own.

"Vince, what's happening?"

"I think the engine just blew and died. That cut the power steering. The brakes feel solid, but no matter how hard I push on the pedal, they don't work."

"There are concrete barriers on both sides. No place to pull off for a couple of miles. "

"Better pray I can horse this crippled car through the curves without power steering. It should stop at the bottom of the hill, near the big intersection with Hobart-Issaquah Road. I'll use the emergency brake if I need to."

With her panic subsiding, the mental image of the man in service coveralls walking away from the car replayed. "Vince, somebody messed with this car."

"What do you mean by messed with?"

"My best guess—with all the high-tech gadgets and connectivity in Paul's car, I'd say it was hacked."

"Come on, Jess. It's me that writes thrillers and has an overactive imagination."

"Bet you four million dollars."

Vince appeared to be digesting her proposition while he manhandled the steering wheel. "No. Patrick wouldn't do something like this. I'll bet your point-nine percent of the company that he didn't."

"No deal, van Gordon. I don't want to cause you to lose controlling interest in Virtuality. And I think you should keep your interest on controlling this car."

"I've got the car under control."

The car slowed as they approached the bottom of the mountain.

"Besides, I like owning a piece of Vince van Gordon. So I'm keeping my point-nine percent."

Vince didn't reply, but he managed to maneuver the car onto the wide shoulder near Hobart-Issaquah Road.

The car stopped.

He blew out a breath and slumped in the seat. "I guess it's time to call Triple A."

"After that, you need to call the local dealer's service department. As soon as you get someone on the line, give me your phone."

Vince turned off the ignition and looked her way. "But why give you—"

"Don't ask. Just do it, Vince."

Chapter 8

Jess and Vince slid into the car Vince had rented and she looked at the controls on the dash trying to determine how hackable the new car might be.

Jess had read about a few car hacking incidents in the IT trade journals. The only thing that would account for Paul's car's behavior was firmware changes made to chips on the Engine Control Module (ECM). That board was the car's equivalent to the operating system of a computer. Seizing control of the ECM would give a hacker complete control over all the digitally controlled systems of the vehicle.

After Vince called the dealer to tell them Paul's car was being towed in, he handed Jess his phone.

She gave several suggestions to the car dealer's service department person for finding evidence of hacking. The discussion left her with an uneasy feeling about the competence of the dealer's mechanics to diagnose any sort of hacking.

If the American automobile industry didn't get serious in a hurry, the lives and well-being of many Americans would be put at risk due to the industry's negligence.

For over a year, Jess had read IT Industry reports of car-hacking tools for sale to anyone with enough money to buy them and the gumption to try using them to take control of a vehicle.

If she was right about the close call they'd had a couple of hours ago, what might have been the intent of the hacker? The hacker could have killed them if he or she had sufficient skills and a motive. On the other hand, maybe the people behind this had only wanted to scare Vince into selling. Murder might not be the organization's preferred *modus operandi*.

Vince pulled his hand from the wheel of his newly rented car and nudged Jess. "A penny for your thoughts."

"So now you want a piece of my mind?"

The look she got from Vince said he was interested in more than just her mind. Whatever his interest, it didn't matter unless it was enough to bring Vince home, permanently.

He looked her way, shook his head, and refocused on the road. "I keep wondering what would've happened if I had been killed when the car went berserk."

Jess wouldn't dwell on that. Couldn't dwell on it. Her life would be over. She would never be as close to another human being again as she had once been to Vince. She didn't want to be close to anyone else. And if she didn't stop dwelling on the past, she would end up crying again.

"If you're talking about the business implications of a death, we need to see that partnership agreement between Paul and Patrick."

The clock on the dash said 12:30 p.m. "Vince, how about getting some lunch then looking in Paul's safe? That is ... if you don't mind taking me home with you."

Her remark drew another warm look from Vince. "Take you home ... does that mean I get to keep you?"

"What do you think?" She gave him her enigmatic smile.

"I think I'm gonna watch Jesse James crack a safe this afternoon."

That wasn't the answer she was hoping for. "And maybe I can watch while you amputate your ear."

"Jess, I—"

Vince's phone rang.

He glanced at the cup holder on the console, where he'd placed it. "See who that is, Jess?"

She picked up the cell and read the display. "It's the car dealer's service department."

"You're the one who wanted to talk to them."

Jess picked up the call.

"Is this Vince van Gordon?"

"He's driving right now. I'm the person who—"

"Yeah. We remember. The computer security whiz. Or is it hacker?"

"What did you find? Did someone flash the ECM's EEPROM?"

"You mean update the firmware?"

"That's what I asked." Jess shook her head and rolled her eyes, not that anyone could see.

"Yes. A chip on the ECM was updated."

This is what she had expected, but they needed to identify and catch the culprits. "Please, don't do anything that might change the firmware on any of the chips on that board. We'll need the FBI and maybe US-CERT to investigate where these hacks came from and, if possible, determine who made them."

"Look, lady ... I can't just call in the Feds and whoever else it was that you mentioned. I don't have—"

"Don't worry. I'll call them. Just don't let anyone mess with that board."

"I've got the board on my desk right now."

"Lock it up for safekeeping. I'll call the proper authorities. We've got to stop this before it becomes widespread and puts you out of business. That's exactly what will happen if you can't guarantee that your customers won't get their cars hacked."

"Jess, what's up?"

"Wait a sec, Vince ... look, doofus, you will lock up that board or an FBI agent is going to show up in a few minutes and spew hot lava all over you and your boss. Do you understand?"

"I understand, Ms. Hacker. Computer geeks—can't live without'em anymore."

"Thanks. We'll have the authorities contact you." She ended the call.

"That sounded ominous."

She nodded. "Paul's car was hacked, and I might have a description of the man who did it."

"What? How did—"

"Vince, when we left Patrick's office, I saw a skinny guy with wild-looking, red hair, dressed in white coveralls, walking away from Paul's car. He reminded me of one of those Three Stooges."

"Sounds like Larry. But, if he could hack a car, it wasn't one of the Three Stooges."

"While you drive us home, I'm going to call the FBI, Seattle Division Cyber Security Task Force. I wonder if they've ever investigated an attempted cyber murder?"

* * *

While Vince rolled the rental car down the steep driveway at Paul's house, Jess still had the phone planted in her ear, talking with someone at the Seattle Field Office.

After he shut off the engine, the car heated quickly on this blistering July day. Vince rolled down the windows and sat in the car listening to Jess's end of the conversation.

Jess mentioned car-hacking tools for sale on the Dark Web, whatever that was. With some mysterious, less than ethical people involved, Paul was probably right about the danger he'd mentioned.

Jess ended the call. "Interesting."

"To you maybe. But it was all geek to me."

"Punny, Vince. Very punny. But the Seattle FBI is chomping at the bit to investigate their first car hack attack."

Vince opened his door. "Let's get into Paul's safe and find that partnership contract."

Jess's mention of Paul brought back the fact that Vince was staying in Paul's house, had been driving his car, sat beside the woman who loved Paul, all with Paul's memorial service scheduled for tomorrow morning. Vince had usurped his brother's place in the world, the place of the incredible man whose shadow had covered Vince most of his life. Would anyone ever recognize Vince as someone other than Paul van Gordon's little brother?

He glanced at Jess, walking beside him up the wide steps to the front door of the big house. If only Vince were her first choice, he would never feel guilty about loving her. With Jess in his life, Vince could simply remember Paul as the good and great man he was, instead of the man who had stolen the happily ever after from Vince's life.

It's high school all over again, dude?

Not if Vince could help it.

Inside the house, the air was hot, still and suffocating. "I'm going to open some windows and the slider. See if you can open Paul's safe."

"I'll need to find the combination first. I met with Paul here to discuss my work contract. He opened his safe to get some papers he needed. He'd hidden the combination in a box on the top shelf of his office closet."

Vince smiled. "As brilliant as my brother was, he couldn't remember simple things like phone numbers."

"And safe combinations," Jess said as she headed down the long hallway.

Five minutes later, Vince walked into Paul's office and plopped down in the desk chair, watching the pleasant sight of Jess standing on the top level of a stepstool.

She had taken off her outer shirt, shucked her shoes, and she stood barefoot in denim shorts and a tank top, rummaging through boxes.

Jess went up on her tip toes, reaching for the back of the closet. "Paul was a bad filer at his work office. Apparently, even worse in his home office."

The calf muscles of her shapely legs flexed as she tiptoed, revealing a level of muscular development one would never suspect from a slender, five-foot-eight woman.

She shoved a box to the back of the shelf. "The box in the back looked like the one Paul used. But it isn't."

"Jess, do that again."

She turned on the step to face Vince. "Do what again?" Jess gave him a bug-eyed stare. "You weren't checking me out, were you?"

"I was just—"

"Vince, you had eighteen years to do that. If you'd found what you were looking for, I would have known."

But she didn't know and now was not the time to tell her. "I just noticed you've got a lot of leg muscle."

"I'm not the feminine, girlie type, remember?"

He scanned her body slowly, trying to get a rise out of Jess. That didn't work, so he tried what he did best, use words. "Five-feet-seven or eight, slender—you look like the feminine type."

"But I'm not, see?" She turned a three-sixty on the foot stool, then put her hands on her hips. "Wanna try me?"

"I'm not sure how to take that." Vince smirked. "What if I say yes?"

Her face turned pink. "Vince, I'm a tomboy. If anyone knows that, it should be you. I climb rocks. I even took some martial arts classes and won a board-breaking competition."

"Oh. How many boards did you break?"

"It's not just the number of boards you break, it's how. It's about style."

"So how many did you break with style?"

"Six in one jump. Two sets of three. One set with my right foot, the other with my left." Jess still stood on the top step, displaying a perfect specimen of the human female body.

His gaze dropped to her board-breaking legs.

"Would you stop staring at my legs? It makes me feel like ... like that time you caught me in my underwear."

"Which time was that?" Vince curled his smirking lips further.

"When kids spend as much time together as we did, there aren't many secrets. You and Paul were my best friends. We did everything together, until Paul outgrew us. Then it was you and me."

Her voice turned to a raspy whisper and broke. Jess stepped down from the footstool, and walked toward him, brushing her cheeks. "I guess we'll have to look somewhere else for the combination to the safe."

One thought of Paul had brought tears to Jess's eyes. He opened his arms to her.

Jess stepped into them, returning his embrace in a way that suggested more than friendship.

But he must be mistaken, unless Jess had begun substituting him for Paul.

And why would she do that, dude?

Because she has no other options.

Chapter 9

Trent had raided various funds in MMI's accounts to come up with the four million dollars he had made available to LACO to offer to Vince van Gordon. Hopefully, it had been enough to persuade the young author to sell Virtuality, a company of which he had little or no understanding.

If he took the money, Vince could retire and write novels to his heart's content. What bright young man would refuse that kind of offer?

Like van Gordon, Trent had been a bright young man once, but no one had ever offered him an opportunity to stop working, except when he'd been fired by a large Hollywood movie studio after a movie deal went sour. The only place he'd found work was making adult movies. But taking the job with MMI had cost Trent his wife and two kids.

Emily didn't want to be associated with a producer of pornography, so she took his two boys and ran. He had never seen nor heard from her since. But he had found where she lived.

With the wealth MMI's virtual reality venture promised, Trent would make her rue the day she left. He could lure his kids away from their mother with all the things he could offer them. And the boys were in their late teens, the perfect luring age.

Maybe money couldn't buy happiness, but it could buy satisfaction ... and revenge. All Trent needed was for Mr. Michaels to deliver on his promises to LACO.

If things had gone as planned, Patrick Michaels should have made the offer to Vince sometime earlier today. But it was 6:00 p.m. and Trent had heard nothing.

He slipped his laptop in its case, along with two half-completed business plans. As he locked his desk, preparing to call it a day, *New York, New York* sounded from his cell.

Russo? Or was it one of the new hires from New York?

"Del Valle here."

"Del Valle, this is Sal Romano. How are you today?"

"Suppose you tell me, Sal."

"You referring to the meeting between Michaels and van Gordon?"

"Yes, I'm waiting for you to give me the good news." It couldn't be good news. Romano would have blurted it out instead of beating around the bush.

"Our contact at LACO streamed the video of the meeting to us. There were some surprises."

Trent didn't like surprises. He played favorable odds and even interfered, when necessary, to improve the odds. And legality seldom played into his decisions to interfere. It was beginning to sound like this deal with Virtuality would require a little interference.

"I take it that Mr. van Gordon didn't like our offer."

"No. But there's a lot more to it than that, Mr. Del Valle. van Gordon got mad and said he was keeping the company. Him taking the four mil—you can forget about that. He more or less told Patrick Michaels what he could do with the money. But the babe van Gordon had on his arm is sharp and she's dangerous. She influences him. One look at her and you would understand why. I'm thinking van Gordon and her have a long history. Closer than close, if you know what I mean."

Sal had rambled on enough for Trent to get a feel for the man's perceptiveness. The guy was sharp enough to cut him a little slack. "So are you recommending a course of action?"

"Yeah. We can try some intimidation and see if van Gordon reconsiders. In fact, we already have."

Already tried intimidation? "Look, Sal. I'm the one giving the orders for anything we do to van Gordon."

"I know that, sir. But Russo said our job description included a little muscle or intimidation. We were just opening the door in case that was needed."

"So you didn't actually threaten van Gordon?"

"Not directly."

"And what's that supposed to mean? Out with it, Sal. What did you and your two friends do?"

"When Vince and the babe went into Virtuality's building, we updated the firmware on his car's ECM."

"Are you saying that you hacked his car?"

"Yeah. But we could activate problems with the car or not, depending on what was needed. When the meeting went sour, we activated the hack and took control of the engine and braking system. Gave him and the girl a bad scare."

"You might have killed him. Then where would we be? That's why you only act on my orders. Got that, Romano?"

"Loud and clear, sir. But it seems the car incident didn't bring van Gordon around. So maybe, with your approval of course, the best way to convince Van Gordon to sell is to use the girl to get to him."

"Tell me about this girl."

"Her name is Jessica Jamison. She has a Master's in Computer Science and she did some programming for Vince's brother a few months ago. So she knows a little about Virtuality. She's not just sorta smart, she's beautiful and she's a genius. Eliminate her and you remove a big problem. But Vince is a hothead. He'd never sell if we eliminated the girl. Threaten her, however, and Vince might play ball with us. Just a thought."

"Hold that thought, Sal. Let me think about this development and I'll get back to you."

Trent ended the call and laid his cell on the desk.

His whole plan could be jeopardized by van Gordon's refusal to sell. Yes, they could try to get to him through the girl. That was a valid option. But perhaps he should try another approach, a bold one.

What would happen if Vince van Gordon were to die in an accident? It wasn't as clean as him selling out to Patrick Michaels, who would cooperate with LACO. Nevertheless, Trent would have his attorneys check out the legal ramifications of van Gordon's death, including any business contract between Virtuality's two partners.

In the meantime, close surveillance might reveal the nature of Vince's relationship with Jessica Jamison. And that could tell Trent how Vince would react if some dreadful turn of events were to place Ms. Jamison in danger.

He picked up his cell, opened the call log, and hit reply on the top entry.

Chapter 10

At ten o'clock the next morning, Vince sat in the front row of Faith Community Church.

Jess, the woman with no other options, sat beside him.

In the left front corner of the large sanctuary packed with people, less than twenty-five feet away, lay a closed casket containing the body of the finest man Vince had ever known.

A large picture of Paul, standing among a group of kids, sat on top of the casket. Taped to the side of the casket was a paper banner with bold writing on it.

I'm not here. Make sure you know where you'll be when you're not here.

Paul's idea and Paul's words. No doubt about it.

Pastor Harding stepped to the pulpit where he would give a room full of friends, people that Paul's life had touched, even more reasons why Vince belonged in Paul's shadow.

The pastor spread his notes out on the podium and the murmurs in the church sanctuary turned silent. "Five days ago, I had a good visit with Paul van Gordon. Paul held to a strong, biblical worldview. In fact, his biblical view of the nature of man led to discoveries which became the technology that brought his company success. Stating Paul's view simply—because that's the only way I can even attempt to understand it—the human mind is only an interface to the real person. Our self-awareness, our identity, and our volition are not physical, but spiritual.

No part of the real Paul van Gordon is in this room. That truth enabled Paul's technological breakthrough. He assured me of it, but please don't expect me to explain that to you."

Put in this context, Paul's words to Vince in the CCU made sense. Vince leaned toward Jess. "This is what Paul wanted me to remember and, eventually, to understand."

Pastor Harding continued. "Let me try to sum up the second part of my conversation with Paul by starting with this question. Why are we here this morning?" The pastor paused for several seconds. "Let's put aside, for the moment, the purpose of honoring this young man's life." He paused. "Now, having done that, I'll ask the question again. As human beings, why are we here?" Pastor Harding paused again.

"If we were wolves, we would sniff, smell death, and go on without a member of our pack. If we were chickens and one of our flock became Sunday dinner, we would hardly notice. If we were vultures, we—maybe we won't go there."

Soft laughter sounded throughout the sanctuary.

The pastor waited until the room quieted. "But we are human beings, the only creature that prepares its dead for something else, for something that comes next. Our being here represents a rebellion against death. We can't stand the thought of death and we fight it literally to the death. James Loder said these words, 'We will not let death have the last word. This is a mark of the human spirit that something in us knows we can overcome this thing.'"

"How do we know this? Isn't it because our creator so loved us, His creatures, that He came and lived among us—Jesus Christ, our hope and light. Christ came. Christ died. Christ rose again. And He said, by relying on Him, we could also rise again. He is our sure hope. And so Paul van Gordon gives us these words, 'I'm not here. Make sure you know where you'll be when you're not here.'"

"Now, for the other reason we're here this morning, to celebrate the life of a man who truly fit the adage larger than life ..."

Pastor Harding continued, enumerating the accolades of Vince's brother—genius, entrepreneur, philanthropist, model Christian. Quality upon quality, deed upon deed, he presented the evidence convicting Vince that he didn't measure up. That he never would. And that Jess was right to prefer Paul.

But Jess couldn't have Paul. And Vince didn't deserve a woman like Jess. The pastor's eulogy made that clear. So he and Jess would both lose. How had their happy beginning as kids ended this way?

That question became a gloomy cloud, darkening Vince's thoughts. It had taken Paul's death to reveal the truth. Vince was an inferior van Gordon, not up to van Gordon standards and he never would be. Even his writing reflected that. His agent couldn't sell his latest novel. Publishers didn't buy inferior stories from an author wannabe.

He leaned forward, propping his forehead on his hand.

Fingers slid under his other hand and curled around it.

Did Jess know? Could she read his mind? Vince had never once told her how worthless and meaningless he felt living in Paul's shadow. But, like Paul, Jess was a genius. And she read people better than Vince could.

Jess interlaced her fingers with his and squeezed.

He raised his head and looked her way, his eyes welling.

No tears in Jess's eyes, only warmth, compassion and something else he couldn't interpret. If she loved Paul, wouldn't this service be as heart-rending for her as it was for Vince? Where were her tears for Paul?

Before he could answer his question, the room went

silent.

What had he missed?

Jess leaned against him. "You need to say something, Vince," she whispered. "You're his only living relative in this room."

The pastor must've opened it up for people to share about Paul. Vince sat up straight and looked at Jess.

She nodded and pushed up on his hand.

While Jess smiled at him with dry eyes, Vince's eyes overflowed. He wiped his cheeks as he stood.

Jess still held his hand and she squeezed, letting him know she intended to keep it.

But Vince offered her his other hand.

She took it.

He turned to face the audience. Vince cleared his throat and waited until the lump stopped choking him. "My brother, Paul, was the finest man I've ever known. He left a mighty big set of shoes to fill. But just before he died, he asked me—no, he told me I needed to try to fill them."

Someone in the back row stood and hurried out of the sanctuary. Patrick. He'd probably heard enough, though Vince had already told Patrick this bit of news, using some sharper words.

Vince cleared his throat again. "So I'd like to ask for your prayers to help me carry out Paul's last request, because those shoes are feeling awfully big right now." Vince's voice broke on the last word. He turned and sat beside Jess.

She pulled his head against her neck and held him as sorrow and regret, mixed with fear and doubt, ran down Jess's neck.

Others spoke.

Vince didn't hear their words.

Sometime later, he lifted his head.

Jess's neck and blouse were wet, and her eyes filled with unshed tears when she smiled at him. She had absorbed his sorrow.

For the moment, they seemed to be two kids again, the closest of friends, heart-to-heart, soul-to-soul, nothing in between. He wished that moment could last for the rest of Vince van Gordon's life.

Jess leaned close to him. "This is the way it used to be. Remember?"

* * *

Jess made sure she stuck to Vince's side through the rest of the memorial service and the short graveside service that followed. On this day, Vince needed her, and he seemed to realize that. Would he need her beyond this day of sorrow? Would the glimpse into their past, a look back to a time when two hearts had been one, change anything? Or would Vince, eventually, return to Denver?

She had to let Vince make that decision. But Jess wouldn't make it easy for him to leave again.

After the graveside service, Vince and Jess had lunch at a local deli. There, Vince's protective shield had gone up again. Through the two services and most of their lunch, it had been down.

The Vince of her childhood, the only person who would bare his soul to Jessica Jamison, had returned for nearly two hours. She would've gladly told him she loved that Vince, but words about love and lifetime commitments would not be discussed until Vince could tell her truthfully that he loved her and wanted her, not just as a friend, but also as a lover and a wife.

Vince pushed back his chair from the deli table and reach out a hand. "Time to meet with Monahan."

She took Vince's hand and waited until he met her gaze. "Are you ready for this? We could postpone it."

"I'm ready. Thanks to you, Jess. We couldn't get into

Paul's safe to read that partnership agreement. But it's probably better to let a lawyer tell us if there are any surprises in Paul's and Patrick's contract."

Vince led her out to his car and opened the door.

She stopped before sliding in. "There's more to this meeting than that agreement."

"What do you mean?"

"I'm guessing that you're the sole beneficiary of Paul's estate. Well, all except what he gave away to the home and the church."

"The home? What's that?"

She slid in. "I'll tell you about it sometime. But, right now, we need to examine our legal weapons of warfare against Patrick. Did you see how he left the service when you—"

"I saw it. When I said I'd be trying to fill Paul's shoes, he left to rally his troops."

"Or maybe his hackers?"

Vince circled the car and slid in the driver's seat. "I hope not. After all, Paul and Patrick were once good friends who became business partners. And Patrick is, supposedly, a Christian."

"But that type of business relationship, partnership, has ended many a friendship."

"Yeah. But, Jess…" he waited for her to look at him, then took her hand. The warm look in Vince's eyes and his set jaw told her that the font of their conversation had just changed … to bold italics.

"Yes." She whispered, then held her breath.

"Nothing can ever do that to our friendship. I won't let that happen again, ever. I promise."

Friendship. One down, two to go. But would Vince's feelings for her ever include the whole package, lover and wife? Her worst fear was that nobody could feel that way about Jessica Jamison. The man she loved more than life

VIRTUALITY

hadn't yet been able to do that. But his bold, italicized words had given Jess a measure of hope. But all he had promised her was to be her friend.

* * *

At half past one, Jess and Vince sat side-by-side in a small law office across a round conference table from Daniel Monahan, Paul's lawyer, a fifty-something man with a kindly face and eyes that radiated intelligence.

The warmth coming from Jess had cooled over the last half hour. What had Vince done and how could he get it back?

One thing had become clear today, he wanted Jess in his life. But she wasn't something that Paul could pass on to Vince in a will. First, Jess had to—he needed to focus on Monahan's words. His future, and probably Jess's, might depend on the legal matters at hand.

Monahan put on his reading glasses, sorted some papers lying in front of him, and placed a legal-size document on top. "Since Paul left his share of Virtuality to you, Vince, you now own fifty-one percent, controlling interest."

"But Jess owns nine-tenths of a percent."

"I stand corrected. You own fifty-point-one percent." Monahan looked at the papers that lay in front of him. He pulled another one out and placed it on top. "The agreement between Paul and Patrick says that Paul's beneficiaries can inherit his interest in the company ... if Paul has a will. Paul had a will, therefore the transfer of ownership to you is uncontestable. But, if the partner doesn't have a will, the agreement says the surviving partner can purchase the deceased partner's share of the company at a fair market value as assessed by a financial organization approved by the National Association of Certified Valuation Analysts. The money goes to whomever the court awards the deceased's estate. You don't have a will do you, Vince?"

"How do you know that?"

"I don't, but your lawyer called and—"

"My lawyer? I don't have a lawyer. Haven't needed one so far, because I can rely on the legal counsel of my agent and my publisher."

"Vince ..." Jess blew out a blast of air. "Their spying on you."

"Who?"

"Patrick and the people backing him."

"Maybe. But let me get this straight, Dan. If I die, Patrick gets controlling interest?"

Daniel Monahan folded his hands in front of him on the table. "He gets complete ownership, providing he can pay the assessed value."

Jess laid her hand on Vince's. "Patrick thinks Virtuality is worth eight million dollars, and he thinks he has the money to buy out Vince."

Vince locked gazes with Monahan. "Paul told me not to sell the company under any conditions. So here's what I want you to do, Dan. Draw up a will that gives my interest in Virtuality and everything else I own, my book rights, my royalties, everything, to Jess."

"No, Vince." She shook her head, sending her long, dark hair whipping her cheeks.

"Jess, you're the best person, the nearest thing to—no, you *are* family." Vince turned toward Monahan. "Can you draw up something quickly? We've already had one close call and now someone is spying on me."

"A close call?" Monahan slid his reading glasses down his nose and peered over the top. "Are you saying there's been an attempt on your life?"

Jess blew out another blast of air. "It sure looks that way. But it could have been a warning instead of attempted murder."

Vince pounded a fist on the table. "Patrick knew about the stipulation in the contract. Jess, he's trying to—"

"Vince, you don't know that. There's a third party involved, the people with the money. We don't know who they are or what they're up to ... other than wanting Patrick to be in control of Virtuality."

"Monahan, draw up the will and I'll sign it as soon as it's ready. I'm going to have a talk with Patrick and I want to see what's going on in my lab. That will tell us what's really at stake here. It will tell us what Virtuality has that would make people murder to get it."

"Vince, they could have killed us both yesterday. In that case, even with a will, Patrick would still get Virtuality. A will isn't foolproof protection."

Jess was right, but he needed to end all the mystery surrounding the company. "All the more reason that I need to see Patrick."

"Then I'm going with you. No way will I let you go out there alone." She looked at the lawyer. "Monahan, please draw up a will for me too? I want to leave everything I own to Vince. And, if he's ... if Vince is dead, I want everything I own to go to Harold Scholes."

Vince shot her a glance. "Who's Harold Scholes?"

"A missionary in Cambodia. He's also the director of the home."

Vince opened his mouth to speak.

Jess cut him off. "I said I'd tell you about it later."

"And your wills will be ready to sign ..." Monahan looked at his tablet computer sitting beside the stack of papers. "The day after tomorrow."

* * *

Jess glanced at the clock on Vince's rental car. 2:45 p.m. He'd had a lead foot all the way out to Snoqualmie, and she hadn't been able to calm Vince down.

Since Jess was a young girl, she'd hated seeing Vince

lose his cool. It had seldom happened. But, when it had, it usually had something to do with her, and it had occasionally resulted in someone getting their face smashed. The person had always deserved it. But still …

If Vince pounded Patrick, like he had the teenage kid who said lewd things to Jess, Vince could find himself in jail. An arrest, even without a conviction, might prevent him from getting a Top-Secret clearance. Not a good thing for the CEO of a company that develops Top Secret products for the military.

After they arrived, Vince got out and strode toward the front door that opened into the lobby. Patrick's office was on one side of the lobby and the entry to the lab on the other. Thankfully, the lab had a cipher lock on the door. Otherwise, Vince might barge in and soon find himself locked up in Leavenworth.

Jess hurried to catch him.

Patrick stood in the doorway of his office, looking like he was blocking the entrance. Evidently, he'd seen them drive up.

"Patrick, since I'm the new majority owner of Virtuality, I want to inspect my company. First, I want to—"

"You want to see the lab. Who would have guessed." Patrick still blocked the door to his office.

Vince turned away from Patrick, walked to the lab door, and fiddled with the cipher lock.

The entry door to the lab was not the place to start this discussion. A war, maybe. But, if a war looked likely, Jess would insert herself before things got ugly.

Vince looked Patrick's way. "Well, are you going to open this door, or—"

"Can't do that. The equipment, the system, its design, and specifications are all classified. Top Secret. You have no clearance and no need to know."

"I'm the owner. Of course I have a need to know."

Patrick sneered at Vince. "Not according to DOD regulations, and I'm the security officer for this facility. If you violate security, I will be forced to call my DOD supervisor, General McCheney. Vince, you don't want the military or the FBI coming after you, certainly not with the security concerns our nation has right now. They would lock you up and throw away the key."

Patrick's warnings seemed to have taken away some of Vince's anger. But this afternoon was far from over, and Vince could be a bulldog when he sank his teeth into something.

Jess hurried to Vince's side. "You know, Vince will need the same level of clearance as Paul had. What does he need to do get it?"

Patrick gave her a crooked smile. "Fill out the forms and I'll submit them."

The scowl on Vince's face faded. "How long will that take?"

"Last time I checked, Top-Secret clearances were taking six months to a year."

Vince's scowl came back, and he took a step toward Patrick.

Jess hooked Vince's arm. "While I was doing research at the U, we sometimes got temporary clearances on an *ad hoc* basis. They didn't take six months."

"You must mean Interim Security Eligibility. That still takes favorable completion of a minimum investigation. I'll check on it."

Vince glared at Patrick. "You do that. And Jess will need eligibility too."

"Why her?"

"Because she's my assistant, my advisor for all technical matters at Virtuality Incorporated. That's why."

"If you say so. Tomorrow I'll check on the requirements

for interim eligibility."

Jess pulled Vince away from Patrick. "Come on, Vince. We wouldn't want to make Patrick call the general."

The lab door swung open.

Vince and Jess turned toward it.

A twenty-something man walked in wearing a strange looking suit with a hat-like contraption that partially covered his head.

Patrick's eyes widened. "Walker, I told you—"

"Patrick ..." The man continued walking toward Patrick. "You said if I took a cut in pay, you'd give me more—"

"Not here, Walker. In my office." Patrick turned toward Vince. "Good afternoon, Mr. van Gordon."

Walker entered the office and Patrick closed the door behind them.

"Wait a minute, Vince." Jess opened and then firmly closed the lobby door. She tiptoed to Patrick's office door.

Vince tried to follow, but she waved him back.

The suit, the head contraption, digitized nerve data transferred using Paul's algorithms, the algorithms she had coded—a picture began to form. Though fuzzy, the picture gave her bad vibes that sent a chill through her shoulders and up the back of her neck. Jess pressed her ear to the door, listening to see if her suspicions about Walker were correct.

Walker argued with Patrick—something about more time. The young man sounded like he was losing it. Almost like—she shuddered.

Jess had seen and heard druggies exhibit the same characteristics as Walker. What in heaven's name was going on in that lab? Or was it more like in hell's name?

Patrick said something about giving Walker more time. But the conversation behind the door grew too soft to hear. The confrontation might be ending.

Jess pointed toward the main entry door and mouthed, "Hurry."

She slipped out the door behind Vince and closed it.

They got in the car and Vince drove across the parking area and toward the road.

At the far edge of the parking lot, Jess looked back at the lab door. It remained closed. "Vince, that guy, Walker, gave me bad vibes. What did you think about him?"

"Looked like a geek to me. Probably a programmer. Didn't care for his geek outfit though. What did you hear through the door?"

"Maybe my imagination is just running wild. But I'd almost swear there are some horribly vile things going down in the lab, things the Army needs to know about." And things that Vince and I need to stop.

"Like what? Did you hear something?"

"It sounded like Virtuality might be doing more than what's in the Army contract. Maybe trying to develop other products at the Army's expense."

Vince turned onto the Snoqualmie Parkway, headed toward Highway 18. "That's why we need to get into the lab. Any ideas about how we do that without ending up in the federal pen and losing the Army contract?"

"From what I've heard, an interim clearance, in your situation, is almost automatic. It shouldn't take long."

"Automatic?"

"You're squeaky clean, Vince. It should be automatic."

"But, Jess, you weren't with me for the past seven years. You don't know what—"

"Yes, I do. I know you're squeaky clean or I wouldn't be here sitting beside you."

Vince's mouth dropped open as realization flashed in his eyes. "You didn't—"

"But I did." She gave Vince her enigmatic smile, the one that used to drive him crazy. "I hacked WSU's administration system and verified my suspicions about your college years, then ran a background check on you. You cost me twenty-five dollars, but you came out clean."

"Did you think I wouldn't? And why were you so interested in me that you would—"

"Not now, Vince." Jess lowered her voice. "When the time is right, we can have that discussion."

Vince's sigh could have been in relief or from frustration. After seven years, Jess couldn't tell. At least he had cooled off. "Back to your clearance. What I did when I checked up on you was about the same level of investigation as the NBIB would do for an interim clearance."

"If that's true, it means Patrick is stalling, stonewalling us."

"Maybe. But there's a guy I went to grad school with who got a job with a defense contractor. He works on classified defense systems, and he lives in Issaquah. When we get to I-90, head west. We can go through Issaquah on our way back. I'll call him and see if we can meet with him after work this afternoon. He can probably tell us what's required for an interim clearance and how long it takes."

"Okay." Vince glanced her way. "But back to that programmer that gave you bad vibes."

"Him?" Jess shook her head in disgust. How could she feel sorry for a person like him? "He acted like a druggie. An intelligent druggie, but still someone who needs something badly, something in that lab, something Patrick controls."

"Patrick's not stupid enough to run a drug operation when he can make millions from a legal business."

"No. He's not," Jess said.

"We need to do some brainstorming about what we might find in the lab. And we need a contingency plan to shut down the work if there's anything illegal going on, or if there's been a breach of contract."

Vince was right. And they would probably need the U.S. Army's help to do that. "Something else you need to do is to get to know the project manager for the Army. Whatever happens, we'll need an ally in the DOD, probably that general Patrick mentioned."

"McCheney?"

"Yes." Jess pulled out her cell phone. "We're almost to I-90. I'm going to call Mike Rothermel, the guy I mentioned. With a little luck, we can be legally inside the lab in a couple of weeks."

"Once Patrick realizes that, he could get desperate and—"

"I know, Vince. From now on, we need to be looking over our shoulders twenty-four-seven. And we need to consider that the person we need to worry about may not be Patrick."

Chapter 11

Vince slowed as he drove down the Snoqualmie Parkway. The on-ramp to I-90 lay only a quarter of a mile ahead. Were they going to Issaquah or going home?

Jess had the cell in her ear, her eyes focused on the dash, and a scowl on her face.

"Jess, I-90 or Highway 18?"

She looked up at him. "Just a sec, Mike ... Highway 18, Vince. Mike is busy this afternoon. But we're talking over the issues now."

Vince sang part of the chorus from that old Simon and Garfunkel song, Homeward Bound.

Jess shook her head and plugged her free ear.

Instead of annoying Jess, maybe he should track the conversation, though he could only hear Jess's end.

Jess continued talking with a finger in one ear. "Mike, who initiates a request for an interim clearance? ... That would be Patrick in our case ... In your experience, how long would that take ... I understand ... Vince is the equivalent of the CEO of the company and he's pure as the driven snow."

Jess looked up at him and her smile tweaked one corner of her mouth. "Well, he thinks he is ... Three or four weeks ... Thanks, Mike. Good luck on your business proposal." She ended the call and her scowl returned.

"So I should have an interim clearance in three or four weeks?"

Jess shook her head. "Should have, yes. But you won't."

The truth about Patrick's actions was becoming clear and heat rose on Vince's neck. "Patrick's sitting on a fortune, so he wants to retain control, indefinitely, right?"

"He's stonewalling. But, Vince, I don't think he's dangerous."

"After my car was hacked and we almost wrecked? He's dangerous. And I've had just about enough of Patrick Michaels."

"You need to settle down, Vince."

"Look. I made a promise to Paul not to give Patrick control of Virtuality, and I'm not going to sit still and let him continue to run the company. Jess, he's stealing control."

"If we put our minds to it, we can come up with some way to stop him."

The heat on Vince's neck reached flashpoint. "Oh, I can come up with a way to stop him. I'll beat the living crud out of that little geek."

"Stop it, Vince. You're out of control. Just like that time when …"

Jess had always hated it when he lost his temper. But sometimes brute force, with a little anger and intimidation, could accomplish a lot in a short time. He tried glaring at her.

The glare she returned hit him like a cutting torch.

Too late. He had pushed Jess over the edge and Vince would now suffer the consequences.

The cutting torch turned icy cold in her pale-blue eyes. "Snoqualmie—been there, done that. Take me back to my apartment, now."

The anger in her voice combined with a reference to the only serious argument they'd had as kids almost pulled an apology out of him. Almost. But he'd promised Paul that he wouldn't let Patrick do precisely what Patrick was doing, controlling Virtuality.

Vince pressed harder on the accelerator and delivered Jess to her apartment in Kent in record time.

Neither had spoken since Jess's command to take her home. And after he stopped in front of her apartment, Jess got out, walked to the door and didn't look back.

That she could do that drove a knife into his gut, followed by the heat, the kind that only Jess could induce.

Vince made a U-turn, with his tires squealing, and headed toward Southeast 256th Street, the shortest route back to Highway 18. Once on 256th, he slowed.

He wanted to confront Patrick alone, and the best chance of that was to arrive in the evening, about eight or nine o'clock. Vince took an alternate route to Snoqualmie, a route that would take at least an hour longer.

* * *

At five till nine, as the sun dropped below the horizon in the northwestern sky, Vince rolled to a stop in front of the Virtuality lab.

Someone in a white lab coat opened the main entryway door.

Vince ran to the door before the man closed it. "I've got an appointment with Patrick."

"He's in." The lab coat looked clean, but the guy's face was dripping with perspiration and he had other personal hygiene issues.

Vince wanted to ask the lab worker a few questions, but the strong body odor changed Vince's mind. He held his breath and went into the lobby.

Patrick's office door stood open.

Vince charged in.

Patrick looked up from his chair behind his desk and froze. "What are you—"

"Shut it, Patrick!" Vince strode around the desk and stood, towering over Patrick.

He rolled his chair backward a couple of feet. "You need to leave. I—I can call the police."

"If you really needed the police, I can guarantee you they would be too late." Vince grabbed a fistful of Patrick's shirt. "You will put in applications for my and Jess's interim clearances, and you will follow up on those applications."

Now it was time to bluff. "We will have our interim clearance approval in four weeks or less, or I'm the one who's going to call the general. And when I do, I think he's going to find certain irregularities in the lab, and the discrepancies in Virtuality's books, extremely interesting."

Patrick's mouth opened, but nothing came out.

Vince shoved Patrick's chest sending him rolling backward, crashing into a wall.

Patrick's eyes searched the room with darting glances. Was he looking for a weapon?

"No more stonewalling. Have I made myself clear?" Vince stepped forward and glared down into Patrick's wide eyes.

He didn't reply.

Vince took another step toward Patrick. "I asked if I made myself clear."

Patrick's breathing had become panting, but the pudgy little man tried to maintain a façade of calmness. "Perfectly."

"Finally, we understand each other ... partner." Vince whirled and left the office, thankful that he hadn't followed through on the impulse to do more than send Patrick rolling across the floor in his office chair.

At Vince's last glimpse of Patrick, before the office door closed, the short man rifled through a file. Maybe looking for the security forms. If not, Patrick would regret it.

Vince stopped inside the lobby when he saw a man in a lab coat headed toward the lab door.

Should I or should I not?

Stupid question. Virtuality was Vince's company and he needed to know what was going down in that lab.

He walked toward the exit door, then turned and followed the lab worker.

The man keyed in a code and the door lock clicked. He entered, and the door closed automatically, but slowly. The man had never looked back.

Vince scurried to the closing door and stopped it with his foot. He pushed the door open a few inches and peered in.

The lab worker disappeared behind a partition near the center of the lab.

Vince slipped inside the lab and moved to his right where five or six cubicle-like structures lined the outer wall. Each had seven-foot-high panels blocking his view of the interior.

Computers lined most of the left side of the large, open-bay lab.

At the far end, on the right, footsteps pounded the floor like someone was running.

Vince strode to the first cubicle on the right and hurried through its open doorway.

A play area? That seemed to be a good description, because the center of the cubicle contained a multi-directional treadmill built into the floor.

The treadmill looked to be about ten feet in diameter. Near the circular treadmill, a strange looking body suit lay on a stool. What appeared to be a TV remote lay on the body suit.

He picked up the remote and studied the icons on it. Play, pause, stop, fast forward and rewind.

Vince picked up the body suit and set the remote down. Underneath the suit, he found a helmet-like headset with goggles attached. The suit had both a shirt and pants made of a highly elastic fabric. He stretched the shirt to the width of his shoulders. It looked big enough for his six-foot-three, two-hundred-twenty-pound frame. And it had built-in gloves to cover his hands.

The question he asked earlier came again.

Should I, or shouldn't I?

The answers to some of his and Jess's questions about possible misuse of the lab likely lay in front of him. Vince stuck his head out of the cubicle and scanned the lab. No one. And, if he closed the sliding partition on the cubicle, no one could see him.

Vince slid the partition closed, picked up the shirt, and examined the metallic buttons distributed irregularly over the fabric.

Something like electrodes? He would soon find out.

Vince pulled off his shirt and slipped into the bodysuit's shirt, pushing his fingers into the gloves. He would pass on the pants.

After scooping up the headset and adjusting its straps, he managed to get it positioned on his head, because it seemed to have only one position that would fit. The goggles were tinted, but he could see clearly through them.

Patrick, it's time to show me what you've been up to.

He picked up the controller, took a deep breath, and pushed the play button.

Lights blinked on a rack of computer equipment that stood against the cubicle's back wall. The floor beneath Vince's feet buzzed sending a strange sensation through his feet and up his legs.

He moved to the center of the ten-foot circle. The treadmill had become an extension of his feet and moved with him as if he were walking across the floor, yet it kept Vince in place.

The lab cubicle around him faded out and, slowly, something entirely different faded in.

A warm breeze tickled the hair on his arm. Vince gasped as a waterfall appeared, directly ahead.

The water cascaded thirty feet downward into a clear pool of water surrounded by palm trees and other lush, green vegetation, punctuated by clusters of flowers—lavender, white, orange and yellow.

Vince approached the water, knelt and dipped his hand into the it. Cool, but not cold. Perfect for swimming.

Water splashed to his left, sending ripples across the pool.

Vince turned toward the splashing and gasped when he saw a young woman in a skimpy swimming suit walking through the water toward him.

His intellect told him this situation was not good. It also told him this appeared headed toward something even worse. Outside of his intellect, Vince was flying high, on top of the world. The same feeling he experienced after an hour of playing racquetball. Not fatigue, but the endorphin-induced high.

Vince's body and brain spoke the same message. This was good. It was right. Go with the adventure and enjoy it.

The young woman smiled and put her arms around him. Vince actually felt those arms on his shoulders.

The intense rush of the high grew stronger. Vince summoned every ounce of will he could muster and took the woman's hands to remove them from his shoulders, but the hands of whatever it was that stood in front of him, gripped his hands and pulled him toward the water.

It had been the perfect temperature for swimming.

Dude, this ain't real.

The message had come from somewhere beyond Vince's physical body and brain.

He knew that with certainty, because everything physical about Vince van Gordon had been seduced into joining the scene and playing role scripted for him.

VIRTUALITY

Paul was right. Vince van Gordon was more than a body and a brain full of neurons. His will and the message about reality had come from his real self, while his physical body was controlled, held captive by nerve impulses and sensory stimulation.

Come on, dude. You need to leave now!

If he didn't, Vince van Gordon was toast.

He yanked the headset off.

But the hands still held his and they weren't letting go.

The controller lay on the floor next to Vince. He jerked a hand free from the virtual Miss Universe, grabbed the controller, and jammed a thumb on the stop button.

All sensations in his upper body ended, leaving him feeling as if he were paralyzed from the waist up. He tried moving his right arm. When it moved, his upper body returned to its normal state, behaving commands from his brain or his mind—however the interplay of will, mind, and brain actually worked.

At some point, the tempo of Vince's heart had increased to allegro, and it hadn't slowed. He pulled the body shirt over his head and threw it on the floor. Vince looked at the wall ahead of him. The lights on the computer equipment mounted on the rack had all gone out.

Good. He stacked the body suit, controller, and headset on the stool, leaving the cubicle as he had found it.

He needed to slip out of the lab without being seen. This game room in a Top-Secret lab, where military applications were being developed, was more like a—he chose not to complete his simile, because the first word that came to mind was one Vince had purposely cut from his vocabulary.

Vince nudged the sliding door. It opened a few inches and he peered out.

The sound of running feet still came from the far end of the lab, but Vince could see no one.

He scampered to the lab door, pulled the big handle, and the thick door opened with the whooshing sound of air rushing from the lab.

Vince slipped through the door, letting it close behind him.

No one in the lobby.

Patrick's office door was closed and the lights appeared to be off.

Vince strode to the exit and left the building.

In the cool darkness outside, his senses seemed to return to their normal state. Thoughts about the alternate reality he'd experienced, and the reasons it had been created, brought revulsion that turned his stomach.

How could he ever tell Jess about this vile, unclean experience he had been led toward? If he described his experience accurately, it would raise a lot of questions in her mind. It had left unanswered questions in Vince's own mind.

Thankfully, the experience was over, and he could deal with how to tell Jess later.

When he turned toward his car, a picture of the pool of water and the girl returned to his mind, vivid and in color. Vince's revulsion had been replaced by a longing to return to the lab and let the scene play out.

He'd invoked his will to take off the suit, and then he turned off the machine. How could this be happening?

What goes into a person's mind stays forever, dude. You're supposed to guard it.

Again, Vince invoked the strong will that he'd developed on the football field, the will to conquer the immediate obstacle, whether that obstacle was fear of a three-hundred-pound lineman, or fear of him running over you ... or fear of being seduced by a virtual babe in a bikini. The tropical-pool scene slowly faded, taking with it the sensual feelings.

There was only one explanation for what he'd experienced. This was virtual reality augmented by remote-nerve and deep-brain stimulation. Its powerful, addictive forces had nearly sucked Vince van Gordon into its prison. And he'd only had on part of the body suit and played the game for two or three minutes.

Should he tell Jess about it?

Yes. Eventually. But could he, knowing what she would think? Knowing what she would do? As kids they had vowed together that they would never cross certain lines unless they were married.

Jess wouldn't consider this a virtual violation of their vow. She would deem it a real one. And instead of breaking six boards, her kick would probably break his head.

Vince climbed into his car, backed out of the parking space, and drove through the parking area back to the highway.

Maybe he'd made some progress with Patrick. And he had learned about one product developed in the lab. But now he faced the most challenging task in a challenging day.

He had lost his temper, completely. Vince needed Jess's forgiveness or there would be no relationship with Jessica Jamison. And groveling wouldn't be a desperate last measure to gain sympathy. Knowing Jess, groveling would be where he started.

* * *

Vince drove home slowly, taking a long route and taking his time. When he pulled into his driveway at nearly eleven, Jess sat on the front steps swatting at bugs that buzzed her under the front door light.

It was three miles from her apartment in Kent to his house and, last he'd heard, her motorcycle was still in the shop for repairs. She had walked, probably alone and in the dark.

He stopped in the driveway, not waiting for the garage door to open. By the time he slid out and stood at the base of the front steps, Jess stood a step above him, hands on hips, eyeball to eyeball.

"What are you doing here?"

"You lost your temper, then you went out and confronted Patrick, didn't you?"

"Jess, I wouldn't exactly say that I—"

"Did you pound poor Patrick?"

"Poor Patrick?"

"Just tell me—did you commit a crime?"

"No. I just sent him and his office chair rolling across the room." Entering the lab, his lab—had that been a criminal act? That was a matter of perspective. At the moment, Vince's perspective said it wasn't a crime, because any other perspective would entail lying to Jess, and that was a capital offense.

She clamped her hands on his cheeks and forced him to look into her eyes. "If you promise me you'll never do that again, we'll both forget it ever happened and I'll—I'll forgive you."

Vince opened his mouth, but the look on Jess's face said he shouldn't comment on her offer, just accept it. She had a temper and Jess held grudges. She was loyal to a fault, but a person did not want to land on her naughty list. She wrote it in indelible ink.

He studied her eyes again in the light of the outdoor pole lamp. Pain had mixed with anger. Vince crumbled. "I promise."

She stepped into his arms and pressed her cheek into his chest.

Was she crying? He wiped her cheek and his hand came away wet. "I'm sorry, Jess. But why did you walk all the way—"

"Why do you think, lop ear?" She looked up at him, tears welling in her eyes. "My motorcycle's in the shop."

"So the truth comes out."

Jess shook her head. "No, Vince. Paul said there was danger. We've got to be more careful. *You've* got to be more careful. If anything ever happened to you, I ..."

He waited, but Jess left her sentence hanging ... like their relationship.

She took a deep breath, wiped her eyes and stepped back out of his arms. "You've had too much to deal with since you came home. And now your business partner is acting more like a business competitor in a hostile takeover attempt. The clearances will take some time." Jess paused, and her gaze bored into his eyes. "I assume you scared and intimidated Patrick into submission."

"We weren't going to talk about that, remember?"

"It's okay. On this starry, starry night, I forgive you, lop ear."

"If you forgive me, why the van Gogh insults?"

"Because you deserve them. Now listen. We, uh, you have been under a lot of pressure. We're going to take tomorrow to relax, wind down, and focus on something other than Virtuality."

He would like to focus on Jess. She had dropped her guard a couple of times, enough to tell him her feelings for him ran deep, even deeper than he had hoped for. They still had a lot to work through, but there seemed to be some light at the end of the dark tunnel of Vince van Gordon's life. "Sounds good. Whatever you'd like to do, I'm game."

"The weather's going to be beautiful tomorrow, so we'll make it an all-day outing. I'm taking you rock climbing near Vantage, at Frenchman Coulee."

"Rock climbing? I thought you wanted to avoid danger and wind down."

"If you listen to me closely and follow my instructions, there won't be any danger. Well, no serious danger. And, if you'll drop me off at the motorcycle shop before midnight, I'll get my bike back and you won't have to pick me up in the morning. You're going to have to get up early enough, anyway."

"It's eleven o'clock, Jess. Who's gonna be at the shop this late in the evening?"

"Carlos Ramirez. He called earlier and said my bike's ready. He'll be there until midnight."

"Oh, yeah. The biker dude from high school. He always did have his eye on you."

"He's actually pretty cute for a … 'biker dude'."

"How many tattoos does this biker dude have?"

Jess shook her head. "I never thought to inspect him. But, if you insist …"

"I don't. But tell me something, Jess. When did you start riding motorcycles, hanging out with bikers, doing karate, climbing rock faces, and cheating death?"

"After you left, when I knew you weren't—" She turned away.

"Jess, what are you saying?"

She turned toward the door. "Let's go inside. I've got some YouTube videos you need to watch. They're about climbing. We can still get to the bike shop by—"

"Jess, look at me, please."

She didn't turn around and didn't reply.

How could his leaving have hurt her as deeply as she implied? Or had she implied anything? After all, she said climbing wasn't dangerous if you did it right. Maybe the videos would convince him that climbing a few hundred feet up a sheer rock wall to sit on top of it was a safe way to experience nature.

Yeah, sure. Safe, like Humpty Dumpty.

Chapter 12

The pressure was building at MMI and Trent needed to calm the fears of jittery board members before they started a coup to oust him and scrap his plans for their future.

Marco and Cunningham had planned their retirement around anticipated earnings of MMI over the next ten years. They stood to lose the most if Trent's virtual adventure flopped.

Trent needed to show his cohorts some signs of progress, or the board could quickly nix the move to Las Vegas. He spun his cell on his desk like—what were those little fidget devices kids played with to keep them quiet—spinners?

His cell rang on the third rotation. *New York, New York*. He stopped the phone and swiped the screen to answer. "Trent, here."

"This is Sal. Got some news for you that you might want to take advantage of."

At this point, Trent would seize any advantage he could. "What have you got?"

"First, we've started electronic surveillance."

"Do I want to hear what that entails?"

"It's probably best that you remain ignorant of the means, if you know what I mean."

"Okay. But what have you found?"

"It looks like Jessica and Vince have planned a little extracurricular activity. They're going rock climbing."

"You sure about that?"

"Yeah. We found out she belongs to a climbing club in the Seattle area and she buys a lot of gear. We won't mention how we got the other details."

"Do you know where they're going?"

"That's just it. We're not sure, but we can follow them if you want us to. However, it will cost more than our three thousand a day."

"Come on, Sal. It's not that expensive to tail them, is it?"

"Depends on what your tailing them with. I, uh, used that contact you gave me at LACO. He said, if we covered the cost of fuel and the pilot, we could use their chopper. Does that give you any ideas?"

"I like a man with your initiative, Sal, but I told you nobody gets hurt unless I say so. If you step out of line at this juncture, you could screw up the whole deal."

Trent's lawyer had called earlier and reported on the terms of the van Gordon-Michaels partnership agreement. If Vince should die without a will, it should be a simple matter for Patrick to purchase van Gordon's share. But, if some van Gordon heir mounted a legal challenge and it got into the courts, all bets were off as to the eventual outcome. And who knew what assets might be frozen in the interim and for how long they would remain unavailable.

"I'm waiting for orders, Mr. Del Valle."

The scenario where van Gordon sold to Patrick Michaels was the cleanest path to control of Virtuality. "Find out where the two are going."

"Using LACO's chopper?"

"Yes, using the chopper." The wild card in the whole deal seemed to be Jessica Jamison. Perhaps she should have a tragic climbing accident. Or should she be used as leverage to force Vince to sell? The answer really depended on the nature of the relationship between Vince and the dark-haired babe. After seeing her pictures, Trent guessed Vince van Gordon would do just about anything for her.

"Sal, how soon can the chopper be ready?"

"LACO said by midnight."

"Get the chopper. Follow them when they leave. Touch bases with me at least every other hour after you take off. When you see where they're going to be climbing, let me know. I'll provide further instructions at that time."

"That kind of leaves us hanging, Mr. Del Valle. Not knowing what we have to do, we won't know what to bring along."

"Bring everything you think you might need."

"That's quite a bit. It will cost at least a grand more."

"At this point, Sal, effectiveness is more important than cost. I want you to be prepared to be effective. And whatever you do, don't lose them."

"You can count on us, sir. But about contacting you every other hour—during the sensitive part of this job, we might not be able to call. Not knowing where they're headed, we might be out of cell service part of the time."

"I understand. Do your best to stay in contact. The moment you know where they're climbing, I want to hear about it. Then I'll tell you what you need to do."

Trent ended the call.

The dilemma Trent faced tied his gut in knots. On a rock face, there was a lot of uncertainty. One of them might fall, or they might both fall. If Sal could only guarantee that one of them would be kept safe, who should it be? Stated differently, who did Trent want to endanger, van Gordon or the babe?

He quickly calculated the odds of getting what he wanted, control of Virtuality's technology. The surest approach was to make certain Jessica Jamison was safe. He could play the babe like a wild card, filling several different roles with a live Jessica. But, if she died, Trent would lose all ability to control stubborn, hot-tempered Vince van Gordon, unless Sal killed the big hot head. But that would be so messy. If, on the other hand, Vince were to have a fatal accident ...

Chapter 13

A motorcycle's engine rumbled as it backed off down the hill on the boulevard.

So Jess had gotten her motorcycle out of the shop at midnight last night. How had she managed that?

If Jess wanted to use her looks to get something, most guys would sacrifice their dignity, making fools of themselves, to please her. But Jess had never done anything like that with Vince.

His thoughts about Jess pulled Vince's mind back from the edge of sleep. He raised his heavy head from the hand that had propped up his head on the arm of his couch and glanced at his watch. 3:30 a.m. Jess was right on time.

He grabbed his duffle bag and studied the bitter cup of coffee on the end table beside the couch. He abandoned the coffee and hurried downstairs to open the garage door for Jess.

When he entered the double-car garage, the door light was on and the garage door had already opened.

Jess stood outside the garage astride her bike with a door opener in her left hand.

So she had access to Paul's house. Though Jess downplayed it, the relationship between her and Paul grew closer with each bit of information Vince acquired.

Jess's right hand clamped tightly on the brake. "I've got to park my bike in your garage. This driveway is only a few degrees shy of a cliff. It's a wonder Paul didn't—" Jess looked down at the concrete driveway.

The specter of Paul seemed to haunt the house now. Funny, he hadn't noticed it while alone in his brother's house. Only after Jess arrived.

Jess eased on the brake lever and let the bike creep down to the level area near the garage door, then pulled off her helmet and hung it on the handlebar. "You know, Paul did slide down the driveway once after an ice storm. He demolished his garage door."

Vince yawned, pushed the ghost out of his mind, and stepped aside to let her pass. "Roll it on in. Your bike will be safer inside."

She pushed the bike by him and stopped between the car and Paul's pickup.

"Jess, remind me again why we had to get up in the middle of the night."

"Don't try weaseling out. We're driving to Vantage and you *will* climb that rock face with me."

"In the dark?"

"We'll be on the rock by 6:00 a.m. It's July and the east side of the state gets hot. At noon, you can fry your fingers on the rocks. Besides, at six we should have the rocks all to ourselves."

Having time alone with Jess was exactly the prescription his frayed nerves needed. But not if she were bringing along her bag full of insults. "To ourselves? Remind me why that matters."

She pulled the kickstand out and leaned her bike on it. "So you won't have to be embarrassed by how many times you fall."

"Fall? Jess, I'm not going to—"

"Yes, you will. You'll fall off the rock. The first time will be on my command."

"Great."

"It's to show you how safe you are, if you do things right when climbing a rock."

"It doesn't sound safe to me. But I guess safe is a relative term for someone who cracks a safe when they rob banks. Or just blows it up."

She folded her arms, leaned back onto her motorcycle seat, and shot him a razor-edged look. "Don't start on the Jesse James stuff, Vincent, because today isn't your day." She shook her head. "Tomorrow's not looking good either."

So Jess had brought her bag of insults. The twin bags hanging across the back of the motorcycle seat were probably full of them. What had happened to the day of relaxation, the day of doing something physical to blow off steam from the pressure of the past two days?

She pulled the bags from her bike and held them up. "This is what makes rock climbing safe, if you know how to use the equipment." Jess opened the back door of his rental car and dropped the bags onto the back seat. "Remember the videos we watched yesterday?"

"Yeah. *Andele, andele!*"

"On belay." She folded her arms again. "Vince, this isn't a joke. It's a protocol meant to keep you alive."

"Excuse me, Jess, but falling on command doesn't sound like a prescription for staying alive." He slid into the driver's seat.

She stood by the open passenger door. "Maybe I should get on my bike and ride back home." Jess had lowered her voice to the soft, intense tone she had used since she was a girl ... right before she erupted. "You know something, Vince? I'll never forget the first time I met you. But I keep trying."

"I'm sorry." Vince slumped forward in submission, head bowed, waiting for hot lava.

A gentle hand came to rest on his shoulder.

What was up with her? He looked up.

Jess had slid in beside him and the dome light now shined into two pale blue eyes that held a much softer expression.

He needed to say something to move things forward, to get beyond all the awkwardness. "You and I deserve this day to unwind, together. We need it." He patted her hand.

She pulled her hand back. "Let's go then."

Why was everything so complex? Why couldn't they just hop in the car and take off together like when they were kids, embarking on their next great adventure?

As kids, they were inseparable. Maybe they weren't kids anymore, but their relationship had been severed while they were still in their teens. And that's where they were picking up the pieces. Two twenty-six-year-old teenagers. That might explain some of the craziness. But a niggling thought said there had to be more to it than teenage immaturity.

"Are you going to drive, or do you want me to?"

"Yeah. Drive—I mean, no. I'll drive."

He backed up the steep driveway and onto the street, shoved the gear shift into drive, but didn't press on the gas. "Jess ... are we acting like teenagers?"

She stared at him for a moment, then shook her head. "I think Vincent van Gogh has completely van gone. Instead of an earlobe, he cut off a frontal lobe."

Vince wasn't the only one acting looney, was he?

What do you think, dude?

That we're two teenagers. Awkward, immature, insecure and ... what was that old '80s song? Trying to Get the Feeling Again?

The obnoxious voice inside had Jess and him pegged, but it wasn't something he could say to her.

Jess huffed a sharp sigh. "Maybe you should let me drive."

He pushed on the gas pedal and rolled toward Fairwood Boulevard.

After he turned onto the boulevard and headed up the hill, Jess swiveled in her seat and snagged her bags from the back seat. She plopped them in her lap and pulled out an assortment of ropes and hardware that Vince vaguely remembered seeing on the climbing videos.

As they passed a street light he looked her way. "I guess we really are going to climb a rock face."

She ignored his comment.

Vince yawned again. His stressed body craved rest. How were they supposed to climb a cliff with only three hours of sleep?

Regardless, if they could park under one of the street lights, just looking at Jess could keep him awake. Since he had to drive, he would prod her instead. Live dangerously. Mess with a volcano. That could keep a person awake too.

Prod number one.

"You didn't cut a deal with Patrick to kill me off on this climb, did you? You know, give him control of the company for a couple of million?"

"That's not even funny. I won't dignify it by answering."

Something had become evident since he came back home. Jess's biting remarks to him were okay, but he wasn't allowed to reciprocate. Since she was a little girl, Jess had had a supercharged sense of justice. But how did she justify all her digs while disallowing his comebacks?

Something had just changed in the car. He could feel it. Vince glanced her way.

It was Jess. Head down. Hands in her lap. She looked like she might cry.

"I'm sorry, Jess. I was only joking. Why do you get to make caustic remarks, but I can't even—"

"That's something you have to figure out." Her head snapped up.

"You've got an attitude problem. Did anyone ever tell you that?"

"No. But you've got a perception problem. Did anyone ever tell you that?"

This wasn't a good start to a day of winding down. Maybe he should change the subject. "Just the two of us again. It reminds me of old times. Of some good times." He reached for her hand.

She moved her hand beyond his reach. "Some good. Some not."

"What do you mean?"

"Vince, you need to listen while I tell you about slings and biners."

"Beaners?"

"It's spelled with an I."

"Doesn't matter how it's spelled. Don't let Carlos hear you say that."

"Punny but not funny. Guess I should expect that from a starving writer who can't write his way out of a story."

Ouch. That was right where it hurt. Had Jess been reading his books?

She drove her barb home with a prolonged glare that Vince could feel, though he could see nothing but a shadowy form beside him.

Doing great, dude. We're staying awake.

Another sharp sigh blasted from Jess's mouth. "You need to listen. I'm going to tell you all I know—"

"This won't take long."

She shot him another zinger with her steel blue eyes.

He couldn't see those eyes now, but he knew them well. And he'd seen that look in them every day of their senior year in high school.

"Okay, Mr. van Gordon. I'll tell you all we both know. It won't take any longer."

"Touché."

Jess had ripped a hole in his front lines in this battle of the barbs.

Vince hadn't a clue where their relationship was headed or if there was anything left of it. But he had gained one thing. He wasn't sleepy anymore.

Silence reigned in the car for the next forty minutes as the car climbed the west side of the Cascades. A ceasefire? Or was Jess waiting to attack?

Vince gripped the wheel with both hands as he steered through the sharp turns on I-90 leading into Snoqualmie Pass.

When the road straightened, a warm hand found his right hand on the wheel, pulled it off, and trapped it between her hands. She held it in her lap.

He knew Jess well enough to realize this was her apology. It's all he would get. It was enough to take the chill off and, right now, that was enough.

For the next thirty miles, he drove in silence. Peaceful silence.

As Vince let the car coast down the eastern slopes of the Cascades, a few miles from Ellensburg, wet drops splashed onto his hand.

Maybe not so peaceful, after all.

Jess released his hand and wiped her cheeks.

In the brightening dawn, a tear glistened as it rolled down Jess's left cheek. She swiped at it.

He looked her way until they approached a sharp turn. "A penny for your thoughts."

"You should know them already." She looked his way. "And if you don't, you haven't got enough money to buy them."

What was he supposed to know? That Jess loved Paul but would settle for his little brother? Maybe he should just stop thinking about it. Women were complicated creatures that he had never been able to understand. But her tears and her words seemed to be in a battle, warring against each other, tearing Jess apart.

He had to react to her crying, and it needed to be something better than a penny for her thoughts. He had already crashed and burned with that approach.

Humility and insanity... if only he could combine them to explain his seven years of silence, of never calling his best friend. "Jess, I was really stupid, inconsiderate ... and, well, I'm sorry for not even calling. I was—"

"Insanity? Is that what you're pleading?"

"I missed you, Jess. It was insanity to abandon the best friend I've ever had."

She sniffled and looked his way. "I wasn't crying ... and you're not going to tell anyone that I was. Got that, lop ear?"

"Loud and clear." He had a Jesse James comeback for her, but the look on her face said that would be a terrible idea, especially since she was going to belay him up that rock face.

"Jess, will you forgive me for leaving you and never coming back. For not calling you?"

"Why? I thought deserters just got a firing squad?"

"Guess the answer is no," Vince mumbled.

"That depends. But in about twenty minutes, we're going to exit the freeway and climb some big rocks. If you don't want any further disfiguration of that thick head of yours, I suggest you listen closely while I review what we're going to do."

Vince bit his tongue. Was he forgiven or not? Regardless, he needed to listen. If he fell off the rock, the answer to his question was moot.

For the next fifteen minutes, Jess repeated procedures she had shown him on YouTube yesterday—securing the harness, anchoring, belaying with her in the lead. Then she asked which knots he should use when tying onto each piece of equipment.

When she finished, Jess went silent, retreating into her melancholy but without tears this time.

Fifteen minutes later, Jess sat silently beside him as they crossed the Columbia River at Vantage.

The twilight had brightened now, and the eastern horizon glowed yellow-orange.

While Vince negotiated the steep hill on the east side of the river, Jess straightened in her seat. "The next exit is ours. It's only a couple of miles from there to Frenchman Coulee."

In another mile, Vince took the exit and followed her directions to Vantage Road which took them down a narrow gorge that widened over the next mile. On their right, a high rock cliff paralleled the roadway a hundred yards from it.

He turned his head to get a better look at the cliff through the side window.

Jess poked his shoulder. "That's the parking area on the left."

He turned in, rolled to the back of the dusty dirt lot and stopped.

Directly in front of them, shrouded in shadows, stood tall columns of rock that looked like gargantuan steel rods welded together on their sides and standing on end to form a shear, mile-long cliff, the Sunshine Wall. It seemed to be two-hundred feet high.

Jess grabbed her bag and got out.

Vince met her at the front of the car. From there, the cliff seemed even more imposing.

"Seriously, Jess, we're going to climb that?

"Don't worry, Vince. No one's been killed here ... well, not for a few years."

"See, I told you this was dangerous. Let's go home."

"Okay. A guy fell when he started to rappel down. Didn't follow safe procedures."

"Safe procedures? I'm not sure there are any. How high are these rocks, anyway?"

"About a hundred feet."

"How are we going to get down once we get up there? If we even do."

"Are you wimping out on me, van Gordon?"

"I'm not a wimp. Just a sane man with an intact skull who wants to keep it that way."

She mumbled something under her breath about his ears. "The most dangerous part of a climb is coming down."

"But it's the easiest part, isn't it?" Vince lifted a hand and whistled as he lowered it until his hand crashed on the hood of the car.

"No, Mr. Andele. We're going to walk down."

"Yeah, right. Just rotate the gravity vector ninety degrees and walk down the cliff. Does God know you're going to make Him do that for us?"

"Vince, we're going to hike around the cliff. It's an easy two-mile hike, downhill all the way. I wouldn't make you rappel down on your first climb. Now, are you satisfied? Don't answer that. Just follow me."

Jess led him along a trail for about a quarter mile.

She was in her element now. Energized, smiling, the gentle breeze animating her waves of brunette hair. Jess was beyond beautiful. She also had a death wish. Or was she a siren, luring him to his death instead of a bunch of sailors?

They stopped at the base of the cliff that towered over them, blocking half of the clear blue sky.

Vince looked up and his insides quivered. "Ho-o-o-ly smoke."

Jess grinned. "Isaiah had the same reaction. But he was looking at God's throne, not some measly little rock formation."

"At least it's got some big cracks between the columns. Maybe ..." Vince cleared his throat, then sang softly. "He hideth me whole in the cleft of the rock that—"

"That's enough wise guy." She started pulling climbing paraphernalia out of her bag.

With slings and things hanging off her, Jess scampered up the base of the rock to about ten feet, then she stopped on some microscopic ledge that would never support his quadruple-E-width foot. She appeared to be creating one of those anchor contraptions.

He had a strong suspicion he would soon be hanging from it.

Jess passed the rope through a couple of biners, pulled through several yards of slack rope and climbed back down.

"Jess, isn't what you just did called free-solo climbing? You told me you don't do that."

"I only went up ten feet. I could have jumped down from that height and been fine."

His gaze went down to her legs, those shapely, well-toned legs, extending down from a nicely filled pair of shorts.

"Vince, I'll be above you, leading. You'll have plenty of opportunity to watch my legs, or anything else your male eyes tend to focus on. You'll have to watch me closely, so you can catch me if I fall off the rock."

"Yeah, the rock. The rock that is higher than I."

"I guess Sunday School sank in after all. I was beginning to wonder about you." She paused. "Put this harness on like I showed you yesterday. After you've got it on and I've checked it, I want you to tie into the rope with a figure-eight knot."

After a couple of corrections from Jess, Vince stood harnessed and tied to the rope.

She clipped on her belay device and threaded the rope through it. Then Jess struck a pose, feet spread and both hands on the rope. "Now you climb up to the anchor."

"I don't attach to anything? Just climb up?"

"Yes, until I yell fall. Then you let go."

"And Patrick gets the business. You weren't kidding about this fall thing, were you?"

"No. You're about to learn how we keep rock climbing safe. This is a confidence builder."

"Yeah, sure. I can feel the confidence just oozing out of me. I think it's all oozed out now."

"One more thing. When I stop your fall, you might swing into the rock. If you do, use your feet to keep from smacking against the rock."

"Smacking into the rock? You said this was safe. But I guess safe is a relative thing." He hurried to the rock and tried climbing rapidly as Jess had done, like a monkey.

She didn't stop him, but Jess muttered a string of unintelligible words as she worked the rope.

Two feet shy of the anchor, his hand slipped from a hold. The extra weight broke a foot loose from its precarious spot. Vince was going down.

"Fall," Jess barked out from below.

As if he had a choice. He broke loose from the rock, struggling to keep his feet below him and wondering if slender, five-foot-eight Jess could catch his two-hundred-twenty-pound body.

Vince braced for the impact, but his body jerked to a stop.

He looked down.

His quadruple-E climbing shoes dangled a few feet above the ground.

Jess had him. All his weight. Now, she fed some rope and lowered him to the ground.

He blew out a sigh, tried to relax, and gave her a grin. "Did I pass?"

She shook her head. "You flunked. What happened to 'on belay'? You know, all of that safety protocol I taught you?"

"Thought I'd try *andele* instead."

Jess pressed her lips together until all the blood was gone.

Pale lips were not a good sign.

"When climbing rocks, it's never *andele*. Everything you do is controlled and calculated, even if that means *retardo*. Got it?"

"Jess, did you just call me a retard, or did you mean *retardar*?"

The look she gave him came full of ambiguous, but threatening nuances.

He needed to stop the word games. He'd given Jess enough grief this morning.

She had already shed some mysterious tears. A lot of tears. It was time to please Jess and gather up the guts to climb this rock.

And pray some EMT doesn't have to gather up yours, dude.

Forty minutes later, Vince stuck a hand above his head and laid it on top of the ledge that would complete the first pitch of a rock column that Jess called Choss Master. But the top of the rock ledge didn't feel like rock. The surface had a different texture than anything he'd felt so far. If he were to describe it, he would call it—no. Something like that couldn't be up here. That wasn't possible, was it?

He pulled his hand back down and wiped it on the rock. What kind of goo had he encountered?

When he looked up at Jess, perched on the ledge belaying him, she grinned. "It's bird poop. There's too much to avoid. But don't worry. By July, most of it is baked so hard you can just pretend it's part of the rock."

"Gross. I just stuck my hand in a pigeon's outhouse. Jess, it wasn't all baked hard."

"You don't sound like the little boy who gave Mr. Potts a beautifully wrapped Christmas gift full of cow manure ...

that you packed in by hand. Climb onto the ledge, clip on your anchor, and rest. In a few minutes, you're going to belay me up the second pitch."

As Jess made her way up the second pitch, Vince was careful to feed her rope while keeping his brake hand ready. They had watched this on video last night, but now he understood the reasons for carefully following the procedure. He had to be ready to catch her in an instant if she came off the rock, especially since the last bolt she clipped into would be below her. As the lead climber, her fall would be farther than his. The quicker he reacted, the shorter her fall.

Everything considered, it was a good excuse to watch a nicely shaped body and a sexy pair of legs. Not that he would tell her. But Jess knew he liked what he saw. She just didn't know the rest of the story, and he didn't know if he had the right to tell her, because Paul, even after his death, still blocked the door to her heart. Jess may not think so, but Vince knew the truth. And he would never make an incredible woman like Jess settle for second best.

The air warmed rapidly as the sun broke the inversion in the small valley at Frenchman Coulee. At 6:35 a.m., Choss Master's north-facing wall still stood in shadows. And Vince still stood in pigeon poop as he belayed Jess to the top of the second pitch.

He watched as Jess scooted onto a ledge at the top of the rock.

"Off belay." Jess's smooth, alto voice echoed softly off the surrounding rocks. She stood and pointed down at him.

Vince cleared the rope from his belay device. "Belay off." He sighed like a deflating tire, releasing the pent-up emotion of having Jess's life in his hands. He had accomplished the most important thing Vince van Gordon could do, keep Jessica Jamison safe.

She disappeared for about thirty seconds then returned to the rock's edge. "Vince, one of the bolts up here is loose. I'm going to rig up something else so our anchor has redundancy. It might take five minutes or so."

"I'll wait here in the birdie outhouse. I mean, it's not like I had any other plans." Clipped on his personal anchor, Vince sat on the ledge in an area of dry pigeon poop and studied the rock cliffs near him.

Jess said July was one of the least popular months for climbing Frenchman Coulee. Too hot. In the sun, the rocks grew hot enough to fry fingers. They hadn't seen anyone since arriving, only a helicopter that flew by an hour ago.

Only a few minutes more and Vince could say he had mastered Choss Master.

He waited a while longer then glanced at his watch. 6:45 a.m. Why was Jess taking so long? Well, better safe than sorry. And sorry, near the top of Choss Master, could mean dead, like the guy Jess told him about.

Trying not to stumble on the coil of rope at his feet, Vince stood to call out to Jess, but a raspy sound came from above.

He looked up toward the source of the noise.

The upper end of the rope slid through the quickdraw attached to the topmost bolt.

Had Jess dropped the rope?

Fifteen feet of rope now dangled from the second bolt from the top. Though the end of the rope was more than ten feet above his head, the reason it had fallen was obvious. It had been cut.

The incident with the car. Patrick's mysterious, hostile behavior. Now a cut rope. It all sent his heart galloping at a presto tempo.

He cupped his hands around his mouth. "Jess!"

"Jess, are you okay?"

Silence.

Chapter 14

If Jess could have come back to belay Vince up the remaining forty feet of Choss Master, she would already have appeared on the top ledge. Only two scenarios made sense. Either she had been injured or someone was keeping Jess from returning. The cut rope indicated the latter.

Vince craned his neck and looked up the column of basalt rock recessed two feet into the wall of the cliff and lined with a crack up the left side. A dull, nauseating ache formed in his gut as he considered what a solo climb up the increasingly smooth rock face would mean.

Maybe he should pull the rope down, anchor it to the bolt in front of him, and lower himself to the bottom. But, even if he made it down safely, it was a long hike around Frenchman Coulee to reach the top. And Jess was up there, somewhere, only forty feet above.

She needs you, man.

Thoughts of Jess in danger drove out all vestiges of fear. He scanned the column up to the top again. Maybe not quite all the fear.

Vince stretched his right arm upward to the limit of his reach. The quickdraw suspended from the bolt above him dangled only six feet above his hand. If he could climb to where he could clip on to the quickdraw, or the bolt to which it was attached, he could reach the cut end of the rope. But he would be climbing unattached for a few feet.

Jess's catchphrase since she began instructing him had been, "Always, always, always stay clipped to the rock."

He would have to violate Jess's cardinal rule of rock climbing to reach the rope. Once there, if he attached to the other end of the rope, he would have some measure of safety as he climbed to the second bolt from the top. But the remaining fifteen feet to the ledge on top—he could think about that later.

Lately, Vince's prayers were about as frequent as a Mariner series sweep at Safeco Field. But, as he unclipped his sling from the bolt in front of him, words slipped out in a hoarse whisper. "Help me get to Jess and I'll do anything you want me to do."

Like trying to bribe God, dude?

Vince clipped back onto the bolt, while his hands shook. Somehow, he had to do this, and his right brain screamed the message that every second he delayed meant more danger for Jess.

He studied the handhold for a couple of seconds, unclipped from the bolt, and climbed several feet to the next bolt, where he clipped back on and waited for his pulse and quivering stomach to settle down. When Vince looked up, the cut end of the rope dangled within reach. He grabbed it and prepared to do something Jess would think was really stupid.

Belaying himself—if one could even call it that—by tying a knot to form a loop near the cut end of the rope, clipping onto it with one of his slings, and then hoisting himself up using a quickdraw for a pulley, would probably have drawn an endless string of insults from Jess. But it worked.

With fifteen feet left to climb, Vince stopped and clipped onto the bolt where the rope hung from the quickdraw.

Now what?

He studied the rock above him. The crack in the seams between the two columns of basalt widened near the top. The last ten feet formed what Jess had called a dihedral. Or was it a chimney?

Regardless, she had told him about the technique of climbing between two rock faces, and she'd called it stemming. Jess said it took a different kind of strength to push feet and hands against rocks on either side of a climber while they worked their way up a rock. And it took a different rhythm.

With only that bit of information, he would have to free climb to the top. One mistake, one slip, would be one too many. Maybe there was a way to partially mitigate the risk.

Vince slid the rope through the quickdraw until he had created a fifteen-foot loop of rope that he could use as a crude sling by clipping the slack end of the rope onto his harness. After he'd pulled enough rope, Vince doubled a three-foot section and tied an overhand knot, forming a small loop that he clipped onto his harness.

Though clipped to the topmost bolt, he had enough rope to reach the top and, if he fell, it would be at most fifteen feet down to the top bolt plus the fifteen feet of his improvised rope sling. But could the combination of rope, quickdraw and bolt absorb the shock and stop his two-hundred-twenty pounds after a thirty-foot fall?

Best not to think about it. Even better not to put his unorthodox safety measures to the test. But it wasn't like he had a choice.

Vince had wasted too much time. He spread his feet and hands to span the gap between the two rock columns, leaned hard on his right hand and unclipped from the bolt using his left hand.

He was stemming, either to the top of the rock or down to his tomb, and that's how it—

A shout rang out from somewhere over the top of the rock face. It echoed through the gorge.

Vince's name. Jess's voice.

He'd only heard desperation in her voice three times in his life. This was the fourth time.

She wouldn't have voluntarily gone so far away, leaving him on the rock face. Jess was in trouble and she needed him. Nothing else mattered.

Vince switched sides with his hands and feet in rapid succession, climbing two or three feet every few seconds. Could he do this all the way to the top? For Jess he was willing to die trying.

Three feet from the ledge on top, with feet pressed into the sides of the chimney, Vince reached for the ledge. His fingertips slid over it, but his left foot slid.

He jammed his left hand into the rock, tightening the wedge to stop his slide. Pain shot up his arm from wrist to elbow. The muscles of his left forearm spasmed.

Vince groaned against the pain and pushed even harder with his left hand. But his hand began a skin-shredding slide down the rough rock.

Desperate now, he stomped his left foot into the basalt column and pushed with all his leg strength.

His slide slowed, nearly to a stop. He added his injured hand to the stemming mix.

With his left arm screaming its complaint, he pulled it from the rock and pressed outward with both legs.

The slide stopped.

Vince looked at his position. He'd slid downward only a foot or two. But the price had been steep.

With his feet holding him in place, he turned his left hand palm up. Blood ran down his wrist. It had come from the heel of his hand which was now missing most of its skin.

He'd sprained a wrist in football. That seemed to be what he'd done to his left wrist when he jammed it into the rock. He'd probably injured it further by jamming it again.

It didn't matter. None of it mattered if he couldn't reach Jess. If he couldn't save her, it wouldn't matter if he fell. Without Jess, life would lose its appeal to Vince van Gordon.

His legs shook. His groin muscles had stretched to their limits. Vince snorted and shook his head to clear it and regain his focus.

If he could only get his fingers on that ledge four feet beyond his reach. If …

His legs felt like they'd been manufactured by Goodyear and his left hand screamed a nerve-shattering complaint about being skinned alive. As he held his jammed body in place, the last bit of strength drained from Vince's leg muscles. He had only seconds left until they would no longer respond.

Shaking, sweating, panting, and with his left hand and wrist shrieking obscenities to his central nervous system, Vince tried to think.

He could stem his way to the top, if only he hadn't ripped most of the skin from his left hand and sprained his wrist. He looked at his hand again and saw the pigeon poop ground into his raw flesh. That sent his stomach quivering as if he might add its contents to the pigeon poop on the rock.

Just concentrate on what you need to do, dude. You can do this.

Vince pressed his injured hand into the rock on his left, gritted his teeth and stepped up the rock with his right foot. Nerves stressed to their limits sent flashes of light through his eyes and into his brain, the precursor to passing out.

He jammed his left foot into the rock and pulled his left hand off, breathing deep, controlled breaths through the pain to ensure he didn't lose consciousness.

Vince needed one more combination of two steps to try for the ledge.

Stemming with his left foot and right hand, Vince took a step up with his left foot and pressed it into the column on his left.

Every muscle in his body quivered now, begging for the torture to stop and threatening to send him downward.

He couldn't let that happen. But, in two or three more seconds, there would be no way to stop it.

Vince twisted to his left and reached with both hands for the ledge.

His fingers found it. He pulled with his arms and his legs pushed.

His palms now lay on the ledge. But pain from his left palm sent more flashes of light through his vision.

His right index finger lay on something hard and round.

Vince reached an inch further and placed three fingers over a biner.

Was it the end of the quickdraw attached to the bolt Jess had been unwilling to use?

Strength gushed from Vince's body like blood from a severed artery. The beginning of his fall.

He bounced upward with his remaining leg strength and clamped his right hand around the biner. The rope portion of the quickdraw ran between his middle and ring fingers. Vince reached out with his left hand and grabbed the quickdraw, while he tried to ignore the pain.

He needed the equivalent of one more chin up.

His mind drifted back ten years to football training camp. Vince had gone for the team chin-up record. If he could pull himself up just one more time, he'd have something much more significant, a chance to find Jess.

Vince pulled hard. With his arms shaking, threatening an unconditional surrender, his upper body slid onto the ledge.

Sweating and nearly vomiting from exertion, Vince lay face down on the ledge, legs dangling over the edge, waiting for the strength to crawl forward to safety.

Jess. He had to find her now.

As Vince's mind cleared, thoughts of his dangerous predicament came rolling in like a storm surge. To help Jess, he may need to go hand-to-hand with her abductors.

He pulled his legs onto the ledge, crawled forward, turned onto his back and sat up. He scanned the area around him. Vince was on top of the rock and he was alone.

Maybe his left wrist hadn't been sprained as badly as he first thought. The pain had backed off a little. But, if he had to fight, his bloody, raw hand was a liability. Vince reached for the roll of tape Jess had clipped to his harness.

He could temporarily replace the lost epithelium on his hand with tape. The artificial gray skin might not feel very good adhered to raw flesh, but it would prevent further injury. After all, isn't that what the Army developed duct tape for, binding up battlefield wounds? The tape might even come in handy if he had to resort to hand-to-hand combat.

He wrapped his left hand with two layers of tape and pushed from his mind all thoughts of the time when he would have to pull that tape off. For now, the tape was his friend. It might save his life and Jess's. When it became his enemy, maybe an emergency room doctor with nerve block and antibiotics could help him take it off ... after he found Jess.

Vince clipped the roll of tape onto his harness and took a deep breath. He had mastered Choss Master. But that was only the beginning of what he had to accomplish.

His taped left hand throbbed from the tape sticking to the raw hamburger that comprised the heel of his hand. But Vince's strength had returned. It was time to find Jess.

He scanned the entire area visible from his position on top of the rock. No one.

A thick layer of dust had blown in, coating the surface on top of the rock. The marks in the dust indicated that Jess had struggled with someone.

He took a closer look. Not someone, multiple people. There appeared to be three unique footprints in addition to Jess's. The intruders must have come from the south.

A strip of duct tape lay on the ground behind the rock crowning this section of the Sunshine Wall. Vince picked up the tape and saw long strands of brunette hair stuck to it. Jess's hair. He could draw only one conclusion. Jess had tape on her hands too. Someone had kidnapped her.

Vince wadded up the tape and slammed it against a large boulder. "If Patrick has anything to do with this, I'll kill the little twerp with my bare hands."

His left hand felt sticky and wet. Blood.

He looked at the blood oozing from the edges of the tape. "Well, maybe I'll kill him with my bare right hand."

A high-pitched whine echoed across the valley to the south.

Vince ran by a rock outcropping to look southward.

From the near side of the desert valley, a helicopter rotor revved. The chopper tilted forward and lifted off, flying southward. A few seconds later, it turned slowly to the right and headed west, toward Seattle.

Vince had begun to suspect why Jess was on that chopper, but where would the kidnappers take her?

Chapter 15

As the chopper disappeared over the mountains to the west, an urge to vomit hit Vince full force. He had always protected Jess, but this time he had failed.

Vince fought off the nausea by trying to answer questions about the identity of the kidnappers. LACO was a multibillion-dollar corporation. They could certainly afford a chopper. But could they afford to risk a crime like kidnapping?

There had to be something more sinister about Patrick's work in the lab than anything he had conjured up. And perhaps there was another potential partner waiting in the wings, an entity that would do the very things Paul didn't want done with his technology.

The potential partner must be a business organization willing to commit crimes for profit. That conclusion begged the question Vince feared to ask. Was organized crime involved?

Had Paul suspected something like this before his death? Was that why he hung on to life until Vince arrived? To warn Vince? Paul said someone was spying on Virtuality.

Paul's intensity in his last few living moments came rushing back at Vince. But he wasn't sure how much he should read into the desperation on a dying man's face. Maybe it only meant that Paul was facing death.

No. That wasn't true. Paul was the most unselfish person Vince had ever known. His concern would be for others, for innocent people, and for the evil this technology might bring. And the evil people it would attract, people like those who had flown away with Jess.

Someone must've been stalking them, spying and waiting for a chance to take her. Were their phones or his car bugged? Regardless, he had to get help to track them down and to free Jess.

Vince pulled out his cell and looked at the signal strength. A single bar flickered on and off. He dialed Paul's home phone to see if he could place a call.

He lost the connection before it even rang. He needed to get back to his car and drive to a location with cell service. But how had Jess said they would hike back to the car? She said it was a two-mile hike around the wall. Which direction? Northeast or southwest?

Vince set out to the northeast, the shortest distance to his car.

After an hour of trying different routes, the Sunshine Wall still cut off his descent. Vince was in no shape to climb rock walls of any height. Besides, he had abandoned his remaining climbing equipment at the top of Choss Master.

After thirty more minutes of encountering sheer drop-offs, he gave up and turned to the southwest to hike around the far end of the wall.

Two hours later, Vince trudged into the parking area. Pulses of pain shot through his left hand with every beat of his heart. His fatigue grew almost as fast as the desperate desire to find Jess.

Vince climbed into his car, tore out of the parking area, and raced toward Ellensburg and phone reception.

The question now niggling was whom should he call, the police or someone else? Maybe he should call someone who was willing to bend the rules to take down the bad guys. Someone like Paul's friend, Dave Craig.

Paul had contracted with his old high school buddy, Dave Craig, for security services before negotiating the contract with the DOD. Craig ran a private security company that performed work for the DOD in places like Afghanistan, Iraq, and in the U.S.

Craig employed ex-military people, nearly all former special forces—weapons sergeants, team daddies, detachment commanders—the kind of people trained to move into any area on the planet without being detected and carry out their mission.

Maybe threatening the kidnappers with Craig's men would—no. It might spook them into dumping Jess's body and splitting. It was best to let Craig handle any discussion with the kidnappers.

First, Vince would try the Ellensburg police.

Thirty minutes later, Vince sat on the edge of town talking to an Ellensburg police officer. Since he was already near the police station, the officer asked him to come to the station.

After fifteen minutes of being passed around, Vince had been handed off to Detective Mooney, who sounded like a no-nonsense sort of cop. Somebody who might help Vince.

"Did you say her name was Jessica Martin?" Mooney looked up from his notepad.

"Jessica Jamison."

"How old is Jessica?"

Jess's birthday was next month. She would be Vince's age. "She's almost 26."

"How long has she been missing?"

Here it comes. Vince stood, ready to bail on the police. "About four hours."

"Look, she's an adult, so we can't declare her missing until—"

"Mooney, she was kidnapped!"

"And you witnessed this?"

"Not exactly. I was stuck on a cliff after the kidnappers cut my rope while Jess was belaying me up a rock face.

After I reached the top, forty-five minutes later, I saw them fly off in a helicopter."

"So it's possible she went willingly."

"Not unless she wanted me dead. This was my first climb and I nearly fell trying to climb solo to the top without most of my equipment."

"Is it possible that ... she intended you harm?"

The surge of heat on Vince's neck drove his fist at the policeman. A split second before he contacted Mooney's face, Vince opened his fist, grabbed a handful of the detective's shirt and twisted hard. "You're not listening to me. Jess and I were as close as two people can be. Best friends. No, she was taken to get—"

The more he tried to explain, the more complicated the story would become ... and less believable. When he got to the missing pieces, Mooney would probably dismiss Vince as a nutcase.

He needed to get out of here. Now.

He released Mooney's shirt.

The detective glared at him for a second, then smoothed the wrinkles from his shirt. "I could have you arrested, Mr. van Gordon. Maybe—"

"I'm sorry. Maybe you could forget that I even came in here. I'll call after twenty-four hours if no one has heard from Jess."

Mooney shrugged like he meant to shrug off the whole incident, including Vince van Gordon. "That I can do. You go cool off. Make some phone calls and, if you haven't heard from your girlfriend by tomorrow evening, call us."

Girlfriend? If only their relationship were that simple. Mooney hadn't a clue about Jess and him. And if Vince stayed here any longer, he was likely to get himself thrown in jail. "Thanks. I'll do that." Thanks for nothing.

Vince walked out the door.

What did the disciples do in the Bible when the people in a town wouldn't listen to their message? Didn't they shake the dust off their feet? It sounded like a great idea.

He looked at his dirty, quadruple-E climbing shoes covered in dust glued on by dried pigeon poop. Shaking anything off those shoes wasn't possible.

Time to recruit Craig. Vince stopped by his car parked at the curb and pulled out his cell to search for the number for Craig's company, Delta Security.

Vince almost dropped his phone when it rang.

Chapter 16

As Vince stood beside his car near the Ellensburg police station, his ringing cell derailed the carefully crafted speech he'd prepared for Craig, the head of Delta Security. But, if Vince mentioned Paul to Craig, he wouldn't need a speech. Paul's name would be enough. Craig would help him.

Paul had opened a lot of doors for Vince in Paul's short life. All except one.

The caller ID displayed an area code Vince didn't recognize. An icy chill ran down his neck as he realized who the caller might be and what he or she probably wanted.

His strategy, reveal as little as possible. "Hello."

"Mr. Vince van Gordon, I presume." The voice was flat, deadpan.

Vince pictured himself talking to a corpse, then realized the person on the other end may have intended such a dead end for Vince earlier this morning when they left him hanging from Choss Master. "Are you the doofus who cut my rope? The man who flew away in a blue Bell Helicopter, tail number—"

"Cut the smalltalk, van Gordon." Deadpan had resurrected as a breathy growler, who sounded like he was about to lose his cool.

Good. Anger might give Vince an advantage in this war of wits and words. He wanted to ask about Jess, but since she was Deadpan's bait, Vince wasn't going to bite. At least not immediately. "Smalltalk? That's all a small man with a small mind can comprehend. You getting any of this?"

The mouth on the other end blew out a blast of air, filling Vince's ear with static. "van Gordon, I'll overlook the insults if you cooperate. And if you don't, a pretty little woman will—"

"Aren't you overlooking something? I'm going to end this call unless you put Jess on the line. Now! You got that?"

Vince hadn't meant to lose it during the call or give clues about how desperate he was to get Jess back safely.

No reply.

You said it, dude. Now you gotta follow through.

"Goodbye, small man." Vince terminated the call.

From a long-neglected place deep inside, the words of a prayer came. But Vince's prayer transcended words. It came as pain, panic, and other feelings too deep to be uttered. His silent petition traveled from Vince's heart straight to the One who knew it best.

Please, God. Let the phone ring again.

Was it ten seconds or ten minutes? He didn't know, but his phone did ring. Same number.

"I wouldn't play that little game again, van Gordon, or a certain little lady will have a painful, life-changing experience."

"Whatever you want, it's no deal unless I talk to Jess now. If she's not okay, you've made the biggest mistake of your sorry little life. Put her on the phone. I get to ask my questions. You're not going to spoof me with voice recordings."

"Take it easy. We're reasonable. We knew you would want to talk to her. We're not stupid, lamebrain."

Vince bit his tongue until it hurt, trying to stifle some choice words he had for this guy.

Raspy sounds and muffled voices came through the phone.

Someone panted into the mic on the other end. "Vince, are you okay?"

Her voice brought reality into context and an ache to his gut. He opted not to tell her about Choss Master's vengeance taken out on a novice climber's hands. "I'm fine, Jess. Have they hurt you in any way? Any way at all?"

"Not really. Only enough to force zip ties on my hands. But they cut your rope, Vince. How did you—"

"You're a good instructor, Jess." That's all she needed to know.

"I ... I've got to go now. Do what they say, Vince. I'll be fine. Pretend I'm captured just like when we played cowboys and Indians."

"But you always—"

"Exactly. Just tell them you'll do whatever they ask."

He caught her implication. Tell them. Don't necessarily do it.

"Enough games." Deadpan again. "She gave you some good advice. You going to follow it?"

Cowboys and Indians. She had given him more than deadpan realized. "Yeah. On one condition."

"You're in no position to—"

"Yes, I am. Now get this, knucklehead. If anything happens to her, your life is over. I'm coming after you with a team of ex-special forces—Navy SEALs, Army Rangers—people I know. They can go anywhere on the planet, slip in undetected, and complete their mission, which will be to take you out—you get the picture. You die, and I guarantee it won't be painless."

"Getting a little worked up, are we? Big talk for a guy who writes novels. Probably fantasies."

"If you want to live, slime face, don't hurt Jess. You got that?"

"This conversation is over, dude. You've got twenty-four hours to sign a sales agreement with Mr. Michaels or your girlfriend's face will get an extreme makeover, and then she'll really start to scream. Don't call us, we'll call you. Have a nice day."

The dirt bag on the other end terminated the call.

Chapter 17

She should have known Vince would make it up Choss Master. Jess had never seen anything stop him when he was determined. And the guys who cut the rope and took her had given Vince plenty of motivation.

The big brute with a shaved head ripped the cell phone from her zip-tied hands, ending her short conversation with Vince.

She would have tried to give Vince a clue about her location, but the blindfold that chrome dome had put on her in the chopper hadn't come off until her three abductors had forced her into this large windowless room. Their flying time, thirty or forty minutes, would put her location somewhere between sixty and ninety miles from Vantage. But which direction?

She had given Vince one clue. She fully intended to escape from the three goons who held her. Vince should have gotten that message from her cowboys and Indians reference.

Chrome dome pushed her onto a folding chair. "Sit and be quiet or those threats I made to your boyfriend will become a painful reality."

The guy wasn't good at intimidation. But his frequent smirks said he thought he was. He could think that for a bit longer while she gathered intelligence from her kidnappers' animated discussion.

"Sal, come over here and explain to Louie why we're just waiting."

So chrome dome's name was Sal.

Sal strode across the room to his two cohorts and poked a finger in the chest of the short guy who had called him.

Jess almost giggled. She was watching The Three Stooges.

But chrome-dome Curly acted more like Moe, the infamous eye gouger. That meant the guy with Moe's bad-haircut must be Larry. By default, the third guy, the one with the wild hair, was—she needed to focus and listen.

This was no comedy, and she doubted this trio was a feckless as The Three Stooges.

"We'll know what he's up to," Sal said. "Joe stuck a GPS tracker under his car."

A GPS tracker. Jess drew a sharp breath. Vince was a bulldog. He would find her if it was the last thing he did. With these stooges tracking him, it might be the last thing Vince did.

Since these men had left Vince dangling halfway up Choss Master, they weren't overly concerned about his health. They would probably kill him if he got too close. Killing wasn't as clean a solution for controlling Virtuality as a signed sales agreement, but it would still give whoever hired The Three Stooges what that person wanted.

The danger to Vince gave Jess an even greater incentive to escape. But what if she died in the attempt? They might still force Vince to sell the company by telling him she was alive and promising to free her after the sale completed.

Vince's name came from across the room.

Jess listened.

"It looks like van Gordon's headed our way," Sal said. "He just turned onto I-90 headed west."

If Vince was headed west, toward them, he must be somewhere near Ellensburg. That would place Jess near Virtuality's lab, or at least on the west side of the mountains near I-90. Lead foot Vince could arrive in an hour, and these guys had already shown they were indifferent to his

VIRTUALITY

potential death. And now, maybe they wanted him dead. That meant they could dispose of her too ... anytime.

Jess needed to act now, or she and Vince might never have a chance at life together. And Paul's worst fears, abuse of his technology, would be realized.

Jess looked down at the zip ties around her wrists, thankful they hadn't tied her feet too. When she looked up, Sal hovered over her with another pair of zip ties in his hand.

"Time to put the ties on the ..." he launched into a vile description of her womanhood.

Jess refused to flinch at his words and returned them with a glare that made silent but similar accusations about his manhood. "Is that the best you can do, slime face?"

Sal pulled his head back. "Slime face? That's the same thing your boyfriend called me. Or is he your pimp?"

She brushed off his crude insinuation. "Boyfriend? Who told you that?"

"That's what the nurse in the CCU thought. You were all curled around him like two—"

"Curly, you need to get a better source of intelligence, or maybe just some intelligence—about 100 IQ points might do it." She'd called him Curly. Hopefully, he hadn't made the—

"Time to shut you up, you worthless piece of ..." While he spewed phrases straight from the sewer, Sal grabbed her ankles.

Evidently, he'd made the Curly connection and didn't see any humor in it.

Having those irritating plastic manacles on her feet would complicate her escape. But with all three men in the room, this was not the time to attempt anything. And what had he meant by shutting her up? Maybe he was going to move her where Curly didn't have to listen to her insults. That meant she'd have at least one less guard.

Sal yanked hard on the ties cutting into the flesh on her ankles.

Jess wouldn't give him any satisfaction by yelping or complaining. But she gasped when Sal grabbed her zip-tied feet and wrists and slung her body across his broad shoulders.

Riding on his shoulders, Jess could gouge his eyes, but that would be pointless and might get her killed.

Sal turned and headed toward a door.

Jess craned her neck to check out the door. It looked like an interior door with a lock on the outside of the doorknob.

"Louie, open the door." The man with the Larry-like hair hurried across the room and opened the door to a small storage room.

Inside were empty storage shelves. There were no windows.

Sal stepped inside the room, stooped, and let her roll off his shoulders, catching her inches before she hit the concrete floor.

Jess looked up at Sal and then at the doorway. A light switch had been installed inside the room on the wall near the doorknob. One naked bulb protruded from a socket in the center of the ceiling.

While she studied the room, Sal had stepped out. He slammed the door.

The room went black.

Lying on the floor on her back, Jess kept her eyes focused on the spot where she saw the light switch, praying that the bulb wasn't burnt out.

She rolled onto her stomach, pushed her body onto her knees, and then stood on her bound feet. After two or three dozen small incremental movements Jess managed to turn a one-eighty. When she reached out her hands in front of her, they both touched the wall. She slid them to the right and her left hand bumped into the molding around the door frame.

Jess slid her hands down the wall to the face plate for the light switch. She found the switch and flipped it.

The light flashed with a muffled pop, leaving the room black.

Darn!

The old light bulb had blown. How long had it been since she said Vince could get here in an hour? Maybe twenty or thirty minutes? She had lost all track of the time of day and could only track time relative to Vince driving onto I-90.

No way would Jess remain here and let them lure Vince to his death. But what she would attempt next, she had only seen done on a video.

Jess raised her bound wrists high over her head and drew a deep breath. In an explosive motion, she drove her hands down and apart.

Plastic ripped into her skin, but her hands flew out to her sides after the zip tie broke. A sharp sting echoed up and down the nerves of her hands and forearms.

She touched her right wrist. It was warm and sticky. Blood. The video said the ties would probably break her skin. A small price to pay for freeing her hands.

To escape, Jess needed to be left with only one guard. She could take one man out using the element of surprise and the powerful kick she had developed. If the door opened before she freed her feet, she'd never get that chance. But how could she free her feet?

She waddled around the room feeling for the shelves. She had seen two sets when Sal carried her in, one on each side of the room. Her left hand bumped one set of the shelves.

These shelves were part of the metal structure. They were screwed or bolted onto it. Nothing she could pull loose.

Jess moved to the other side of the room. The shelves here were wooden boards, lying across shelf brackets. She measured the length of the shelf. Twelve hand widths. About eight feet.

The corners of the boards were milled with a moderately sharp edge. Maybe she could sit on the floor and saw through her ankle restraints. But she feared she had only about fifteen minutes left before Vince arrived and her situation changed.

Footsteps sounded by the door.

She didn't need this. Jess swept the floor with her hands and grabbed the broken restraints that had bound her wrists. She put them around her wrists, pressing her hands together as if she were still bound.

The door rattled and opened.

Jess dropped to her knees, blinded by the light now stabbing her eyes and flooding the room.

"Looks like you've been busy." Louie's voice.

"I have orders to move you. Sal can carry you if he wants. But for me, you're going to walk." Louie pulled something from his pocket.

Each blink of her eyes gave Jess a stabbing pain from the light. She forced her eyes open to minimize the adjustment time because she needed to watch Larry. This might be the only time she would have a single guard while the room door was open.

Larry, AKA Louie, opened the pocket knife. "Sit down and give me your feet."

She wanted to give him her feet right on his big crooked nose.

Jess rocked back onto her rear and shoved her feet toward Larry.

He cut the ties on the fourth try. Larry wasn't the most coordinated of the stooges.

She stood, a better posture for attacking.

"Ms. Jamison, you are in luck. We're all alone and, despite all the names Sal called you, I think you are one hot babe. How about a kiss for luck?"

They were alone and he wanted a kiss? How about a foot in the kisser? But she had only about ten minutes to accomplish that and get away.

Louie moved close.

Jess drew a breath, planted both feet solidly on the floor, and shoved Louie's chest.

He stepped backward to gain his balance, opening six feet between them.

Jess prayed it was enough and leaped, launching her body toward Louie with her leg retracted, preparing to kick his head into orbit.

Chapter 18

Vince flew down the west side of the Cascades at least twenty miles-per-hour over the speed limit. As darkness blanketed the valley below, what the caller said he would do to Jess replayed as a nightmare that Vince couldn't shake.

The man had succeeded at pushing Vince's buttons. Was that slime face's intent? Maybe he was only trying to intimidate Vince like the trash talkers he'd heard on the football field? But his gut told him these guys could do trash as well as talk it. For that reason, Vince would go after them, no holds barred. He would be violent, brutal, whatever was needed to rip Jess away from their filthy paws.

But Jess had mentioned playing cowboys and Indians. Each time they played, she was the Indian maiden whom Vince captured. When he tied her up, his knots were never good enough to hold her. Jess always got away. Was that what she was telling him? That she could escape from these men?

Jess was smart, strong, and she knew some karate, but these men were likely pros at what they did. If she tried to escape and got caught, they might make good on their threats. And, as the man had said, they could do worse things to Jess than killing her.

The police wouldn't help him for twenty-four hours. By then, it would be too late. The people who had Jess knew the laws. Whatever these guys' game, it would be over by then.

Twenty-four hours. The clock was ticking, but so was Vince ... like a virtual time bomb. And Patrick would soon catch the brunt of Vince's explosion.

The people behind Jess's abduction wanted Patrick in control of Virtuality. That meant the pudgy little punk should have some clout with the kidnappers. And Vince's threat of immediate, severe bodily harm should convince Patrick to wield that clout.

After the threats, if Patrick refused to cooperate, Vince would beat the little geek, who likely started all this mess, until he spilled everything he knew.

Fifteen minutes later, Vince exited I-90 at North Bend and drove through town headed toward Snoqualmie and Virtuality's lab.

Rumors he and Jess had heard said Patrick had been living at the lab twenty-four-seven since Paul went into the hospital. The clock on the dash read 11:30 p.m. Hopefully, Patrick would be up.

Vince pulled into the old mill site in Snoqualmie at 11:35 and cut the car's lights.

The window by Patrick's office indicated he was still up.

Vince eased the car to a quiet stop almost fifty yards from the lab. He locked his car and made his way along the windowless side of the big building, where he couldn't be spotted from Patrick's office window.

Vince tried the lobby entrance door. It was locked. He could smash Patrick's office window, but that would probably set off the security alarm. And Vince van Gordon pounding on the door at midnight probably wouldn't get a positive response from Patrick either.

With Jess in danger and the lab locked, a big rock through the window was about to get Vince's vote.

The lab door opened.

Vince pressed tightly against the building and froze in the semi-darkness of the dimly lit area.

A man in a white lab coat stepped out, pinching a cigarette between two fingers. The man reached back and fiddled with something the inside of the door. Then he lit the cigarette and walked across the parking area toward a parked vehicle.

Vince moved to the door behind the man and waited until he was about thirty yards away. When Vince tried the door, it opened. A small wad of paper fell to the floor.

The lazy worker had stopped the door from locking. If the guy got locked out when Vince entered, it served him right.

Vince slipped inside and tried the office door.

The door was closed and locked.

Time to wake Mr. Michaels. Vince beat on the door loud enough to wake Patrick out of a dead sleep.

Footsteps sounded on the other side. The door opened. "Walker, I told you—" Patrick looked up at Vince and froze. Panic filled Patrick's darting eyes.

Vince clamped his hands around the short man's neck and squeezed, choking off a whimper. He shoved Patrick across the office and pinned him against the far wall.

"I want you to listen, carefully, because one chance is all you're going to get."

Patrick squeaked out a pitiful complaint.

Vince choked it off. "Somebody nearly killed me today. They kidnapped Jess and flew off with her in a chopper. Where is Jess, Patrick?" Vince eased off his choke hold.

"What do you mean kidnapped—"

Vince choked harder. "That was a question, not an answer. Now, if you value your larynx and that tube in your throat that you suck air through, I suggest you give the correct answer. Where is Jess?" Vince relaxed his grip slightly.

"I—I don't know. I don't know anything about a kidnapping. You don't think I had—"

"That's where you're wrong. You had everything to do with it. Kidnapping and threatening Jess. Demanding that I sign an agreement to sell Virtuality to you. Mr. Michaels, that's what the goon on the phone did. And if I refuse to sign, he said some bad things would happen to Jess."

Patrick's eyes bulged as Vince squeezed again. "I want the truth, Patrick. Tell me where she is and call off your dogs, now, or some horrific things are going to happen to you. Do you know what it's like to choke to death on your own larynx?"

Patrick waved his hands wildly and sucked in a raspy breath.

Vince relaxed his grip.

"Please, man, don't kill me." Patrick moaned out the words. "I swear I don't know anything about a kidnapping. Jess was one of Paul's friends. I would never hurt her."

"Then suppose you tell me who *would* hurt her and why."

Patrick blew out a ragged breath.

Vince let go of his throat, grabbed a fistful Patrick's pajama top, and pinned him to the wall. "If anything happens to Jess, I'm holding you personally accountable. Now, for the third time, who took her?"

"Vince, you know I've had discussions with LACO. Paul probably told you that. I didn't know it until a few days ago, but LACO has some shady, third-party partners. I think they're planning on making a lot of money if I gain ownership and if they can force me into seeing things their way."

"Who are these shady characters? The Mafia?"

Patrick's eyes bulged again, without any choking. "Why would you ask about the Mafia?"

"Hyperbole for effect. Now who are the shady characters?"

"You may be right about Mafia connections."

It had been hyperbole for effect. But, if there were an element of truth to Patrick's words, things were spiraling even further out of control. Organized crime wouldn't think twice about murder—Jess and Vince both—if it got them what they wanted. "Tell me what you know. All of it!"

"I did some checking with what little info I had. These third parties are connected with the adult entertainment world out of Southern California."

"You mean porn companies?"

"Something like that."

"And you, the Christian partner of my Christian brother, were good with this?"

"I didn't say that."

"Everyone involved wanted to make money doing the very things Paul was trying to prevent."

"LACO and the others evidently want to. And they'll do things Paul didn't even know existed."

After slipping on that shirt and the goggles, Vince had an idea about what existed. "How much money are we talking?"

Patrick massaged his neck and pointed at Vince's fist still grinding into Patrick's chest.

Vince loosened his grip.

Patrick drew a breath and blew it back out slowly. "LACO told me I might become the next Bill Gates, if I cooperated."

"Which you were ready to do, provided you could remove the obstacle, me."

"No. That's not—"

"Cool it, Patrick. Let me think for a minute." Vince released his hold on Patrick. "And you think Mafia-type thugs have Jess?"

"That's my best guess."

"Can you use LACO to call off the Mafia mongrels?"

"Vince, these guys do whatever they want. They have their own reasons. Nobody can control them."

Patrick still wasn't telling Vince everything. If this DOD project were Top Secret, how would LACO and organized crime know enough to strike up a deal with Patrick? Something about this project had been either leaked by lab workers or by Patrick.

Unlocking that mystery required inspecting the lab more thoroughly than the two or three minutes Vince had been inside. If he were correct, there already had been serious security breaches. At this point, one more wouldn't matter.

The evidence said Patrick was making a big-time gamble for wealth. It was time to call him on it, even if that required some speculation and bluffing. "I want to see what's going on in the lab. And I need a tour guide." Vince grabbed Patrick's pajamas again and stared down into the short man's eyes.

"But I can't let you in, Vince. The work in the lab is classified."

"I'm not officially cleared, but that's only because of your stonewalling and negligence. Punch the cipher code into the door lock or I'm going to break your neck and then break down the door."

"But—but, that would cost us the Army contract." Patrick sputtered out the words.

"Patrick, I don't give a rip about the contract you're using to fund the R&D to develop products that will damage people, damage our society—probably the entire world—to make you filthy rich."

"But it's not like that. It's—"

"But it *is* like that. And I'll bet the Army has no clue about your plans for their technology or that they're already funding them."

"They aren't stupid. They know there are other applications for remote nerve and—" Patrick stopped. The look in his eyes said he had just smacked himself on the forehead for his unintentional disclosure.

"What were you saying?"

"I can't say. It's classified."

Patrick wouldn't voluntarily open the door. Vince decided to go with plan B. He grabbed Patrick's arm, twisted, and forced it behind his back. Vince pushed up on it until Patrick moaned.

Then Vince pushed harder.

Patrick wailed.

Vince shoved him toward the locked door. "Open it. Now!" He forced Patrick's arm near the breaking point.

"Okay! Okay. I'll open it."

Vince eased up on the arm.

Patrick slumped into a broken heap, gasping for breath.

What about Jess? You aren't thinking, dude.

The voice inside was right. He needed to learn more about the lab, but he could do that later. If Patrick's arm needed to be broken, it should be done to keep Jess safe.

Vince huffed a blast of air, then spun Patrick around. "First, you're going to call LACO, their CEO, and tell him everything you planned with them is about to go down the toilet. If LACO can't convince the thugs to free Jess, unharmed, it *is* all down the toilet, because I'm the person who's about to flush it. I want Jess freed within the hour or that's exactly what I will do. I'll flush this whole project, the technology and your billion dollars. And I'll kill anybody who gets in my way. So call! Now!"

"But I can't just demand—"

"Yes, you can, Mr. Michaels, or you won't be around to see what happens with your precious little project and its technology." Vince pushed Patrick into his office and closed the door. "There's the phone. Pick it up and call."

"But it's after midnight."

"Call their emergency contact number. Companies always have one for important business. Consider this an emergency, a life-threatening one, because that's what I'm making it. Do you understand?"

Vince clamped a hand on Patrick's throat and squeezed.

Patrick choked.

Vince relaxed his grip and pointed at the phone.

Patrick coughed three or four times and then reached for it.

Behind Vince, a thump came from the office door.

He whirled toward it.

The door swung open.

A slender form leaped into the room.

Jess. How had she gotten away from—

"Vince, I took out Larry. But Curly and Moe have assault rifles." Jess's strong, slender arms gripped Vince's shoulders. "We've got to get out of here."

Chapter 19

Somehow, Vince and Jess had slipped out of the lab, dodged a few bullets and beat the thugs to the river. They had nearly reached the other side. But now the glacier-fed water of the Snoqualmie River was beating Vince.

Though he stood in three feet of water near the shore with his good hand gripping Jess's tank top, a torrent ripped at Vince's lower legs and thighs. The current slid him downstream, along the river bottom.

He slid at least a foot every second. If he raised even one foot to take a step, he would lose this duel with the river.

How could three feet of water exert so much force?

Jess's body created most of the drag. He needed to get her out of the water.

The black void lay only two steps to Vince's right.

Though his arms had turned to rubber, he bent down and shoved his arms under Jess.

Bending sent Vince's body shooting toward the precipice.

He lifted hard and, with Jess in his arms, dove toward the shore. But would he land on the bank or on the rocks three-hundred feet below?

The pain came as a relief when his shoulder and side smashed on river rocks in six inches of water. His deep, violent gasps threatened to rip something loose inside his body.

During their final assault on the current, Vince had somehow managed to keep Jess's body upstream from his.

Now, she lay beside him, pressed against his body by the current. Her right arm curled around his waist, holding on with whatever strength remained.

Vince raised his head and looked to his right into a black hole that rumbled back at him, sending a cloud of mist coating his head with an icy chill, a chill colder than the river water, the chill of fear and imminent death.

He lay only a step away from where the river plunged three-hundred feet to the churning cauldron of angry water at the base of Snoqualmie Falls.

"D-did we m-make it, Vince? A-are we—" Jess shook violently as she tried to talk.

He needed to get her out of the water and out of possible gunshot range. The opposite side of the river wasn't easily navigated on foot this close to the falls. But this was no time for taking further chances because, if such a thing as luck existed, Vince had probably used up his life's quota over the past fifteen minutes.

He scooped Jess up in his arms. "We made it ... sweetheart. We—"

Jess stopped moving, except for her shaking, then drew a sharp breath.

It had slipped out. The word he'd used in his mind a thousand times. The first term of endearment that had ever passed between them, other than friend, buddy, pal or occasional BFFs in a text message.

With Jess in his arms, Vince stumbled into the darkness of the forest lining the west side of the river.

Jess had buried her face in his neck. Now his neck seemed wetter than when he was in the river. Maybe that was because, now, he could feel his neck and the wetness was no longer numbing. It was warm.

Vince set Jess on her feet and wrapped her up in his arms to keep her from falling. Thankfully, his arms were regaining strength by the second.

Jess leaned against him, her body shaking, partly from shivering, the rest from her sobs.

Was this relief that they had made it? Or was it his choice of words? He would bet money that it was his words.

Next question—was she happy or hurting? After the awkward way the day had started, he couldn't be sure.

Somewhere between one and two o'clock in the morning, exhausted from the ordeal, Vince couldn't sort it all out. Maybe Jess would eventually say something and—

Jess cupped both of his cheeks and pulled his face down to hers.

For a few sweet seconds, Vince poured the pent-up passion of years of loving this incredible woman into his kiss. But the real wonder was that Jess returned it the same way.

An almost miraculous escape from gunmen through a deadly river that claimed several lives each year, his first kiss from the only woman he'd ever loved—maybe Vince's meaningless life of living alone in the shadows was ending. Maybe …

One thing he was sure of, now that it had warmed up, his taped hand hurt like heck. But that didn't keep him from using it to pull Jess snugly against him.

* * *

After Jess pulled her lips from Vince's, she hid her face against his neck. But that was stupid. He couldn't see her face under the blackness of the forest canopy. She seldom showed her deepest feelings, but she shouldn't be embarrassed for doing so.

Jess raised a hand to touch her warm cheek. How could a freezing, hypothermic face become a hot, flushed face in a few seconds? An easy question to answer. She'd finally gotten the kiss Jess had looked forward to, the one she had expected all those years in high school. And the man who made his living using words had finally found a word to describe his feelings toward her, sweetheart.

Had he always thought about her that way but just hadn't said it?

Jess put on the brakes to her analysis of Vince's words, before it could make her angry and destroy the moment. But she had to do something to break the awkward silence. "I thought we were going to die ... one way or another. I didn't want that to happen, Vince, before ..."

Maybe she had said enough. And she had initiated it, so maybe the kiss wasn't as meaningful as she thought. Still, it was a kiss from Vince, and the passion behind it was undeniable.

She pulled her head back. Vince's gaze had grown so intense she could feel it, even in the darkness. Jess couldn't meet that gaze after exposing her heart more than she'd intended. She couldn't chance being disappointed again. One more time of dying inside from his rejection would be too much. It would be easier to leave and never be sure than to get that final rejection from the only man Jess had ever loved.

"Jess, I'm so sorry."

Big mistake, girl.

"It's my fault." Vince put a hand under her chin and tilted her face up toward his.

She let him raise her chin. Probably another big mistake.

Vince drew a deep breath. "You and I should never have waited until we were twenty-six, about to be shot, or drowned before ..." Vince kissed her, a kiss he initiated.

They had started over again. Vince had erased years of pain in a few seconds. And for the first time in more than eight years, Jess had no insult ready for him.

For years, she had turned the pain and frustration that lay just under the surface into words that lashed out at

Vince's rejection. Words he seemed to take as a joke most of the time.

She hadn't meant the van Gogh digs as a joke. But they were no longer needed.

Vince pulled his arm from her and slipped out of his shirt.

"Vince, what are you doing? We're still freezing from the water."

"Speak for yourself. I'm much warmer now."

"No matter how warm we are, we're not going to take off our—"

"Jess, how could you think—"

She pressed a finger against his lips. "Vince, would you like to tell me everything that was going through your head a few seconds ago?"

"Yeah. I mean, no. I mean—guess we did get caught up in the moment." Vince paused. "But the gunmen will leave if they think we went over the falls. We came so close that they'll have to consider that possibility. They'll probably check below the falls."

He rolled his wet shirt into a ball and turned toward the river. "So I'm going to give them some evidence." He threw his shirt into the water.

Vince was thinking about their safety while she clearly had other things on her mind.

Vince returned from the water's edge and poked a finger at the neckline of her tank top. "If you really want to contribute something to the cause …" The teasing tone had returned to his voice.

Instantly, they were two kids again. And Vince would not get the better of her.

Jess pulled an arm down inside of her tank top, then her second arm. She slowly lifted the bottom.

"Jess, you wouldn't—"

"Wouldn't what? Contribute to the cause? I'll tell you what. If you cut off an ear and contribute it, I'll keep my clothes on."

"What am I going to do with you?"

"That's up to you. But, right now ..." She slipped her arms back through the arm holes. "... I think we need to get out of here before they decide to drive over the bridge and check out the forest on this side of the river. But what about your ear—I mean your car?"

"It's a rental. We leave it. Who knows about these dudes. They might booby-trap it to kill us. They've already hacked my ear once—I mean my car."

Jess giggled. How could she find anything humorous when they were in so much danger? The answer to that question stood beside her.

Vince had never failed to protect her. His size, strength, and his heart had always prevailed, no matter the size of the obstacle or the power of the enemy. She had watched his WSU football games on TV and heard his football nickname. At strong safety, the announcers called him ...

Invincible Vince.

Jess looked up at him and smiled. It fit. She curled her hand around his right hand. He seemed to be protecting his left hand.

Vince kissed her forehead, then turned and led her through the forest, upriver, toward the town of Snoqualmie.

He looked like he was cold. But, if the Snoqualmie River couldn't freeze him, this warm, summer night surely wouldn't.

"We've got two miles of forest to get through and you don't even have a shirt."

"I'll be okay. The temperature's in the upper sixties tonight, and we'll be moving the whole time."

"I—I can keep you warm, Vince." Why had she said that?

Through an opening in the forest canopy, the crescent moon lit Vince's face. The look in his eyes said, now that the ice had been broken, she could keep him warm just by being in eyeshot.

He cupped her cheek with his left hand, sending a strange sensation across the side of her face.

"You already are, Jess." Vince said. "Now, let's follow the edge of the trees back to Snoqualmie. I saw a twenty-four-hour convenience store when we drove through town. I can probably snag a Seahawks or Mariners T-shirt and call a taxi while you watch for three stooges carrying guns."

Vince paused and looked at her. "Jess, those guys were mafia-type enforcers. Did you really take them out by kicking them when you got away?"

"Remember what your dad used to say to me when I was just a kid."

"You're avoiding my question."

"No, I'm not. He said things that *my* dad should have said to me, but never did."

"You mean like inside of every girl there's a princess?"

"Yes. And inside of every princess—waiting for just the right time to get out—there's a warrior."

"So the warrior got out tonight?"

"I guess so. But the princess waited until there was only one stooge guarding her before she let the warrior out."

"Smart princess. Strong warrior. How did you the leave the lone stooge?"

"With a flat nose. Like you left Jimmy Grant on your front lawn. But, Vince, I never thanked your dad for all he did for me during those growing-up years. Now he's gone."

"You can thank him when you see him ... up there. But let's not do that tonight. And as much as I'd like to focus on other things ..." Vince's gaze locked on a location a little south of her nose. "... let's concentrate on getting to

Snoqualmie and then getting back home. We've got a lot to talk about."

It was nearly 2:00 a.m. when they found a convenience store in Snoqualmie. While Vince paid for his Mariners t-shirt with a twenty from his soggy wallet, Jess watched the main street through the store window.

Vince slipped his shirt on, but he had barely used his left hand. And it was covered in duct tape like the tape they had carried on their harnesses.

Something had happened to his hand. Jess had been too preoccupied to notice, and Vince hadn't mentioned it.

He came up behind her and laid the taped hand on her shoulder. "I'm going to call a cab, now. Have you seen any sign of them?"

"No. But the SUV that just passed the store slowed and—Vince, it's making a U-turn and coming back."

"Follow me. Jess." Vince shot a laser look at the cashier. "We were never here, dude. Got it?"

Chapter 20

Jess glanced back before she and Vince slipped out the back door of the convenience store.

Headlights of the SUV beamed through the glass door in front of the store.

She closed the door behind them. "They just pulled in."

Vince led her at a trot past the delivery area behind the building and into the dark shadows of a grove of fir trees.

Thirty yards in, Vince stopped.

She craned her neck, trying to see the rear door. "I can't see the store, but I haven't heard them."

Vince took her hand and pulled her close to his side. "We wait here. After they leave, we'll go back in and I'll call."

"But what if—"

"Jess, the guy in the store wants to help us."

"How do you know that?"

"His eyes told me. And he couldn't keep them off you. Do you really think he'd hand you over to those Three Stooges?"

She didn't reply.

Somewhere an engine revved. Tires squealed, and the vehicle took off down the street, headed toward the Snoqualmie Falls end of town.

"They left. Let's go."

"How can we be sure they left?"

"It's 2:30 in the morning. How many vehicles have you seen on the street?"

"Just one."

Vince led her to the store's rear entrance. He tried the door.

It was locked.

"The dude locked us out. We can't go around to the front. They might spot us."

"Accept it, Vince. Some days you're the pigeon and others ... well, you're Choss Master."

He looked at her then shook his head. Maybe Vince was out of comebacks. And maybe Jess needed to break her habit of spewing insults at the man she loved.

The squeak of rubber-soled shoes on a clean floor came from inside the door.

Vince pushed Jess away from the door, and they flattened against the rear wall of the store.

Jess reached for his hand, but Vince had clenched his fists.

A head popped out of the door. The store attendant.

Jess took a calming breath.

Vince's balled fists relaxed.

"I thought you two might be here. Those three dudes left in a big hurry. One of them pulled a gun. But I've been robbed before, so I could see he had something other than robbery on his mind. I told him you had left and the last time I saw you, you were headed north, keeping a block off Main Street."

"Thanks for covering for us," Vince said. "Can I use your phone?"

The attendant pointed to a phone on the counter.

Vince reached for the phone with his left hand. "Doggone it!" He pulled his hand from the phone and cradled it in his right hand.

"Vince, what's wrong with your hand? I've heard you can fix anything with duct tape but, seriously, a hand?"

"Uh, I slipped on the rocks."

"On Choss Master?"

"Yeah. It's just a little abrasion."

The picture came into clear focus of Vince on Choss Master and what it would take to produce such a wound. Vince would never cover his hand with duct tape unless he needed it to continue climbing.

"How did you do that?"

"Just took the roll of tape that you hung on my harness and wrapped—"

"No, Vince. How did you get the abrasion?"

"Thought I'd try a little stemming, but I slid a little."

"You slid while stemming, ripped the skin off, and had to cover your hand or you couldn't—"

"Something like that."

"Let me see your hand." She reached for it.

Vince pulled it away, but rotated it, showing her both sides.

"Real funny, van Gordon. I want to see what's under that tape."

"Can't let you do that, Jess. Nobody touches that hand until I get to an ER or some other place with nerve block."

"If it hurts, I'll bet it's getting hot and inflamed. You know what could happen? You could end up in the hospital fighting for your life or lose your hand if you just let the infection run wild. How much skin did you lose? Was it the size of a quarter? A fifty-cent piece?"

"It was the size of a dollar."

"You mean like a silver dollar?"

"No. A paper dollar."

Jess sucked in a sharp breath. She looked over at the store clerk. "I've got to dress this, now. Have you got iodine, antibacterial ointment, gauze and bandages—maybe some small scissors too?"

"I think so. Try the aisle beyond the candy."

"Jess, I didn't agree to let you—"

"Either you let me, or I'll knock you out with a kick and do it anyway."

"I—I don't know about this, Jess."

"But you do know what could be under that tape, don't you?"

"Yeah. A real microbial mishmash."

She huffed a sharp sigh. "Precisely. It's full of pigeon poop."

In the first-aid section, Jess found a liquid disinfectant with some iodine in it, a tube of Polysporin, gauze, scissors and tape for bandaging. She grabbed Vince by his earlobe and followed the sign pointing to the restrooms.

The fact that Vince didn't try to break her hold on him told her this "little abrasion" was killing him. If she didn't dress it, it *could* kill him. No telling when they could safely get to a doctor.

Vince pointed at the door labeled, men.

"No way. Men's restrooms are gross."

"And how did you get to be an expert on that subject, Ms. Jamison?"

Jess didn't reply, but she opened the women's restroom door and pulled on Vince's ear.

Despite her pulling on his ear, Vince turned to look at the clerk. "Dude, let us know if any suspicious-looking characters show up. You know, guys carrying AK-47s—anything like that."

"Don't worry. I've got your back." The clerk pulled a handgun from under the counter, held it up, then tucked it away.

"Thanks. When this is all over, we'll have to come back and thank you properly."

Jess pulled Vince into the women's room and pointed at the small, vinyl-covered couch. "Sit and don't speak."

"Sounds like doggie obedience training," he muttered, then looked up at her. "But no Husky is gonna make a Cougar sit in the doghouse."

"All you need to know is that Jess Jamison is going to make Vince van Gordon sit still until she's done with him. Got that?" She pushed him onto the seat.

While Vince sat, staring at his taped hand, Jess opened her supplies and lined them up on the edge of a sink. "Now to get that tape off. I'll take it slow and easy. I promise, Vince."

"How about promising me you won't hold it against me if I smack your head when you pull that tape off?"

Jess stopped. Her eyes welled. "Vince …" She wiped her eyes. "… you've already smacked me on the head twice tonight. I didn't hold it against you either time."

Vince reached out, brushed her lips with his fingers, and nodded.

It was her go-ahead signal. She pulled on the edge of the tape, then blew out her relief when another layer of tape appeared below. Soon, Jess had peeled off the tape, leaving a single layer covering the abrasion on the palm and heel of Vince's huge hand.

After the filthy rocks, swimming the river, and fifteen or sixteen hours of time, the skin at the edges of the wound had turned an angry red. Adjacent to that, there would be raw flesh that looked like hamburger. Ugh.

"I've got to get this tape off now, but …"

Jess looked into Vince's eyes and tears rolled down her cheeks. "I don't know if I can do this to you."

Vince curled his good hand around the back of her neck, pulled her toward him, and kissed her forehead. In the next moment, his hand was gone from her neck.

Jess looked down as Vince ripped the tape from his hand in one quick motion.

He sucked in a lungful of air, blew it back out, then breathed hard, his nostrils flaring with each breath as his gaze bored into the raw, red flesh.

Blood flowed from the deepest part of the abrasion. It was Vince's blood. Blood that he had shed for her, trying to save her from the kidnappers.

Jess looked up when she sensed Vince's eyes focused on her face.

"I wouldn't have done this for anyone but you, Jess. But I could say that about a half-dozen things I've done in the past twenty-four hours."

Jess wiped her cheeks and picked up the iodine solution. "If you've got any other nice things to say to me, say them now, because this might draw a few words from the other end of your vocabulary."

"Jess, I write for the CBA, so I don't use—"

Jess doused the wound with iodine.

That pulled one word from Vince that was definitely not CBA-compliant.

"This time will be a lot easier."

Vince sat, breathing hard, clenching and unclenching his right hand. "You mean, there has to be a next time?"

He hadn't noticed. She had already poured the rest of the small bottle onto his hand.

"See?" She lifted Vince's injured hand and kissed it well above the injury and the iodine.

Vince cupped her cheek and nudged her head up. A crooked smile tweaked one side of his mouth. "There's no abrasion there, Jess." He glanced down at the spot she had kissed. "But, a while ago, it was covered with pigeon poop."

Why didn't he—how could he—

He grinned the mischievous grin of twelve-year-old Vince.

She picked up the scissors and reached for his ear. "This just ain't your starry, starry night, Vincent."

In an instant, they were two pre-teens with fun and excitement filling their present and a future filled with each other.

She lowered the scissors.

Vince cupped her cheek again. "This is the way it used to be. Remember?"

He had repeated her words. And it was the second time they had found the magic from the best days of Jessica Jamison's life. Once this present danger passed, maybe she wouldn't have to look for the magic. Maybe the old normal would become the new normal. Maybe ...

Jess finished dressing Vince's wound, using half the tube of Polysporin and most of the gauze and tape, ensuring that the next time she dressed the wound, there would be little or no pain.

Vince made the phone call and twenty minutes later, and with no more visits from the stooges, Vince and Jess climbed into the back of a green and white cab.

"Fairwood, please. Highway 18 is the shortest route," Vince said.

The cabbie tapped on his GPS for a few seconds. "Fairwood it is."

Jess sat as close to Vince as her seatbelt allowed. She hooked his arm and waited for him to speak.

"I'm not sure what Patrick plans to do with Paul's breakthrough technology but, evidently, he thinks he can become the next Bill Gates." Vince took her hand. "Have you got any idea what application of Paul's technology is worth that kind of money?"

"I already told you that the algorithms I coded for Paul were for lossless compression and decompression of digitized nerve impulse data. Does that give you some ideas?"

"Are we talking about the next generation of video games, Jess?"

"I think it goes far beyond what video games do. There's a sociologist at the University, Dr. Scoggins. Paul met with him twice that I know of in the past two months. This guy studies technology's impacts on American society. For several years, he's focused on video games and virtual reality."

"Are you suggesting that we go meet with this stuffed shirt?"

"Come on, Vince. We both have master's degrees. Just because somebody gets a PhD doesn't mean they're pompous. Besides, we can ask Scoggins what he told Paul. Maybe it will tell us more about the danger Paul mentioned."

"I think we've seen the danger, Jess. More than enough of it."

"Maybe. But Paul couldn't have known about the three stooges. But he might have realized the kind of potential business partners his technology would attract when it tempted people with obscene amounts of money."

"Sounds like you know more about this than you've been letting on."

"Nothing in between, Vince. Remember? I've told you all I know. When I finished coding the algorithms and helped integrate them into the other software, my job was done. I didn't see Paul again until he called and told me he was losing his battle with cancer. He wanted me to persuade you to come home. I did. And I put you in a lot of danger. You know the rest of the story."

"Yeah. As far as the story has gone." He paused and squeezed her hand. "I think you and I need to meet with this Professor Scoggins, tell him what we know, and see if he can shed some light on what kind of deal Patrick might be brokering with LACO and its nefarious partners. Maybe then we'll know why we have people acting like mafia thugs trying to kill us."

"Vince, if we slip up, even once, these people *will* kill us. Are you sure you wouldn't rather take me to Alaska, marry me, and live off the grid in a little cabin for the rest of our lives?"

Vince lowered his voice. "Are you trying to tempt me? You've never done that before."

"You've got a bad memory. There was one time ..." She whispered the words softly and leaned closer to Vince. "But, you know, you would get a lot more than just temptation with the Alaska deal."

She had tried to tempt Vince once, seven years ago. It happened when Vince started slowly withdrawing from her. Women with Jess's INTJ personality type don't make friends easily. And she feared losing the only person she felt close to. The only one she could confide in, her very best friend. But, for Jess, best friend had become much more.

The events of that evening came storming back into her mind and heart. It was the night of the National Honor Society dinner and dance. Vince and Jess were both members, and he had asked her to go with him.

She wanted it to be a real date, not just two buddies attending together. She even bought a little black dress and carefully applied makeup, which she seldom wore. And Jess had her hair done.

When she stood in front of the mirror in her room, Jess hardly recognized herself. She had become what Mr. van Gordon had called her, a beautiful princess with a warrior inside. Surely, Vince would notice how she looked.

Vince picked her up but, though his eyes said he noticed a difference, he never commented on her appearance or her clothes. They attended the dinner, but he made an excuse to skip the dance and they left early. He took her straight home. Didn't even walk Jess to her door. He just left ... and broke her heart. And on that starry,

starry night, the insults started. van Gordon became van Gogh and Jess made sure Vince got an earful.

But Vince had cut off a lot more than an ear. He had cut off his best friend and ripped out her heart in the process.

"... I would, Jess."

Would what? What had Vince said while she was dredging up the past? The last three words sounded like he might take her up on the Alaskan adventure.

She tried her best to forget the past and to give Vince a smile. "Before we do anything rash, we probably should solve the mystery of the mill site."

Idiot!

Why had she changed the subject? She might have gotten some of her questions about Vince answered.

He released her hand. "Questions like what is Patrick really building in the lab and who's trying to kill us to get it?"

According to the clock on the dashboard of the taxi, it was nearly three o'clock in the morning when they turned off Petrovitsky Road and rolled into Fairwood.

Vince had nodded off about fifteen minutes earlier and his head now leaned against hers.

"Vince, we're almost home." Home. She wished they shared a home, shared their lives. The two kisses they shared had revived old memories and old dreams. Did Vince share her dreams? More importantly, would they live long enough to realize those dreams.

Vince raised his head. "Nice pillow. Maybe I can borrow it again sometime."

"That depends on what questions you ask ... and what answers I give."

"I see." Vince looked down into her eyes then sighed and looked ahead down Fairwood Boulevard. "We need a vehicle. Paul's pickup is in the garage. It's an older model. Looks like he used it for house and yard projects. With nearly four thousand square-feet of house and a yard full of bushes, trees, and grass, it probably got a lot of use. I think we should give it some more use tonight."

"But these guys know you're staying at Paul's house. They might be watching it."

"Yeah. I thought about that too. Driver, take the boulevard to 140th and go south into Kent."

"But they could be watching my apartment too?"

"We can find another place to spend the night. But won't you need clothes and such from your apartment?"

"Yes. And I can probably sneak into my apartment through the back entrance and get what I need."

Fifteen minutes later, Jess sat beside Vince in the back of the taxi with a duffel bag by her feet. She had carefully tucked some clothes and essentials inside, essentials like her .38 Special.

Vince instructed the driver to let them off where the Fairwood Golf Course crossed the boulevard, by the fifteenth green. They would cross the green and enter the adjacent greenbelt. They could sneak into the back yard of Paul's house by following the creek through the greenbelt, then get into the house through the side garage door. If they were careful, no one watching from the front of the house could see them until they pulled out of the garage in the truck. That would be the dicey part of their plan.

Vince curled an arm her around her shoulders. Maybe we can get a motel room in the valley for tonight."

"Don't you mean two motel rooms?"

"Jess, we just spent the better part of a night together."

"It was more like the worst part of a night. And we didn't sleep together."

"We came pretty doggone close at the falls. The *big* sleep."

"Don't remind me. But I've got a better idea."

"Better than sleeping together?"

"Uh, Vince, that would require those questions and the right answers ... and then a little ceremony." Vince had no idea how tempting he was as her heart reopened seriously to the idea of *them*. But she wasn't going to tell him. Not yet.

"I was just testing the waters. Checking you out."

"Checking me out? You've already done that ... at Paul's house and on the rocks at Choss Master. If you found what you were looking for, you'll get around to telling me, eventually. Though Vince van Gordon is a bit slow."

"I'm not slow. I was the second fastest guy on the football team in high school."

"That's right. Body by Bowflex, brain by Babys"R"Us. Like I said, slow."

"Jess, when are you—"

"Don't you want to hear my idea?"

"Please. If it will stop the insults."

"My grandparents own a cabin by Lake Retreat. They let me use it when I'm studying for finals or just want to get away for a while. It has electricity and even Internet access."

"Sounds like a good place to hide out while we come up with a plan to turn the three stooges into the three jailbirds." Vince's arm gave her an assuring squeeze.

Jess nodded. "It is a good place. As long as we make sure they don't follow us there."

Vince's free hand went to his chin, massaging it as if it were Aladdin's lamp. "And that could prove tricky since we've got to back Paul's truck out of the garage."

They could use a genie and a few wishes if the house was being watched. "I hope you've got a contingency plan for an ambush about the time you back out onto the street."

"Working on it, Jess."

Chapter 21

3:00 a.m. Trent's high hopes for Sal Romano's team were declining with each passing hour. Now, Trent's plan might have to incorporate serious crimes, the kind that could get a person locked up for life.

The nauseating cramp in his gut had kept him awake, and now it threatened to send him to the bathroom to puke. What about *every other hour* did Sal Romano not understand?

Sal had called around six o'clock in the morning to say Vince and Jessica were headed toward a popular climbing area called Frenchman Coulee. Since that time, Trent had heard nothing from Sal.

Trent checked his recent call log again. Nothing. No text messages either. It had been at least fourteen hours.

If they crashed LACO's chopper, Trent doubted he could scrape up enough to pay for it and still keep the cash reserves he needed. It was LACO's own pilot at the controls. That might get Trent off the hook for the chopper, but he would still lose his three men. What would Russo want as compensation? Their agreement hadn't covered that contingency.

How the New York underworld might decide to handle such events, perhaps an eye for an eye, brought back Trent's urge to vomit.

Regardless, no news was no longer good news.

Trent hit the speed dial for Sal's cell phone. It rang until Trent got the voicemail prompt.

Should he leave a message? Not a good idea. If Sal died in a chopper crash and a cop had Sal's cell, Trent would have incriminated himself without the opportunity to plead the fifth. He would be pleading stupidity to leave a message. Trent ended the call.

He had calmed the jittery nerves of MMI board members a couple of days ago, but if this turned out to be bad news—no, he couldn't allow that. Trent still had valid options, even if Vince, the babe, and Sal's team were all killed. Well, he had some good options provided Patrick retained control of the company. And, if Virtuality's ownership got hung up in the courts, Patrick would probably be allowed to keep running Virtuality, so it could deliver on the Army contract.

That thought settled Trent's stomach, but only a little. Instead of going head first to the throne, he might be able to back in.

New York, New York played on Trent's cell. His pulse revved from andante to allegro. He drew a slow breath and answered.

"Sal, here, Del Valle."

"Where is *here*, Sal? And what happened to calling every other hour?"

"I said we would try, but that there might be other factors affecting our calls."

"Let's cut the small talk. What happened on the climb?"

"That part couldn't have gone better if we had scripted it, Mr. Del Valle. When the babe, uh, Ms. Jamison, reached the top and was ready to hoist up van Gordon, we came in from behind and took her out of the play. We flew away with her in the chopper, and left van Gordon stuck half way up the rock. And he was obviously a novice climber."

"Did he make it off the rock?"

"Yeah. He managed to get off, somehow."

That still left the most desirable option open. "So you took the girl and gave Vince your ultimatum?"

"We did, sir. But he went ballistic and we had an interesting phone conversation."

"So where do things stand now? Is van Gordon playing ball?"

"Well, sir ... it's like this. Uh ... we don't know where he is."

"What? Did he go to the police?"

"Maybe. In Ellensburg. But they wouldn't help him yet. She's an adult and it hasn't been twenty-four hours."

Trent waited, but Sal remained silent.

"Tell me about this babe, Jessica. She seems to be the key to van Gordon's heart and his will."

"Well ... we found out some things about her."

A stream of vile words exploded from Trent's mouth, words he could no longer hold back. He punctuated his outburst with, "Where is the girl?"

"Like I said, we learned—"

"Enough, Sal!"

"It seems she knows karate. She kicked Louie's face in, flattened his nose, nearly knocked him out, and got away near the Virtuality lab."

That wasn't even possible. "Are you telling me that three of the best Russo has to offer let a slip of a woman take you out?"

"She's a lot stronger than she looks. Incredibly smart and she knows how to fight ... the martial arts stuff."

"I can't believe you three. Who did I hire? The Three Stooges?"

Trent paced his study iterating through his considerable vocabulary of vile descriptions of idiots. It didn't help. The only thing that would help was to find both the girl and van Gordon.

"Sal?"

"Yes, sir."

"Where is the girl now?"

"She's with van Gordon."

"Do you mean I paid for a helicopter, so you could track them, and we're right back where we started this morning?"

"No, Mr. Del Valle. They both might be dead."

This story had more twists and turns than an Agatha Christie mystery. But, if Sal was right ... "Dead? What makes you think that?"

"We chased them from the lab to the Snoqualmie River. They tried to swim it above the falls."

"What falls?"

"Sir, the whole Snoqualmie River goes over a three-hundred-foot cliff, Snoqualmie Falls. The water in the river comes right off the glaciers in the Cascades. It's ice water. We took a road below the falls and came up the river with our flashlights. van Gordon's shirt was in the water."

The first bit of good news Trent had heard in this whole sorry conversation.

"If you saw these falls, you would realize that, if they went over, they're dead."

"Is there any chance they didn't go over?"

"Not much. Last time we spotted them, they were hanging onto the safety line just above the falls in a strong current. Louie fired a burst at them. They let go of the line and went under. I don't think Michael Phelps could swim his way out of that situation."

Trent sighed. His knotted gut eased its cramping and he stopped staring at his bathroom door.

"Mr. Del Valle, should we continue looking for—"

"No. Absolutely not. Stay away from that area. We'll just wait. Someone will report them missing. If not, we'll ask Patrick Michaels to report them missing. If they're dead, their bodies will turn up. But we don't want you three associated with them. If they're not dead, one way or another, we'll hear about it."

And, if that not-dead scenario turned to reality, the path to control of Virtuality's technology might go directly through Vince van Gordon's funeral. But killing Vince created the mother of all plan killers, complexity. Worst case, Trent might have to instruct Sal to steal the technology. If so, MMI might have to hold onto it for months, maybe a couple of years, before it became safe to use it in any products. Competitors would gain on them, cutting into their profits. But, if they had to steal everything, there would be no other alternatives because, if found, Trent could be implicated in theft and possibly a murder or two.

"Watch Patrick Michaels' office and the local news. Let me know the minute you hear anything."

Trent pressed the red icon on his phone. Then he began two parallel tasks. First, he fabricated the story he would tell the MMI board if things went awry. Second, he created a mental list of the foreign accounts he had access to, places he could squirrel away funds in case he had to run and hide.

All these problems could be traced back to that babe, Jessica Jamison—beautiful, smart, a martial arts expert, a woman who climbed rock faces for fun—where did van Gordon find her? In some James Bond movie?

Chapter 22

"Remember, you haven't seen us since you took us to her apartment in Kennewick." Vince handed the cab driver a hefty tip before getting out at the fifteenth green of the Fairwood Golf Course.

"You got it. Good luck, dude. Take care of the young lady, you hear."

Vince nodded and smiled. The cabbie was pushing seventy but, during their time with him, the man spoke a mixture of Millennial, Generation X, and Baby-Boomer slang. Obviously, he tried to make all his passengers comfortable. It was a good sign that they could trust him.

Jess ran behind Vince across the fifteenth green toward the far side of the creek. The stream flowed through a huge culvert and under the fairway.

"Take care of the young lady, the man says." Jess snorted a soft laugh. "I've been doing that all day."

"Yeah. You did take care of yourself." Vince stopped at the creek's edge. "Until the river."

She curled an arm around Vince's waist. "I didn't forget about the river. You saved my life. I'd like to forget it, because I'm probably going to have nightmares for the next year."

"So the princess doesn't always have her warrior inside? Maybe you need someone to help you with—"

"Help me with nightmares? Be careful, Vince. You wouldn't want to get flagged for illegal procedure."

"Jess, I played defense. Strong safety. They can't flag me for that. But princess warrior..." He studied her shadowy form for a moment. "Though she be but little, she is fierce."

"Where did that come from? And I'm not little."

"It came from Shakespeare. And little ... that depends on what I'm measuring."

She cupped his cheeks and twisted his head until he faced the creek. "If you want to measure something, measure that cliff we have to climb."

"Yeah. The creek's almost dry, but it does look a little like the Grand Canyon behind Paul's house."

Vince led Jess fifty yards up the creek bed, then stopped and craned his neck to see the top of the cliff against the moonlit sky. It wasn't rock climbing. But, in the darkness, it wasn't much easier. Just a little safer. No rocks. And the soil was soft clay. A person would tumble and slide down it but wouldn't get hurt unless they cracked their head on one of the large stones that lay in the creek bed.

Using cedar saplings and large ferns as climbing aids, Vince worked his way up the steep bank lining the creek.

Jess followed close behind him.

After they reached the top, Vince moved to the edge of the greenbelt. The backyard lawn and west side of the house looked safe.

He pulled the key ring from his pocket and pulled Jess with him across the lawn to the small garage door on the west side of the house. "I haven't gotten the hang of the alarm system. I didn't turn it on, so we can go in without alerting anyone who might be watching the front."

Vince unlocked the garage door and they slipped inside.

The lights on both garage door openers lit as the sensors detected them.

Vince ran to the opposite side of the garage and flipped off the switch powering the doors.

The lights went out.

He walked to the freezer on the side of the garage and cracked the freezer door giving them some light, but not enough to be visible outside the garage.

"I need to see if anyone's watching from the street. If they saw the garage door lights, we could be in trouble."

"You're not going anywhere without me, Vince van Gordon." Jess hooked his arm. "And you said you were working on a plan to get us out of here. How's that going?"

"Working on it, Jess."

"That's what you said an hour ago. That's a little slow for the second fastest guy on the football team."

"Does Jess, the genius, have a plan?"

"As a matter of fact ... "

Jess had left the plan hanging, nebulous and, as Vince's rigid posture said, worrisome.

"As a matter of fact? I haven't heard any facts that matter, Jess."

"You flipped the power switch for the doors, so we have to manually open them, then get in the truck, back up onto the street, and try to get away in the truck. That will take twenty or thirty seconds, minimum. With the guns they have, if they're out there, they'll kill us before we leave the cul-de-sac."

"I still haven't heard any facts about your plan." Vince's sarcastic tone indicated he wouldn't like her proposal.

"Vince, I know how to find out if they're out watching without driving out there and getting shot."

"Yeah. We can *walk* out and get shot."

She ignored Vince's sarcastic remark. "I assume Paul's clothes are still in the house."

"You're changing the subject."

"No. You're not cooperating. Are Paul's clothes still here?"

"Where else would they be? I've been in Seattle for four nights, but we've been on the run since the memorial service. I haven't had a chance to—"

"Paul loved wearing oversized sweatshirts with hoods. I'll put on one and sneak out the back, cross a few backyards to the end of cul-de-sac. If it looks I'm coming from one of the houses, disguised by a hoodie, I can walk out of the cul-de-sac to the boulevard and—"

"No way, Jess. I'm not letting you expose yourself like that."

"But, Vince, I can slip into a pair of Paul's jeans and shoes. They're not going to know it's me. I'll just be some guy going to the bus stop on the boulevard."

"King County Metro doesn't run out here until the commute starts."

"But they don't know that."

"No. I'll do it. Not you, Jess."

"Sure. Six-foot-three, Invincible Vince can just masquerade as a midget and see if they're watching the house." She was right and Vince knew it.

He shook his head, but the resignation grew on his face.

"Come on. Let's go in and get my costume."

"Yeah." He had agreed, verbally, but Vince wasn't moving toward the door.

She took his hand and tugged.

Vince pulled the key ring from his pocket, closed the freezer, and followed Jess to the house door. "While you steal my brother's clothes, I'll get the pickup keys. They're upstairs too."

He unlocked the door to the downstairs, then led Jess inside and they trotted up the stairs. Vince stopped at the door to the family room off the kitchen.

The moon's faint light shining in through the big slider revealed the top of the roll-top desk against the near wall of the family room. Vince picked up a small flashlight and turned it on, then rummaged through a basket of miscellaneous items on the desk.

"Here are the pickup keys. But ... Jess?" Vince stared at an eight-by-ten picture sitting on the roll-top. "This is the same picture that sat on Paul's casket. Who are all these kids?"

"That was taken at the home."

"You've mentioned that place three or four times. But—"

"I'll take you there, Vince, when there's no one shooting at us."

"Provided we're still—"

"We will be." She circled his waist with her arms. "We've got to be. If we don't make it through this—there's more to lose than you think." Jess headed down the long hallway to the master bedroom.

"Time to make your fashion statement?"

"Help me find a big hoodie."

Vince slipped by her into the master bedroom and slid open the mirrored doors of the large closet.

Jess started pulling sweatshirts off the shelves lining the top of the closet.

Vince knelt on the floor. What was he doing?

In the peripheral glow of the flashlight, it looked like he was pulling inserts out of running shoes.

She grabbed the bulkiest hoodie she could find, then rummaged through the hanging clothes for a pair of jeans. Jess snagged a pair of slim-fit jeans and pulled a belt from a hook on the side of the closet.

Vince rose beside her and shoved a pair of hiking boots at her. "Here. Paul wore size eleven shoes, so I stuffed his hiking boots with inserts from his running shoes. Along with the boots, these will make you about three inches taller."

Jess took the boots and pointed at the bedroom door. "Out, Vince. I'm getting dressed."

"That's silly. You're just putting these on over—"

"I don't care if it's silly or not. You're not watching me dress. That's ... uncomfortable."

"Not as uncomfortable as you're going to be with all this stuff on you." Vince walked into Paul's office across the hallway. "I'm going to peek out front to see if there's anything suspicious."

Jess pulled on the sweatshirt and slid her legs into the jeans. The belt was elastic, so it should work. The sandals she'd been wearing were strapped on and had somehow survived the river. She pulled them off and stuffed them in the front pocket of the hoodie. After putting on a thick pair of Paul's socks, Jess managed to fill the hiking boots enough to walk with a near normal gait.

She stepped into the hallway, pulled the hood over her head, and stuffed her hands in the hoodie pocket. When she turned sideways, the moon shining through the bedroom window should give Vince a shadowy profile of her from where he stood across the hallway. "Well, do I look like a six-foot man with a medium build?"

"No. Jess ... you, uh ..."

"What?"

"You need to keep your hands out of the pockets. They pull the sweatshirt down and stretch it over ... well, it's obvious you're a woman when you do that."

"With all I've got on, no one would notice that, unless they were really focusing—"

"Exactly." He paused. "I don't think you should go out there, Jess."

"I'll be fine. You watch me from the living room as I go by. I'll slip out the downstairs slider."

"What if I say you're not going out there?" He moved toward her.

"I can kick a lot harder with these boots."

"I'm an injured man, Jess. You wouldn't kick me after you doctored me."

"Wanna try me?"

"As a matter of fact—"

"Vince, I'll be fine."

His strong arms wrapped her up and squeezed the breath out of her. "Be careful out there. If anyone tries to stop you, run straight into the green belt and come around to the back door. I'll leave the downstairs slider open."

She pressed her cheek into his chest. "Okay. But, if nothing happens, when I reach the boulevard, I'll go into the next cul-de-sac and come back through the green belt. We leave in the pickup, immediately, if I don't see anything suspicious."

Vince pushed back her hood and kissed her forehead. "Please, be careful out there, Jess. I'll be watching you all the way to the boulevard."

Vince released her.

Jess hurried down the stairs and slipped outside through the slider to the back patio.

Two minutes later she walked beside a house at the end of the cul-de-sac.

A small dog in one of the houses started yapping.

She had to walk normally, not act suspicious, and not let a dog deter her.

154th Place Southeast was a short street connecting a cul-de-sac to the boulevard. The few cars parked on the street sat directly in front of houses and all the cars appeared empty.

Jess passed by Paul's house, the second one in from the corner, and continued her slow walk toward the boulevard. As she passed the house on the corner, she looked to her left, up the steep hill on the boulevard.

A dark-colored SUV had parked about thirty yards up the hill. To her recollection, she'd never seen a car park there. Parking on the outside of a downhill curve could get a person's vehicle sideswiped.

It looked like the SUV she had seen across the parking lot from Virtuality's lab.

Now what? Jess was supposed to be a resident out walking for some reason. Her heart revved up to somewhere near her redline.

You've got to think, Jessica Jamison.

What would a resident do if they saw a car parked on that hill? They would think it odd to see a vehicle parked there and would wonder what the driver was up to. But, at this time of night, they wouldn't investigate.

Jess stopped, put her hands on her hips and turned toward the SUV. After she had stared at the vehicle for four or five seconds, its headlights came on and it pulled away from the curb.

She held her breath until it passed her.

The SUV continued down the boulevard.

It had to be one or more of the thugs. Vince and Jess needed to get away before it returned.

As soon as the SUV rounded the turn and disappeared, Jess turned, ran back to the house and came in through the downstairs slider.

Vince met her at the door. "It was them, wasn't it?"

"I think so."

"What did they do?"

"They left, headed toward the main entrance to Fairwood." Jess pulled out her sandals and peeled off the extra clothing.

"So I can't watch you put your clothes on, but I get to watch you take them off?"

"Vince, this is no time for smart remarks. We've got to get out of here before they come back. Open the garage door. I'll be there as soon as I can strap on my sandals."

Less than a minute later, with Jess beside him, Vince backed the pickup up the steep driveway to the street, put it in gear, and rolled down 154th Place toward the boulevard. "If we see no headlights, I'm going to head up the hill and leave Fairwood the back way. Watch behind us, Jess. If you don't see any headlights, we're home free."

She saw no headlights.

Fifteen minutes later, Jess looked at the pickup's clock. 3:50 a.m. After the events of this night, she was exhausted. But they would be at the cabin in about thirty minutes.

She looked at Vince behind the wheel.

His head had nodded twice in the last minute.

Jess put her hand on his shoulder.

Vince glanced her way then sat up in the seat. "Tell me where to turn when we get to the lake."

Jess smiled.

* * *

Vince had nearly run off Kent-Kangley Road when he fell asleep at Y intersection with Retreat-Kanaskat Road.

But Jess had punched his shoulder in time to make the turn.

He fought off another attack of drowsiness and managed to stay awake for the next mile to the cabin on the south side of Lake Retreat.

The cabin was a small, rustic log house well-hidden in the trees across the street from the lake. The gunmen would never find them here. First, they wouldn't be able to spot the pickup from the lane. But, more importantly, they would have to find out about the cabin's existence and location from some other source. That was highly unlikely, unless they managed to hack Jess's email and she had mentioned the cabin in a message.

He and Jess would be safe for the night.

It was 4:30 a.m. when Jess pulled out a key hidden under a landscaping brick and unlocked the door. She headed straight for the shower.

Vince couldn't blame her after climbing Choss Master, getting abducted, escaping from kidnappers, then swimming the river and tramping through the woods.

But some things were more important than personal hygiene. Vince headed straight for the couch and crashed.

"Vince ... Vince, you need to take a shower."

He heard her words, but was he awake, dreaming, or somewhere in between?

His legs wouldn't move. Neither would his arms. And his mouth wouldn't cooperate.

Vince lay in that twilight-zone stupor of semi-consciousness. Slowly his tongue returned from paralysis to conscious control. "Jess, I'm beat. Take the bedroom. I'll sleep here."

Jess sat beside him on the couch. "You need to shower. You're a mess."

He reached for her shoulders.

Jess leaned away from him. "First, you need to take a shower. You're soiling my grandparents couch."

He sat up. "I haven't soiled anything since I was three."

"That's not exactly what I meant. I'm clean. You're not." Jess raised her eyebrows.

"Oh." Now that she was clean, she wouldn't let him touch her in his current state. "Unclean. Unclean." Vince stood, scooped up his small duffle bag and stumbled toward the bathroom.

The clock in the hallway said 5:00 a.m. when Vince shuffled out of the bathroom, clean but rapidly slipping into that stupor again. He collapsed on the couch and noticed it had built-in recliners. He pulled a lever on the side, leaned back, and his feet rose. "Take the bed, Jess. I'm crashing here ... now ..." Vince's head rolled to one side and he gave in to his exhaustion.

* * *

Vince cracked his eyes. Sunlight flooded the cabin through the living room window. Something tickled his nose each time he inhaled. He raised his right hand to scratch his itching nose, because his left arm was pinned down by one-hundred-fifteen pounds of the most beautiful clay on the planet.

He could see through the open bedroom door. The covers were turned down, but there was no sign that anyone had slept there.

Jess lay on her side, facing him, arms around him. Several strands of her hair lay against his nose.

He'd been inhaling them then exhaling them, while they tickled his nose, until he'd been forced to scratch it. He had also been inhaling the sweet fragrance of Jess. Vince had done that many times as a kid, but never in this context and never as an adult.

Her deep, steady breathing attested to her exhaustion from the physical and emotional stress of the night and the previous day. Maybe she'd had nightmares about the falls and couldn't rest peacefully alone in the bedroom. But she was doing just that curled around him.

Paul's words replayed. *Jess needs you, Vince.*

Had he been reading Jess wrongly? Even if Vince was second in line behind his brother, maybe Jess really did need him? Maybe ...

She stirred. Her eyes popped open and widened, inches from his. She drew a sharp breath, then let it out slowly. Her lips curved ever so slightly, forming her enigmatic smile.

At least that's what the blurry face too close to focus on appeared to be doing.

"We did it, Vince." She blew out a blast of air and put a pout on her lips. "We broke all the rules. We both swore we would never sleep with anyone until—"

"Not *all* the rules, Jess."

His remark turned her face pink. She turned away and looked across the room toward the wall clock. "It's nine o'clock. Shouldn't we—"

"Call the professor?" He kissed her forehead and nudged her up with his left arm.

She sat up on the couch. "Are you going to call Dr. Scoggins now?"

"Yeah. But first, we need to decide what to say when we call. Then we need to come up with a list of questions that we want him to answer when we meet. What do you think I should tell him?"

Jess studied the wall on the other side of the room as if the answer to his question were written there. "Tell him ... Paul gave you his share of Virtuality and that there are people who want to take it away from you so badly they have tried to kill you. Then mention that you know Paul talked with him about the technology. You're not a geek, so you're looking for an explanation of why anyone would be so desperate to gain control of Virtuality that they would kill for it."

"That's some heavy stuff to hit him with out of the blue. I don't want to scare him off with my phone call."

"It *is* heavy stuff," Jess said. "But I think Paul already discussed some serious issues with Scoggins. And because of what the professor researches, I'm guessing he'll be more intrigued than alarmed."

"I grabbed Paul's cell when I picked up my bag at the house. Hopefully, he has the professor in his contacts." Vince stood, raised his arms and stretched out the kinks in his shoulders and neck. When he lowered his arms, Jess had stepped inside their reach and rested her cheek against his chest.

She spoke softly and her voice dropped to her low alto. "If this meeting with Scoggins doesn't lead to a plan of action, one we think will work ... then it's time for us to go to Alaska, sweetheart." She looked up into his eyes.

Vince had already melted at the sound of that sultry voice but repeating his term of endearment with that look in her eyes, the look that had always been reserved for Jess's most solemn revelations, opened the flood gates holding back long pent up emotions.

There was no going back to the fractured relationship that had put a thousand miles and seven years between them.

Jess reached up and wiped a tear from his cheek. "You're a big softy, Vince van Gordon. But I love you for it."

Loved him? "Jess ... how did I ever walk away from—"

She pressed her fingers over his lips. "It never happened. Remember? We're starting again as two kids, soulmates, who are ready for whatever comes next for us."

For there to be a *next*, he had to find the source of the danger to them and eliminate it.

Since they were eight or nine, Vince had always eliminated danger to Jess. Not that she couldn't take care of herself. But Vince had always been there to blacken eyes, bloody noses, and, in general, beat the living crud out of anybody who threatened her. For years, no one in South King County would bother Jessica Jamison out of fear of Vince's brutal sense of justice and his ability to enforce it.

Their pursuers, however, hadn't come from South King County. And Vince had to begin protecting Jess again, without the aid of fear and intimidation. That protection would start with this phone call. "You said, 'whatever comes next'. Right now, the phone call to Scoggins is next. You'd better pray he has some good advice or some light to shed on our situation. If not, we might be headed for Alaska sooner than you think."

Jess cupped his cheek. "If it didn't mean the technology falling into the wrong hands, I'd vote for Alaska right now."

"Yeah. Me too." He wrapped up Jess in his arms and let the realization sink in that Jess wanted what he wanted, apparently as much as he wanted it.

He released Jess and reached for his duffle bag, while he pictured a for-sale sign in front of his Denver townhouse.

Vince picked up his duffle bag and pulled out Paul's cell. He booted the phone and waited. When the home screen lit, he opened the contacts and jumped to the S section. "Bingo." Vince pressed the call button.

"Scoggins, here."

The voice was pleasant, not pompous. Vince already like this man. "Dr. Scoggins, this is Vince van Gordon."

"Paul's brother? I wondered if you might call. I'm so sorry about Paul. Our whole community lost a wonderful man."

"Yes, we did." A lump in his throat choked off his last word. Vince paused until he could control his voice. "Professor, I'm just a writer, but Paul left me controlling interest in Virtuality and I have—we have run into some serious problems."

"May I ask who *we* includes?"

"Jessica Jamison has been helping me. I've known her for a long time."

"Ms. Jamison—one of the brightest students to graduate since your brother. Consider yourself blessed to have her on your side."

Blessed? This man sounded like a believer. Certainly not a typical professor of Sociology. Maybe that's why Paul sought him out. "Yes, sir. I am blessed to have Jess working with me."

Jess stepped to his side and draped an arm around his waist.

Vince toggled the speaker phone for Jess to listen.

"The problems I mentioned—are you, or others connected with Virtuality Incorporated, in any kind of danger?"

Why would Scoggins mention danger? Was it something Paul said or something Scoggins's research uncovered? And how much should Vince reveal at this point? Vince went with, "Yes."

"I feared that might happen, but not so quickly. How soon can you and Jessica meet with me here on campus?"

"How about this afternoon?"

"That works. Meet me at my office at 4:00 p.m. It's on the second floor of Savery Hall. Do you know where that is?"

Jess poked his shoulder and nodded to him.

"Yeah. Uh, yes, sir. We'll be there." Vince ended the call.

Jess looked up at him, concern etched into the lines on her face. "Don't you mean we'll be there if those three stooges don't find us first?"

"Jess, the whole time we were growing up. Did I ever let anyone hurt you?"

She took his hand. "But this is different. These guys have guns, automatic weapons, and they seem to enjoy shooting them at us."

She was right, but Vince could feel his fingers curling around Curly's neck. It would take more than a bullet to stop Vince from wringing it. And something deep inside told him this drama would not end until Vince had done just that.

Chapter 23

If Vince took the shortest route to the University of Washington campus, it would take Jess and him through areas where they had encountered the three gunmen. To minimize the chances of being spotted, Vince had driven south, through Auburn, and then cut over to I-5 using Highway 18.

Jess, sitting beside him in the truck, pointed at the dashboard clock. "We're going to get to campus at least an hour early. Take the 599 exit. I want to show you something." She pointed ahead to the rightmost lane.

Vince exited onto 599. "Where are we going?"

"Take the first exit. It drops us onto Interurban. Then go right."

"Go right to where, Jess?"

"The home."

He glanced her way. "So I'm finally going to see the house of mystery?"

"It's not really a house, but it is a home. It's hard to describe. You have to see it for yourself." She paused. "Vince, there are some things you probably didn't know about Paul. I live here, but I didn't know them until recently. Here's the exit."

Jess directed him down Interurban and across a bridge into a residential area bordering on commercial property. "Turn in here." She pointed at a gated driveway. The gate was closed.

After he stopped the truck, Jess climbed out, pushed the gate open, then hopped in beside Vince.

"This looks like a big place and it's set back off the street at least fifty yards."

"That's not all. The backyard borders the Duwamish River. It's peaceful here, except for a little road noise from the cars on I-5 across the river."

The house had been expanded until it looked like a single-story school. Or maybe a hospital. "Must be a big family."

"You could say that." Jess touched his arm then pointed to their right. "Park beside the van."

Vince pulled in and cut the engine.

Music came from the house. And voices, singing. The voices of children?

"Chapel time is almost over." Jess slid out and closed her door. "Let's go in so you can meet them."

She led him to large double doors and opened them.

"What kind of family has chapel time? They must have a lot of kids."

"You got that right." Jess pulled him inside.

The large entryway opened to a huge room. Ahead, to their right, seemed to be the source of the singing.

Jess led him into that room.

Vince drew a sharp breath after they entered on the side of the spacious room.

Four long rows of chairs, more than a dozen chairs per row, faced a platform to their left.

The singing was led by a large man playing an acoustic guitar, but Vince's gaze quickly focused on the boys. He scanned them, slowly.

Their ages might have ranged from seven or eight up to late teens. Some looked healthy. Others had no hair. Several had gaunt faces with dark circles around sunken eyes. But one thing they all had in common, they sang, holding back nothing.

Vince scanned the boys again. They had another thing in common. The intensity in their eyes was unmistakable, determined, almost fierce.

He looked at Jess. "Tell me what I'm seeing here."

"First, listen to them for a moment. It's beautiful, Vince."

The voices crescendoed on the next line. "We'll fly away when Jesus calls our name. No more chemo no more pain."

Jess leaned close to him. "They changed the words a little," she whispered.

"Fly away on angel's wings, to meet our God to meet our King."

Their words were more than praise. They were telling a story. "Are they all sick?"

She nodded. "Terminal, according to the doctors. But the survival rate here is about forty-five percent after two years."

The song ended, and the leader slid out of his guitar strap, set it on the stage and began speaking to the boys.

"Where did they all come from?"

"Paul's spies. He has a network of informants at hospitals, clinics, schools, shelters, and on the streets. These are all boys with no one either able or willing to take care of them. All dying. But what did you see in their eyes and hear in their singing?"

"Determination. Fierce determination."

"Yes. They know the stakes. Did you see any fear?"

"No. They looked like soldiers going into battle ... well, it's how I've always pictured sold—." The lump in Vince's throat choked off his words.

"They get the finest medical treatment, good nutrition and spiritual nourishment. A formula for health. Paul told you everything he left behind is yours. So what do you intend to do with this?"

Vince's eyes blurred. He wiped them before—too late. He swiped at his cheek.

Jess wiped his other cheek. "You're a big softy, Vince van Gordon. Paul was smart."

"Everybody knew that about Paul." Vince took Jess's hand.

"He was also right. He knew what he was doing. Now, what are you going to do with the home?"

He drew a breath, half-choking on it. "No matter what, Jess. We've got to keep this place open. Otherwise ..." Otherwise was unthinkable.

"You're a good man, Vince van Gordon. And that's why Paul gave everything to you."

That was debatable ... the good man part. But Jess was right about Paul trusting him. For whatever reason, his big brother had trusted Vince with the things most dear to Paul's heart. Then he put Vince in charge of Virtuality. It was too big a burden for too small a man.

"Jess ... I can't do this without you."

"What can't you do without me?" She studied his face and waited.

"Any of it. I guess that's why Paul said ..." Paul hadn't finished, but the words that remained unspoken when Paul ran out of time Vince had clearly understood.

"Why Paul said what?"

"That I should trust you, listen to you, because I needed you."

Jess hooked his arm and laid her head against Vince's shoulder. "And ..." Her voice had turned to a hoarse whisper. "I can't be that person without you."

They slipped out during the leader's closing prayer.

Jess walked silently beside him, still hanging on to his arm.

For the moment, it felt good and right to have Jess on his arm, knowing they would be a team. But Vince had a lot of questions about what he'd seen, starting with ... "Jess, how's the home financed?"

"I think it's supported eighty percent by Paul and about twenty percent by other donors. If Virtuality were to go out of business, the home would probably have to close."

"Then we've got to make sure that doesn't happen. Whatever it takes."

As they approached the truck, Jess looked up and smiled. "You know, you're more like your big brother than you think."

It was quiet in the truck as Vince headed up Interurban Avenue and took the on-ramp to I-5 north, headed toward the UW campus.

Forty minutes later, Vince and Jess entered the first floor of Savery Hall, five minutes early for their 4:00 p.m. meeting.

Jess stopped after entering the building and studied the two intersecting hallways. "This building has had a facelift since I took my Sociology classes." She pointed at the stairs. "Modern stairs that a student can walk up without fearing they might fall down."

"Falling down? The stairs or the student?" Vince gave her a smirky smile. "When you use pronouns like that, the antecedent isn't clear, especially when a person is speaking rather than someone reading the words on a page."

Jess started up the stairway. "Look, I may have taken my liberal arts classes here, but I never claimed to be an English major. I write code, not trashy novels."

"Are you insinuating that—"

"If the shoe fits, Vince."

"Have you ever read one of my novels?"

"Yes." Her voice had softened and deepened.

"How many?"

"All of them. Bad endings and all. But, Vince, we should be focusing on Dr. Scoggins and what we're going to ask him."

While he was trying to forget her, trying to abandon Jess, she had been following him and his writing. How much more had he gotten wrong about this woman?

Vince took the steps two at a time until he caught Jess at the top of the stairway. He hooked her elbow.

When she turned to face him, curiosity filled those pale blue eyes.

"Well, did you like them?"

She gave him her enigmatic smile. "What do you think, Vince?"

What he thought was entirely inappropriate for two people trying to stay alive and looking for clues about who wanted to kill them. Those two plump, unpainted lips he had focused on lay at the center of his thoughts. But this wasn't a good time or place for—

"Well, what do you think?"

What did they call women like her? "Femme fatale. That's it."

"What did you just call me? And quit looking at me like that." She put her hands on her hips. "The professor's office is right behind you. Are we going in or are you going to keep gawking at me like some adolescent boy who's going to grow up and cut off his ear?"

It would only get worse if he took the bait and played her game. Vince turned and knocked on the door to Dr. Scoggins' office.

On the third rap of Vince's knuckles, the door swung open and he stood face-to-face with a thirty-something, dark-skinned man who stood around five-foot-ten and consisted of at least two-hundred pounds of muscle. Scoggins didn't wear glasses, had no beard, and looked more like a wide receiver or a corner for the Seattle Seahawks than Vince's stereotype of a college professor.

"Mr. Vince van Gordon, I presume." Scoggins stuck out a pink-palmed hand.

Vince took it, then nodded toward Jess. "And this is Jessica Jamison my ... uh ..." What should he call Jess when things were still awkward and tentative?

"Hello, professor. I'm Vince's technical advisor," Jess said, rescuing him.

"Your reputation precedes you, Ms. Jamison. Good to finally meet you. Come in and have a seat."

They walked into a mid-sized office where dozens of stacks of journals, magazines, books, and stapled papers surrounded them, some on a small table, others on the floor. Hundreds of books filled the shelves lining two walls of the office. But, on the professor's desk, were only a closed laptop, a copy of some scientific journal, a pen and a notepad.

Vince and Jess took seats across the desk from the professor.

Jess took Vince's hand. She squeezed and nodded.

"Dr. Scoggins, when Paul died last week, I inherited controlling interest in Virtuality Incorporated. I'm an English major and an author, so managing a growing high-tech company is way out of my comfort zone. That's why I hired—"

The frown Jess gave him stopped Vince. He hadn't hired her. There had been no talk about pay or any such thing. She had simply started helping him because he needed her.

"Please continue, Vince." Scoggins waved him on with an open hand.

"I understand Paul had discussions with you about Virtuality's technology. Jess and I have serious concerns, probably the same concerns as Paul. We would like to know what you told him and then get your take on some things that have happened since I took over Virtuality."

"I suppose you also want to hear about my latest research findings?"

"Yes. Especially what your research has revealed about virtual reality, video games, and any related applications of virtual reality?"

"First, let me say that video games are becoming a big problem, particularly with young men ages twenty-one to thirty. About fifteen percent of these men worked zero weeks last year. Thirty-five percent of them are living at home with their parents or a close relative, which helps enable video game abuse. These and other statistics clearly indicate that many young men are choosing to stay at home and play video games. And now the abuse is impacting young women as well."

"About the young men—I can believe those statistics based on what I've seen among my friends in Denver. Dr. Scoggins, you know Virtuality has an Army contract for an advanced training system. Are you aware of other research or development that the DOD is performing in this area?"

"Fortunately, the DOD seems to be focusing on the positive side of this technology, trying to isolate and identify the elements of video games most conducive to human learning. The Navy and Marine Corps are interested in using the technology where jobs require substantial training time on simulators, such as sonar technicians, radar operators, pilots, and even surgeons. The Space and Naval Warfare Systems Command is already using augmented reality—referred to as AR—to train some of their gunners."

"Augmented reality?" It was the first time Vince had heard that term. "Can you give me an example of an AR application?"

"Okay. Here's one scenario. You wear a headset, including goggles to provide enhanced visual display. Your GPS guides you, visually and by voice. You walk down a street looking for a certain restaurant, a yellow line appears on the sidewalk and leads you to the restaurant. That's AR"

"Cool. Can it keep me from being hit by a car?" Vince grinned.

"Perhaps, someday. But, consider this about AR—it can enhance your life and it doesn't necessarily lock out other people while doing so. But, with virtual reality, you're in your own world, closing out reality. Real-world social experiences are gone. Over time, VR will cause people to drift apart. Social skills will vanish. Perhaps the ability to socialize, and the desire to do so, will also vanish. Some may permanently drop out of society, preferring their own virtual world to the real one."

"With all the VR gadgets and games coming on the market, that doesn't bode well for America," Vince said.

Jess folded her hands on the professor's desk. "I don't understand what's so addictive about video games that people would prefer a game to life in the real world?"

Scoggins rocked back in his big office chair. "Video games meet some of the needs that are being neglected by modern society."

"Not any of my needs," Jess huffed.

"But think about this, Ms. Jamison. The complexity and high-population density in society doesn't allow full expression of human cultural needs—you know, things we experience only in close groups. There are simply too many people in our individual social networks—one-hundred friends on Facebook, a hundred more on Instagram and Snapchat, the thirty or forty people we frequently text or email. There are so many people that individuals don't see their own existence or their work as being impactful or being important or meaningful. That feeling of not really mattering is amplified if one works for a large corporation. Nothing these employees do seems to matter. Consequently, they seek a world where they can be important, where what they do matters, and where they can see immediate positive results of their actions. A bad guy pops up and you shoot him, saving all your buddies and racking up record scores."

Scoggins paused. "Video games came along like a perfect storm for our times, sweeping people into virtual worlds because the real world wasn't meeting their needs. The short answer to your question—video games tune in to basic psychological needs."

"Dr. Scoggins, we suspect that some of the third-party people who want control of Virtuality come from the adult entertainment world. They may even have ties to organized crime," Vince said.

"I hadn't gotten to the baser appeals of games—violence, power, and sex. Most games provide immediate rewards for certain behaviors, giving positive reinforcement when a person makes progress in the game. If you add in the satisfaction of our basest proclivities, it will produce an even stronger addictive force. I don't believe I need to provide graphic descriptions of what we're talking about here."

"Please don't," Jess said. "Sex sells. Let's just leave it at that. But I worked for Paul, coding algorithms for lossless compression and decompression of recorded, digitized nerve signals. I heard him talking about remote nerve stimulation and deep brain stimulation. Couldn't they play a role too?"

Scoggins nodded. "Brain stimulation has been used for medical applications for some time now. We're making many advancements in this area. Over two-hundred thousand people with Parkinson's have had surgery to receive deep-brain stimulators, implants that send pulses of electricity through areas of brain tissue to control their tremors. This has given back their lives to many people, people who were in diapers, confined to wheel chairs, and barely able to talk."

Vince could see where Jess was headed with her questions. He let her take the lead.

"As I mentioned, I wrote code to handle nerve signals," Jess said. "Has anyone been recording and playing back nerve signals?"

"Let me start with what I know, and we'll see if we can answer your question," Scoggins said. "Brain-Computer Interfaces, BCI, are being developed to control robotic limbs for people who have lost arms or legs. These show great promise, if we can record enough of the right neural signals."

"So it has been done to some degree," Jess said. "I've been thinking … maybe that's where Patrick comes in. He was a medical student, and now he has a graduate degree in Computer Science."

"Based on my discussion with Paul, I believe you're correct about Patrick's role. But beyond restorative medical applications, some companies are working on building brain implants to try to give superhuman powers to healthy people. That I consider to be an unhealthy application."

"Superhuman powers?" Vince said. "Could that be what the military is doing?"

"That's possible," the professor said. "But it's unhealthy and unwise."

"Terribly unwise," Jess said. "I don't think that's what's going on at Virtuality, because Paul wouldn't have agreed to it. But could artificial intelligence have any role in all of this? I didn't have enough visibility into Virtuality to know if they're also using AI. But I do know Steven Hawking warned that AI could bring about the end of the human race."

Scoggins chuckled. "That would seem to be true only if one has the wrong model for the human brain—actually a wrong understanding of who and what a human being is."

Jess gave him a crooked smile. "So you're claiming to know more than Stephen Hawking?"

Doctor Scoggins raised an eyebrow. "We all have our own opinions, Jess. And each of us thinks we know better than the others do."

"Nice dodge, professor." Now, Vince was the one giving the crooked smile.

"I wasn't trying to dodge the question," Scoggins said. "An equivalence of biological intelligence with digital intelligence—it's never going to happen. But then I base my conclusion partly on my worldview, which includes a biblical definition of who we are as human beings, *Imago Dei*, created in the image of God. Perhaps my biblical understanding isn't quite correct, but I would stake my professional reputation on it." Scoggins pointed to a journal lying on the corner of his desk. "As a matter of fact, I already have."

"So that's what Paul meant when he told me he didn't exist in his brain. It was only an interface to the real person."

"Exactly. It's part of our dualistic nature—physical and spiritual."

"Physical and spiritual," Vince said. "I think I understand what you mean by dualism, but could you explain, once more, exactly what you mean when you use the term?"

"Sure. Let me state in another way the differences between materialism and dualism. Dualism says that our mind—where we think and exist—is separate from the matter that comprises the brain. Mind and material are separate categories. Neither one can be reduced to, or can be said to contain, the other."

"If that were true ..." Jess massaged her forehead, then looked up. "Couldn't we demonstrate it, somehow, in a lab? I mean, we could have mental states that don't correspond to physical states of the brain and vice versa."

"And that's a brilliant deduction, Ms. Jamison. Yes, we have demonstrated in a laboratory that mental function and brain function don't always correlate. Which means that mental function is not identical to brain function."

Jess shook her head. "Then why aren't we hearing about this from some source—science, the media?"

"Journal articles have been published about this. The evidence is out there. One researcher even demonstrated that acts of the will, making choices, have no corresponding brain activity. Volition does not require a brain."

"That has been demonstrated in a lab?" Jess's eyebrows nearly touched.

"Yes. But, to someone who has literally sold their soul to a materialistic view of the universe, it takes more than a little evidence to convince them to change their mind and admit that there is more to us, and this universe, than just the physical. For goodness sake, we might find that we're accountable to some higher being." Scoggins chuckled. "It's frustrating, but such is the world of academia."

"Let's see. Where was I?" Scoggins paused. "Unfortunately, here's what's happening in mainstream brain research, trying to understand how our minds store and recall information." The professor paused again. "Do you really want to hear this, or should we move on to stimulating nerves?"

"I think we both need to hear it," Jess said.

"Yeah," Vince said. "Evidently, Paul thought the subject was important enough to tell me about it only seconds before he died."

"I see." Doctor Scoggins sighed heavily, looked down at his desk, and rubbed his chin. "Okay. You asked for it." He looked up and grinned, then pointed to a large picture of the human brain mounted on his wall. "Our brains have a little shy of a billion neurons in them, highly interconnected. There are several thousand connections to each neuron. Current research is going bottom-up to study the shape, size and interconnections of these neurons in hope of finding their role, behaviorally and biologically."

"With all those connections and possible paths through the brain, good luck with that approach," Jess said.

"Besides all that complexity, that's a materialistic view of human beings," Vince said. "Mind equals matter."

Dr. Scoggins nodded. "That's what this research incorrectly presupposes. But the problem with modern research goes even deeper. Suppose our theoretical models of the brain don't reflect reality. And that could well be the case if, as Paul thought, the brain is an interface to something else, the real self, a spirit, which many who study theology believe to be the case. The mainstream research, studying neurons, might improve our efforts to help people with certain, specific brain dysfunctions, but we would never reach a complete understanding of the brain. And robots with human intelligence—you can forget that, unless you write the fantasy form of science-fiction."

Jess leaned forward in her chair. "What you're saying is that the problem with current research isn't even a scientific issue, it's worldview-based. It's the application of science to philosophy, you know, physics, to metaphysics?"

"Bingo, Ms. Jamison. Most modern-day scientists are so steeped in their materialistic philosophies that they are completely close-minded about anything outside the domain of science. But their real problem is that they try to stretch science to include things outside its domain—applications of science that violate its metaphysical presuppositions."

"And they're too stupid to see that!" Jess pounded her fist on Scoggins' desk. "Sorry. I got a little, uh ..."

The professor chuckled. "Me too. It's frustrating when these geniuses won't even consider that human beings may have a spiritual component that explains things like self-awareness. And we can see that their bottom-up approach, and materialistic philosophy, will cause them to beat their brains against a brick wall they have built, while they work on problems they can never solve if they hold strictly to their materialistic worldview."

"They're caught in a trap." Vince shook his head. "A lab-rat trap."

"You're right, Vince. It's a trap with only one escape, an awareness of, and willingness to listen to, the God who made us."

Dr. Scoggins paused and sighed. "Well, I didn't mean to take you so far afield."

"I think you kept us right on target," Jess said. "How can Vince run Virtuality if he doesn't understand the true reality behind the virtual reality of his company's products?"

"Well put," Scoggins said. "But back to stimulating nerves in the body and the brain. Some scientists envision a day when we can upload our thoughts to a storage medium and download the thoughts of others. Many think this is purely fiction. But it isn't entirely fiction, because people are doing some things today that require computer-brain interfaces, like the robotic arms and legs I mentioned."

"Vince, remember that guy, Walker, the one who gave me bad vibes?" Jess said.

"The one you said acted like a druggie?"

"Yes. Him." Jess turned to the professor. "Has your research discovered any work being done that directly stimulates the brain in a manner similar to drugs?"

"Well, the influence of transcranial, pulsated ultrasound on neuron activity is being researched with some success."

Vince straightened in his seat. "Ultrasound? You mean they actually blast people's brains with ultrasonic radiation? I'm not going to volunteer for that experiment."

"It's not as bad as it sounds. Pulsed ultrasound can produce mechanical bioeffects with no heating or tissue damage. To stimulate a brain circuit, you must hit the target within approximately two millimeters. However, if you can do that, you don't have to do surgery to do brain stimulation. This has implications for the treatment of diseases like Parkinson's and some types of depression."

Dr. Scoggins' comment on brain stimulation brought them to the salient question, the one most troubling to Vince. "Professor, that Psychology 101 rat with the electrode in the pleasure center of his brain—can we hit that same part of the brain with ultrasound and produce euphoria?"

"Unfortunately, yes," Scoggins said. "And that is a big problem. Can you imagine having a product that gives one an intense high, all the euphoria of the strongest drugs on the street—crack, meth, heroine—but without all the adverse health impacts of drugs?"

Jess shuddered, visibly, at Dr. Scoggins' words. "If that were turned loose on our population, wouldn't nearly everyone become an addict? Who could resist something like that once they had tried it?"

"You're right, Jess. People may behave just like that rat. Sit there and push the lever, over, and over, and over, and over again. That's the danger," Scoggins said.

Vince shook his head. "There's more danger than that. A lot more."

Jess gave him her bug-eyed stare. "And what has that writer's imagination of yours conjured up now, Vince van Gordon?"

"A product like that could put the drug cartels out of business."

"Maybe out of the drug business," Scoggins said. "But the cartels are masters at reinventing themselves. They've morphed to new drugs, to human trafficking, anything people demand that's illegal."

"That raises two more questions," Vince said as he looked at Jess. "Has someone leaked what Virtuality is doing and, secondly, are they trying to get in on the ground floor of the action?"

"Vince, if you're thinking it's some cartel visionary that's trying to kill us, you've got to consider other forms of organized crime," Jess said. "Or it might even be someone from the porn industry."

"Well, we seem to have opened up a real can of worms," Scoggins said.

"What were we thinking?" Jess shook her head. "By having this meeting, we may have endangered you too, Dr. Scoggins. We were so intent on solving our own problems that we didn't think about you."

"Yeah." Vince said. "We should have thought this through and been more discreet about meeting with you."

"Don't feel badly. I always knew that my research would eventually lead to this juncture. You've simply accelerated things a bit. And that's probably good for our society. Well, it's good if the powers that be will make the right decisions."

"And if we can keep the three stooges, and whoever else is after us, from knocking us off."

Scoggins raised his eyebrows and opened his mouth to speak.

"Don't ask." Jess blew out a blast of air. "We've had some unpleasant contact with some very unpleasant people."

Vince chuckled. "And Jess always gives nicknames to people she doesn't like. That's why I'm Vincent van Gogh."

Jess shot him a glaring glance. "That's a categorical error, Vince van Gogh—I mean van Gordon."

"See what I mean, professor."

Scoggins smiled but didn't reply.

"I don't think we've solved any mysteries," Jess said. "We just muddied the waters about who wants to kill us. We've identified at least three components of the underworld who would want our technology and that doesn't even include the *upstanding* members of our society who might be willing to kill, or commit other crimes, to become obscenely wealthy."

"Professor," Vince said, "Do you have any idea what kind of money we're talking here if video games suddenly morphed into an addictive form of virtual reality?"

"If you add addiction to the mix, the first company to bring a product to market could make fifty billion dollars the first year and nearly 200 billion by the second year—that is if they can keep their software engineers from getting hooked on their own product and dropping out of the real world. I'm only extrapolating from the current market for video games. But, if the porn industry got involved, and the government didn't stop them, they could make a trillion dollars annually, a few years down the road."

Jess looked at Vince. "Well, now we know what the discussion between Patrick and Walker was about. You know, cutting his pay to get more game time."

"That's it, Jess."

"What's what?"

"I've been trying to figure out how Patrick could fund his research and development. How he could misuse Army funds to develop these games where everybody gets to be king of their little virtual world—be an NFL quarterback, a Hollywood star, whatever a programmer can code into a scenario."

Jess folded her arms across her chest. "And?"

"He's cut his labor costs down to almost nothing by paying his programmers with game time. They code up a few games. Whatever suits their fancy. And Patrick lets them play. But I'd bet this is getting out of control, about now, and Patrick's back is against the wall."

"Regardless," Jess said, "I can put a stop to this ... with a little help from you. But it will mean defaulting on our DOD contract."

"That's gonna happen regardless," Vince said. "We've got to tell the general what's going on. He needs to know before he discovers it and sends me to jail."

"Even if you stop this project, eventually, others will do what Virtuality has done," Scoggins said. "It may take a few more years, but the technology and the problems it brings won't go away."

The professor was right. The problem with this technology was not going away on its own. "And we're talking about the addictive equivalent of a drug so powerful it will be impossible for normal people to stop using it," Vince said. "They'll have no desire to do anything except play their games until they die of neglect. That's the end of society as we know it."

"Maybe we can stop this if we can bring a convincing case to the government," Jess said. "If they view this as the end of American civilization, they'll stop it."

Vince's laugh sounded like a snort. "What if they view it as a huge increase in tax revenue?"

Jess shook her head. "That increase in taxes will disappear when everybody stops working to live in their fantasyland."

"The amount of money involved, and the powerful people who will stop at nothing to profit by the technology, means the stakes are high," Scoggins said. "If you want to stop this, you need to move quickly. The players will know that being first to market is paramount, because it could make them the wealthiest and most powerful people on the planet. Many will kill for a chance at that kind of power."

"Yeah." Vince shook his head. "So we've seen."

Jess clamped her hand on his arm. "This is spinning out of control, and it's happening way too fast. I can buy us some time by stopping Patrick's work. Once I've done that, it will get the Army's attention. Then we can call a meeting with the contract administrator, General McCheney, and let the problem escalate until we get the attention of the Secretary of Defense."

Scoggins dropped his fist on his desk "Count me in. If you need testimony at your meetings with the DOD, or at congressional committee hearings, I'll make myself available."

Vince drained his lungs with a long sigh "One way or another, it's going to come to that, congressional hearings. If I'm still alive, I'm going to make sure it does."

Chapter 24

Vince and Jess had almost reached the truck and she hadn't said a word during their five-minute walk from Dr. Scoggins's office. Had the professor's revelations upset her?

Time for Vince to prod. "How do you plan to stop the work on the project? Patrick's not going to let you waltz in and power the lab down."

The blank stare his question drew was clear enough. Jess was deep in thought, INTJ mode, and didn't want to be disturbed.

When they reached Paul's truck, Jess stopped in front of the passenger door and waited.

Good. She wanted him to open her door. It was Jess's invitation into her thoughts. She was ready to talk.

He walked around the pickup and opened her door.

"Thanks, Vince." Jess tiptoed and kissed his cheek.

Vince wasn't going to complain but … "You have a wonderful way of saying thank you. What do you want, Jess?"

"Is that all you got? I don't bribe people to get what I want, like some people I know."

"And what are you insinuating, Ms. Jamison?"

"Remember that time when—never mind. But I do need something."

He nodded. "See what I mean."

"You need to take me to Paul's—uh, to your house."

"Not gonna happen. The bad dudes, the stooges—whoever they are—know where I live. They might be watching."

"Do you want to shut down the project or not, Vince?" The look she shot him stopped his reply.

"Look, my gun is in my purse. We pray they won't come, but if they show up, we can use it to hold them off and get away. The stooges I saw are cowards. They'll run from a real firefight."

Jess read people well but ... "And how do you know this?"

"I just do." She set her jaw and stared him down.

"Okay. Now why do you need to go to my place?"

"Let's get in and go. I'll tell you on the way."

Jess had always been willing to take risks. But generally, only carefully calculated risks. Vince listened for an explanation, while he pulled out of the parking garage and worked his way southward toward 512.

He was still waiting when Jess placed her hand on his arm and squeezed.

When he looked her way, she smiled. It wasn't the bewildering, enigmatic smile that threatened mischief, but a warm smile that stirred Vince's heart, bringing his deepest feelings to the surface. Jess could ask for anything she wanted, right now, and get it.

The look in her eyes said she knew that. But Jess had never taken advantage of the sway she'd always had over him. Whenever it came to a war of the wills, she barked out commands. Jess never played the femme fatale. Will and logic were her weapons of choice.

But why the change? Maybe everything really had changed between them after they swam the river and escaped the falls. Maybe ...

"Here's the plan." She sat quietly, evidently waiting for his reply.

"I'm listening, Jess. But you could probably pull this off by yourself."

The warm look in her eyes faded to a frown. "You need to listen. This will take both of us, Vince."

"Okay. How do we shut down this operation?"

Jess blew out a sharp sigh. "I coded all of Paul's algorithms. I created the high-level language code and the firmware that's in assembly language. When we moved that code to the lab, I used Virtuality's software configuration management tool, TeamTech, to compile and distribute the binaries and to update the embedded code. I also used their DBMS to—"

"Their what?"

"Database management system. It contains the nerve impulse data and the system configuration data."

"Does all that mean you know how to distribute software and data to the lab?"

"Yes. I can do it correctly or incorrectly."

"What do you mean by incorrectly?"

"Paul had a manual for TeamTech. It's at your house. It has all the commands available from the command line when you're not using the graphical user interface. I'll use that information to gin up a script that logs me in as administrator—"

"Administrator? I thought you didn't have direct access to the lab."

"I sort of, accidentally, got the administrator's password."

He gave her his best attempt at an evil eye.

"Vince, don't look at me that way. I wouldn't hack a Top-Secret lab."

"Oh? Isn't that what you're proposing we do?"

"I'm proposing that I write a script that walks the code directory, randomly twiddling bytes, scrambling all their source code. But I will first, back up the code and data to my USB drive. Oh, I forgot to mention, the system design documents are also stored in TeamTech. So we'll rip off the entire working system, including its design documents, and scramble the source code and all the binary executables from the latest compilation. Then we'll distribute the nonworking code to the lab, delete everything in the system and get out of Dodge." She paused. "What do you think?"

"I think you're gonna hack a Top-Secret lab. But, Jess ... can't they use a system backup to roll back to previous working configuration?"

"Since when does a writer know about software configuration management?" She gave him her bug-eyed stare.

"Well, I do have to manage different versions of my manuscripts as we edit them to produce the final manuscript. It's not a million lines of code, but it is nearly a million characters. And sometimes I have thirty versions before a novel is completed."

I've never thought about that." Jess poked his shoulder. "Maybe it does take a little intelligence to produce a novel. I just assumed wordsmiths were like blacksmiths. You know, they just pound on things until—"

"You mean like codesmiths hack on things? Or should I call them geeksmiths?"

"Touché."

"Jess, you still haven't answered my question about how you prevent them from rolling back to an older version and going forward again."

"There are probably periodic backups stored offsite. Maybe on some DOD server on the East Coast to protect against catastrophic events. Recovery from those backups would take a while and we would have time to contact the DOD to get this place shut down and locked up."

"Yeah. That works."

"Here's something else, Vince ... something I'm not sure Patrick has thought through. At least he hasn't mentioned it to me." She paused. "Now that Paul is gone, no one knows the nerve-impulse code or the algorithms. They're just like black boxes to the application programmers. They don't know what's in the boxes. It's the most complex code in the system. They could never replicate the part of the system that I wrote. They can't take the product forward. And they might not even be able to use it in production if the last DOD backup didn't include my latest bug fixes."

Jess was probably right about her part of the system, but ... "Jess, when I write a story, I start with a synopsis and an outline. It's like the design documents for Virtuality's system. Won't they have something like that?"

"I told you the design documents are in TeamTech. They'll be wiped out."

"Don't they back it up to the cloud?"

"No, silly. This is classified code and data."

"That didn't stop some other people from putting stuff like that on the Internet."

"That would probably be a violation of some military specification for classified systems. Paul and Patrick would never do that. But here's where I need your help, Vince."

"Something tells me I'm not going to like this job." He gave her a corner-of-the-eye glance from behind the wheel and signaled to exit from 512 onto 405 South.

"You've wanted to pound poor Patrick several times. Well, here's your chance. But he's a wimp. So, hopefully, it won't come to that. You just keep him occupied while I make backup copies of everything in TeamTech and then distribute the crippled code to the lab just before I wipe out the entire repository of code, the data, and the documentation."

"And you can write a script to do all that while you're at my house?"

"It's not that complicated. A Perl script can be written at any level—even like a stream of commands given to an application from the UNIX command line."

"Whatever you said sounds fine, Jess. I just hope it all works."

"Oh, ye of little faith. I'll test it at your house. It's not that hard to do."

"But you don't have Virtuality's system at my house."

"I don't need it. I'll have the TeamTech manual to give me the commands, and I can dummy up the directory structure on my laptop." She paused. "My laptop. It's at my apartment. You need to swing by and—"

"And give the stooges another shot at finding us?"

"We don't have any choice. The UNIX shell, my Perl installation, and everything else I need is on that laptop."

This was not a good idea. These guys had almost killed Jess and him several times. He changed lanes then looked at the major frown on Jess's face. "I guess we'll just have to pray they aren't watching your apartment."

Jess leaned against his shoulder and gave him a side hug. "Pray? It's good to know that you're doing that again. When you walked away from me, I thought maybe you walked away from …"

"No, Jess. I didn't. And weren't we starting over again? Like the last twelve years never happened?"

"We are. But are you praying and trusting Him again? More than you trust in Vince van Gordon?"

"Yeah. Can't trust that van Gordon guy. He did some pretty stupid things."

Jess gave him that look that knocked down all his defenses, the look that made total surrender his only sensible option. "Maybe sometime soon, you can help this girl understand why you really walked away. Because no matter what you thought, it wasn't what I wanted, Vince." Her voice broke.

But had she wanted him to stay as her best friend or something more? If he could only be sure, Vince could put the past completely behind him. "Sometime, Jess. But for right now ... can we just say it never happened."

Jess turned away, looked out the passenger side window at the Bellevue traffic crawling down 405 and wiped her cheeks.

He would give anything for a do over of those high school years. And since he returned home, the evidence suggested that he and Jess could have been married by now, living their dreams together. They still might have a shot at that if Vince could keep them both alive.

"Back to the subject at hand." Jess cleared her throat. "You've been dying to look inside the lab."

"Dying? That's a poor choice of words. But, yeah, I want to know what's really going on in there. And I can force Patrick to open the lab door."

"Then you can kill two birds with one stone—see what's going on in the lab and keep Patrick occupied while I'm in his office copying everything, scrambling the executables, and shoving it into the lab just before I blow away everything in TeamTech."

"But, Jess, can they unscramble what you scrambled?"

"It's not likely. I'm doing it randomly, and I update my seed from the system clock at random intervals. Unless they get some people from NSA to help them, they'll never figure out what I did before we have the DOD and the DOJ after them for fraud and breach of contract."

"How long do I need to occupy Patrick in the lab?"

"Uh ... you may have to occupy more than just Patrick."

"What do you mean? Who and how long?"

"When I distribute the nonfunctional executables, programmers, and anyone else using the lab, will know something's up because things will start failing. You know, things like the games Walker might be playing."

"Great," Vince said. "If they realize what we've done, they'll be hopping mad. How soon can we leave after that happens?"

"You should take my gun, because you may need to control the lab by force for ten or fifteen minutes so that no one can come into Patrick's office and try to stop me."

Vince moved into the HOV lane and sped up to near the legal limit. "Any other surprises?"

"Let's hope not."

"You mean you're hoping the three stooges don't show."

"Yes. Let's pray they're out somewhere looking for us and not anywhere near the lab," Jess said. "And when we leave the lab, we have to make sure they're not following us."

"Last question—when do we do all this?"

Jess pointed to the clock on the dash. "It's 6:00 p.m. It will take me three or four hours to write and test the scripts and about an hour to drive out and sneak into the building. We'll do it around midnight, while it's dark. That gives us our best chance of pulling it off."

"And what if something goes wrong?"

"Whoever sees it first notifies the other. Then ... I guess we both jump in your pickup and head for that cabin in Alaska."

Chapter 25

Jess glanced at the clock on the dash as Vince exited the freeway at North Bend. 10:45 p.m.

"Are you sure your script will work, Jess?" It was the third time Vince had asked that question since she tested it over an hour ago.

"No, I'm not sure. But if it fails, it will do so with an error message that tells me what went wrong. I'll fix it and rerun it."

"You can do that? Just restart a program wherever it failed?"

"More or less. It's a Perl script that I wrote. I'll know where to restart it."

"How are we going to get into the office? The building's locked."

Vince had been like a caffeinated cat in a kennel full of barking dogs since she started writing her scripts. "You need to relax. I can get us in, Vince. I know some of the programmers."

"You know some programmers. That's supposed to relax me?"

"Relax and prepare to be amazed."

The lights in downtown North Bend lit Vince's scowling face. "Jess, how can you joke at a time like this?"

"I can handle my part, including getting us into Virtuality's office. And you can handle forcing Patrick into the lab. I do my damage and we're out of there. It will be okay, sweetheart?"

Vince's head turned her way. He took her hand as they headed out of North Bend toward Snoqualmie. His thumb massaged the back of her hand slowly, softly. It was quiet for the next several minutes.

Vince pulled into the old mill site, turned off his headlights, and let the pickup roll slowly toward Virtuality's building.

"Don't park by the front door. There's Patrick's SUV in the corner. Park by his car. We don't want to draw attention."

"We could break the office window in front of his SUV. But it would probably set off the security alarm."

She looked up at Vince's eyes in the dim light of the parking lot. We're not going to break in."

"So Jesse James is gonna pick the lock?"

"No." Jess pointed behind them across the parking lot. "One of those programmers is going to let me in. But you've got to get down, out of sight."

"Great. How do I know when to come up for air?"

"Wait a couple of minutes, then you peek. If you see a flickering light in the office window, it will be me at a workstation on the server. Tap on the window and I'll let you in."

Jess grabbed her computer bag and slipped out of the truck before the three programmers reached the main entrance.

Chip Gentry, a fellow computer science student she had recruited for Paul, was in the group.

Jess hurried toward the three as one of them unlocked the door.

"Chip, wait for me."

"Jessica? What are you doing here?"

"You know those bugs in the decompression firmware?"

"Yeah. Didn't you patch those a few weeks ago."

She stopped beside Chip. "I did, but there's an error condition I didn't handle correctly. I need to distribute the update to the lab. It could crash the system if anything triggers that error condition."

Chip pulled the door open and motioned her in.

She pulled a flash drive from her computer case. "I'll need to use the office to get on the server. I only need twenty or thirty minutes and I can let myself out."

"No problem," Chip said. "Just don't mess up the lab configuration or Patrick and some of the other programmers will have my hide. Yours too, if they thought that you, uh—"

"I get the message. I won't leave until everything is configured to my satisfaction, and you know how particular I can be." Technically, she hadn't lied to Chip. But every word had been full of deception. Deceiving the deceivers. That raised ethical dilemmas that she didn't have time to sort out.

Chip unlocked the office door. "Don't wake up Patrick. He's sleeping over tonight. Actually, that dude's been doing that for the last month. He locks his apartment door, because there's no alarm on it. And he's a heavy sleeper." Chip opened the door.

Heavy sleeper was good. "I'll be as quiet as a mouse. Thanks, Chip."

Jess closed the door and walked straight to the rack of blinking lights along the wall adjacent to the lab, sat down in front of a workstation, and plugged in the flash drive containing the Perl script.

She logged in to the server and then to TeamTech's administrator account.

A tapping sound came from the window.

The dim parking lot lights created a silhouette of Vince's tall frame. He pointed toward the main entry.

She stepped into the light of the monitor, so he could see her, and waved him toward the door.

Thirty seconds later, Vince stood beside her while her script walked the source code directories, ripping off the code and design documents for Virtuality's entire system.

Jess spoke softly over the whir of computing equipment. "When I've got the entire system on my flash drive, I'll start Twiddle and—"

"Twiddle?"

She looked up at Vince's wrinkled forehead. "It's what I named the sabotage script. That's when you need to wake up Patrick."

Vince studied Patrick's room door for a moment.

"Yes, Vince. It's locked. Just knock on the door and wait until he replies."

"Then what?"

Jess turned to face Vince. "If he opens the door, he's all yours. If he asks who you are, say you're Chip and that you've got a problem he needs to see, now. He'll open the door. Then you pull out my gun and tell him what we rehearsed."

"Jess, are you—"

"I'm sure, sweetheart. This will work." She squeezed his shoulder, then turned her attention to the script that was spitting out copied filenames to the monitor.

Five minutes later, Jess had the entire system source code, makefiles and design documents on her 512 GB USB drive. She plugged in the flash drive containing Twiddle and launched it from the command line.

Twiddle began living up to its name by employing a moderately sophisticated byte twiddling algorithm. It traversed two directories without any problems. The script was working fine and shouldn't need any further attention.

She turned to Vince. "Time to wake up Patrick. And, Vince, don't forget to give me the cipher code to the lab door before you go in. Once inside, I won't be able to contact you. The door is soundproof, and your cell won't work in there. The walls block all radiation—the entire spectrum."

"I understand, Jess. But if you sense trouble, come and get me, immediately."

* * *

Vince stuck his right hand into the pocket of his shorts and pulled out Jess's .38.

She glanced at the gun in his hand. "Remember, it's a Smith and Wesson, a five shooter."

"I know."

"I just didn't want you to make a one-off error, you know, like programmers do sometimes."

"I'm not a programmer. And quiet, Jess, or you'll wake up Patrick."

"Isn't that the idea?"

"Let's just—"

"It doesn't have a safety either."

"You already told me that."

"I just didn't want you to actually shoot off something ... like your ear."

"What's gotten into you, Jess. This isn't a game we're playing."

"You're wound up a little too tight. You need to relax, get into your role, and intimidate Patrick. If you do that well, you shouldn't have to shoot anybody."

"You, who can't act, telling me to get into my role?" Vince shook his head, then took a calming breath, pointed the gun at the floor, pounded on Patrick's door, and listened.

Nothing.

He pounded again.

"Just a minute." A weak voice, barely audible, came from inside.

The doorknob rattled, then stopped. "Who's there?"

"It's Chip. We've got a problem. You need to take a look at this, now."

The door opened. Patrick stood, facing Vince, wearing basketball shorts and a Star Wars T-shirt. Patrick's eyes looked up at Vince's face and went wide with recognition.

Vince hooked Patrick's neck with an arm and jammed the gun against his forehead. "I'm through playing games. You are going to open the lab door and give me a tour or what few brains you have will—"

"Okay, okay. Just don't shoot, Vince." Patrick glanced back into his room.

"Eyes this way, Patrick. Do exactly what I tell you and no tricks. If you do that, you might survive the night. Now, I want to see my lab."

"I know you wanted to shoot him, Vince." Jess's voice came from a workstation near the wall. "But, if you can, let's do this without killing anyone. That's so messy."

Jess's words came wrapped in cold indifference, the perfect intonation for intimidation.

Patrick's body trembled.

Vince stepped behind Patrick, clamped a hand on his upper arm, and shoved the .38 against his back. "To the lab door."

"W-what's sh-she doing here?"

"Questions like that could get you killed, little man. Now, open the office door and walk straight to the lab door. Got it?"

"G-got it."

When they reached the lab door, footsteps sounded behind Vince. He shoved Patrick's face against the door and twisted to look back.

Jess.

He blew out a blast of air, trying to calm himself. "I might have shot you, Jess."

"Hurry, Vince."

Maybe her work was going more quickly than she anticipated. If so, he needed to hurry if he wanted to inspect the lab thoroughly.

Vince grabbed a handful of Patrick's t-shirt, twisting Darth Vader into Vince's bandaged hand. It hurt, but not nearly enough to stop Vince. He jerked Patrick to the side of the lab door. "Give me the cipher-lock code."

"Now you're really committing a crime, Vince. A federal crime."

"A federal crime? I was thinking of committing a simple Washington state crime. You know, one like murder? Give me the code, doofus!" Vince growled out the words and prodded Patrick with the barrel of the gun.

"Two, zero, one, six"

"How ingenious. The year you and Paul started Virtuality." Vince punched in the numbers. The lock clicked and the hiss of rushing air escaping from the lab rippled Vince's hair. He opened the door.

Behind Vince, Jess's footsteps retreated across the tile floor.

Good. Jess had heard the code. Now for a tour of his lab. But with all the high-tech gadgetry, would he even recognize what he was looking at?

Vince pulled Patrick to the door and poked the gun into his back. "Just so any workers in here don't get overly excited, the gun is going into my pocket, but my hand will be on it. You lead exactly like I tell you, and answer my questions without hesitation, and you might not get shot. Like Jess said, not shooting you isn't my preference, but it could happen. Now, let's go."

After they stepped into the lab, the door closed and locked behind them.

Vince scanned the large open bay lab. Five or six workstations lined the left side of the lab. A long row of cubicles lined the right side. He saw only two other people. Two men.

One sat at a workstation in the far-left corner, typing furiously. The other man sat inside one of cubicles near the far-right corner.

Vince spotted a third man in the second cubicle to Vince's right, adjacent to the one where Vince had encountered the waterfall scene. The lab worker wore what looked like VR goggles made into a helmet and had a contraption attached to the helmet that looked like what that programmer, Walker, had worn. He also wore a black body suit that molded to his shape like spandex, but with small white circles distributed across the legs, back, shoulders and arms. The man ran on a round device like the treadmill Vince had stepped onto. The surface moved any direction the man ran. And run he did, cutting right, then left, until he fell to the floor. The man got up again.

"What's that guy doing, Patrick?"

"That's classified information."

Vince pointed at the runner. "Look at that. He took a handoff, ran left, then cut back and fell. He's playing football. The Army doesn't train people to play football, except for a few guys at West Point. You're developing games for retail sales, aren't you? Next-generation video games, using virtual reality and remote nerve stimulation."

Patrick's head snapped around toward Vince. "Who told you that?"

"You just did. I'd say you're developing next-generation video games to be sold by LACO, and the Army is footing the bill but doesn't know it. That's fraud, Patrick. It's the DOD and the taxpayers you're cheating. You'll be an old man before they let you out of Leavenworth, if I don't shoot you first."

"It's not like that, Vince. The Army will get what they paid for at the price we agreed on."

"So how are you—wait. That Walker guy was asking you to cut his pay so he could have more time. You're keeping the costs off the books by not paying your developers. But you're using the Army hardware and money to develop this stuff for LACO. It's still fraud, Patrick."

"Don't you see, Vince? Everybody wins. Nobody's getting cheated here."

"Nobody? Then why did three thugs try to kill Jess and me? We were getting cheated right out of our right to life."

"I don't know who those people are. Honest," Patrick said. "LACO said to ignore them. I think some business associate of LACO sent them in and ... everyone seems to be afraid of them."

"Gee, I can't imagine why. If you make them mad, they come after you with AK-47s. But that's hardly more than a squirt gun. Like LACO said, just ignore them." He paused. "You know, I think LACO needs to re-associate."

"But those people are not part of the business deal. They are—"

"Oh, but they are, Patrick. You've brought organized crime in on your sordid little rip-off scheme."

"Mafia? You're crazy, Vince."

"I didn't say Mafia. You did. And you were right, weren't you?" He didn't wait for Patrick's reply. "Let me guess. These people either represent, or are being paid by, the adult entertainment industry. Let me be more specific—the porn industry. They want the technology and are willing to kill to get it."

Patrick was shaking his head and backing away as Vince advanced. He grabbed Patrick's throat. "But there's still a missing piece."

"You're all wrong," Patrick said. "We're not making anything for the adult entertainment industry."

"And you are full of it, little man."

"No, that's not so."

"Couldn't prove it by me. But I'll let you try. Tell me what that guy's been doing at the far end of the lab. He laid down on his side after we came in. Now, every few seconds he reaches out a hand, like he's touching something, then sprawls out on the floor again."

"I—I hadn't noticed."

"You are a liar, Patrick. I'll tell you what. We're going to walk up to him, and you're going to tell him to stop what he's doing or you're gonna pull his power plug."

"No. You can't do that. He might get upset."

"Upset? You mean like dangerous?"

"Maybe." Patrick started shaking again.

"Which is more dangerous, my gun against your skull or your order for him to stop before you pull the plug on him?"

"Your gun, of course."

"Then your choice is clear." Vince pushed Patrick toward the prone man.

When they approached the man, Vince recognized him. "Walker. Who would've guessed. It's your deep-brain stimulator junkie, Patrick."

"Who told you that?" Patrick's eyes widened again.

"You just did. Let me guess. You're using ultrasound to target the pleasure center of the—"

"Who have you been talking to, Vince?"

"It doesn't matter. You've reduced Walker, a human being, to that lab rat they show in Psych 101, the one with the electrode in his brain. Hopelessly addicted to something better than the strongest drugs. Only your little experiment has gotten out of hand. People can't stop. Don't you see how stupid this is? Sure, you can get them hooked on your product, but they're so helplessly, hopelessly addicted, you'll never sell them anything else. They'll tune out the world and drop out of society. You do that to enough people and society itself will collapse. I'll bet you're just now realizing that, aren't you, Patrick."

"There are certain problems with the device Walker has been using. That's not anything we would ever sell to—"

"But the adult entertainment industry would. Wouldn't they? And they'd kill for the chance to do it. They'll even kill you, Patrick, if they think they can steal the technology from you."

Patrick didn't reply.

"You've only got one option. Turn yourself in and stop this disaster before it destroys everyone it touches."

"You wrong, Vince. It doesn't have to be that way. In fact, if you knew the truth, you wouldn't be doing this. Because ..."

Vince waited.

Patrick didn't continue.

"The truth about what?"

"About Jess."

"I know she coded the algorithms for the nerve—"

"No. About her and Paul."

Vince felt his gut knot up. "Get to the point before I lose my patience with you, little man."

"Maybe you should reconsider who you're calling little man." Patrick paused and studied Vince's face. "Jess and Paul had an intense relationship going, until—"

"That's enough, Patrick." Vince's gut tightened to a nauseating cramp. Patrick was lying, trying to—trying to what? Get even? Maybe, but Vince didn't have a good answer. Patrick had found the chink in Vince's armor and he had no defense for it. But Patrick couldn't have known that, could he?

Patrick continued. "Paul put the brakes on the relationship when he got the bad report about his cancer. It broke Jess's heart. I guess ... you're the next best thing to Paul."

Patrick's words came like Vince's blow to Jimmy Grant's solar plexus, stealing his breath, leaving full-fledged nausea in its wake. And, like Jimmy, Vince wanted to throw up.

Patrick's eyes—Vince couldn't read them. But Patrick wasn't a good liar. Vince had already seen that. And before Paul's death, Jess had cried more than he'd ever seen her cry. The crying stopped after Vince had been with her for a few days. But that didn't prove that Patrick wasn't lying. It might even validate—no.

Vince needed time to sort out what he'd just heard. He couldn't jump to conclusions. Only one thing was certain. He would vomit if he didn't stop thinking about what Patrick had told him.

Patrick cleared his throat. "I'm sorry, but I think you should—"

"Vince ..." Jess's voice came from the other end of the lab, by the door. "Time to go."

Before Vince could focus on Jess, a movement from the other end of the lab caught his attention.

Walker. The man leaped to his feet growling like a raging animal. His gaze was laser focused on Patrick and Walker strode toward him.

Red lights blinked from electronic equipment all around the lab.

"What's happening?" Patrick's voice had jumped up an octave.

The running back had stopped running. He pulled off his headset and looked their way.

They had to get out of the lab before Walker reached them, or Vince might have to shoot the guy.

Vince ran toward Jess. By the time he reached her, she had slung her computer bag over her shoulder. But Jess had, somehow, changed.

"We've got to get out of here, now, Vince."

"I know, the guys in the lab—"

VIRTUALITY

"Forget the guys in the lab. A car just pulled into the site and parked by the building where the stooges held me. Three men got out and they were looking our way."

"Once they see the lab door open, we'll have to hustle. Get in the truck, keep down and I'll get us out of here."

He had to keep them alive. Vince needed questions answered, questions that would tell him where Vince van Gordon belonged, Seattle or Denver.

His promises to Paul, his promise to Jess, the boys at the home—everything important was on the line now. If Vince let these thugs kill him or Jess ... that would be the ultimate bad ending to a Vince van Gordon story. A huge, gut-wrenching question mark.

Chapter 26

Vince glanced back as the lab door swung shut behind him. The scene etched an image in his memory, a graphical depiction of panic and frustration, an image of Patrick scurrying about, trying to fix every piece of equipment that screamed, *failure* with its piercing tone and blinking red lights.

Patrick would soon realize his effort was futile. But what Patrick had said about Jess might also render any attempt to resolve Vince's and Jess's relationship an exercise in futility. That possibility brought cramping nausea. However, for the moment, the Vince-Jess-relationship jury remained in a place where Vince's dinner might be any second ... out.

Jess gave him her hand. Paralyzed, Vince stared at the same hand he'd held and massaged as he drove here forty minutes earlier. But thoughts of what might happen if the lab door flew open overcame Vince's paralysis.

He took Jess's hand and pulled her to Virtuality's front door. "As soon as the door opens, we break for the truck. Then climb in and get down."

"You already told me that."

Vince opened the door a crack and peeked out. No movement from the car across the lot. Maybe the men were inside the building, but Vince couldn't count on that.

"Let's go, Jess."

He slipped out the door with Jess close behind.

In five more seconds, he had unlocked his pickup and they slid in. Vince hit the ignition and the tail lights came on advertising their leaving. He shoved the gear shift into reverse and backed out in a semicircle, ending with the truck facing the mill site exit.

The door of the building across the site flew open. The dark forms of three men appeared. They scurried out of the building.

Vince pushed the gear shift into drive and punched the accelerator. While the tires screamed their complaint, he tried to keep the nose of the fishtailing truck pointed at the exit.

No shots. But the SUV's lights came on.

Vince's truck shot out onto the street.

In a few seconds, the headlights of the SUV appeared in the rearview mirror.

Since there had been no shooting, the thugs' plan must be to catch Jess and Vince, not just kill them. Had Patrick tipped them off? Maybe they knew they would need Jess to fix the mess in the lab.

Vince turned onto highway 202 and headed toward Fall City.

Jess stared at him but remained silent. She knew something was different.

But this wasn't a time for serious talk. "Jess, we're going to Fall City and up through that winding stretch of road to Preston. I know the road, they probably don't. We should be able to beat them through the curves. They'll roll if they take it too fast."

"What's wrong, Vince?"

"The three stooges are after us. They probably want to force you to fix the lab, if they can catch us."

Jess sat quietly while the tires of the pickup screeched through the turns near Snoqualmie Falls.

When he approached Fall City, Jess spoke softly. "I guess you'll tell me what's wrong when you're ready. What did you see in the lab?"

Dr. Scoggins' predictions swirled through Vince's mind like a crazy nightmare. "Some guy, a programmer, was on a multidirectional treadmill, acting like a running back in the NFL."

Vince stopped talking to break for a sharp turn. He checked the rearview mirror. No lights.

He exited the turn. "Jess, will you watch for their lights in the side mirror. I need to focus on the road ahead."

"I'm watching. Now, tell me more about the football player."

"It was like he was playing in a game. Running, cutting, getting tackled. Grunting. He rubbed some muscles in his legs after a couple of tackles. Jess, they've got to be using RNS and virtual reality to enhance these games. And the Army is paying for the next generation of video games but doesn't know it."

Vince accelerated down the last straight stretch before the roundabout on the edge of Fall City.

"Anything else?"

"Yeah. Our friend, Walker, was ... Jess, he was the lab rat in the Psych 101 movie. They've got to be using deep brain stimulation. It was pitiful. He just kept reaching out, pushing some invisible button, and sinking back onto the floor. The guy wouldn't stop. But he grew furious when the lab stopped working. From euphoria to hydrophobia in about ten seconds."

Vince stomped the brake pedal. "Hang on."

They slid partway around the roundabout.

Vince slowed the truck as they entered Fall City.

"I see headlights. At the far end of the straight stretch."

Vince cut his lights.

"Vince, what are you—"

"I don't want them to see us turn here."

He sped through the east end of Fall City without his lights, and turned left, toward Preston and the three-mile stretch of twisting, winding road. So far, no police in sight. A police stop could get them killed, maybe get a policeman killed too.

Vince punched the gas and hit the lights, then sped through three turns in rapid succession. "Any signs of them?"

"No. I haven't seen them since they entered that last straight stretch east of Fall City."

"Then maybe we've lost them. To be safe, I'm going to keep our speed up until we reach I-90. We'll double back to Highway 18, exit onto Hobart Issaquah Road, then come in the back way to your cabin. Watch for them, Jess. We're not home free yet."

It was silent for the next five minutes.

Jess sat twisted away from him, focused on the side mirror of the truck.

After Vince turned onto I-90, eastbound, he relaxed his grip on the wheel and coaxed the truck up to seventy-five miles-per-hour. With a speed limit of seventy, it wasn't enough to get them stopped by the state police.

"Did you get everything done, Jess?"

"I wondered when you'd ask. What you saw in the lab was shocking, horrifying. Especially after Dr. Scoggins explained it to us. You know, this was Paul's worst nightmare, and they're doing it right in Virtuality's lab. But maybe we've ended it."

And now it was Vince's worst nightmare. Paul was back and his shadow larger than ever. Vince couldn't stay in Seattle, so he couldn't run Virtuality as he'd promised. He was a loser, losing on all fronts. The jury had come back, the verdict was in—Vince van Gordon, guilty of inadequacy in the first degree.

Patrick had told Vince the truth. A dozen little things confirmed it—Jess's crying, her reluctance to—but what about that kiss and the words they exchanged after escaping Snoqualmie Falls?

Jess had finally settled for him. That's all it was. An inadequate man was her last and only option.

Vince took the Highway 18 exit, ran the stoplight at the end of the off-ramp, and turned onto the highway.

"Is this a good time?" Jess stared at him, studying him. He could feel her eyes, though she was only a dark shadow on the seat beside him.

He couldn't come up with an appropriate reply. His stomach was a mess. A dark cloud had settled over him, worse than when he left Seattle seven years ago. So much for happy endings. And his writing—maybe he should write horror stories. Jamie said that a writer can only write what they've lived.

"How could what you saw in the lab have upset you like this, Vince. What is it?"

"I'm just thinking, Jess." A lame reply, but it wasn't a lie. "Did you finish your work on the server?"

"Everything is on my little USB drive. You can hold the whole project in the palm of your hand."

"Did you get a chance to clean up afterward, so they can't undo what you did?"

"Yes, all except the logs that the server maintains. The logs will show them that I ran some Perl scripts and they'll know what I accessed, if the logs weren't blown away. But the logs won't tell them exactly what I did."

"When should we call McCheney to give him the bad news?" Vince needed to keep her talking. No way did he want the discussion of their relationship to take place while he was driving.

"We should call him first thing in the morning. He's on Eastern time, so we should call about 6:00 a.m. our time."

Somehow, Vince kept Jess talking all the way to the cabin. They would be safe at the cabin. Certainly, long enough to have their discussion. And once they did, what then? Vince couldn't run back to Colorado while Jess and Virtuality both remained in danger and with his promise to Paul unfulfilled.

Vince turned in and drove down the cabin's long driveway.

Being around Jess after he ended their relationship wasn't his only problem. Eventually, the thugs would find Jess's cabin by talking to the right people, searching for relatives and looking through county records. Before that happened, hopefully, the DOD, FBI, and local law-enforcement would all be engaged to catch the guilty parties.

After that, the project would die and Virtuality along with it. Vince would fly back to Denver to stay. And do what? Become the next Alfred Hitchcock? Write thrillers with horrifying endings?

He parked the truck behind the biggest trees beside the cabin.

Jess slid out and headed for the cabin door before Vince could climb out. Why was she in such a hurry?

Vince caught up with her inside, where Jess was working furiously on her laptop?

"Why the hurry?"

"Vince, we only had one copy of the system. It only existed on my USB drive. That was driving me crazy. What if we had an accident and I lost the drive, or it was damaged? Well, in about five minutes, we'll have a backup copy on my laptop. I'll hide the USB drive in the storage shed out back."

"That's good thinking."

"Looks like it's already done. My laptop has a faster USB port than Patrick's workstations." She pulled the drive from the port. "Be right back. I'm going to hide this little drive, then I can relax."

No. Jess wouldn't relax. Not after Vince began his questioning.

The back door closed and Jess was gone, hiding their prize.

Success. Mission accomplished for Paul and for Virtuality. For Vince, disappointment and failure. He should have realized that the last few days were too good to be true. There were no good endings for losers like Vince van Gordon. And he couldn't pretend everything was fine and continue a relationship with Jess. She hadn't been truthful with him and probably not with herself.

What if you're wrong, dude?

The thought struck Vince with a jolt to his nervous system. He couldn't be wrong. Patrick lying to Vince didn't make sense. Vince and Jess had won. Patrick had lost.

Was that it? Could Patrick have wanted revenge for what Vince and Jess had done to him? No. Vince was going under for the last time, a man just grasping at straws.

Jess opened the door and interrupted the heart-rending questions and agonizing answers swirling through his mind.

She drained her lungs in a long, lip vibrating sigh. "Finally." She headed toward him, arms out, eyes focused on his.

Vince broke eye contact and stepped back from her.

"Vince, sweetheart, what is it?" Her eyes narrowed in a deep frown.

Like a dull knife the word, sweetheart, ripped through his heart. Jess had Paul, then lost him. She'd been in love with him only weeks ago. How could she love Vince? Using the word, sweetheart, didn't mean Jess loved him. It meant Jess had settled for a man who was only second choice, second best, second rate. And she had lied.

Their gazes locked. Jess's eyes widened. Her mouth dropped open. Recognition flashed in her eyes. Then horror.

He had seen that look in her eyes only a few times, but Vince had never been the cause of it. Not until now.

She had read his mind, the entire devastating story in one glance

"Don't do this to me again, Vince. I can't—" Her hands covered her face. Tears ran through her fingers. Soon her body shook with each guttural sob.

Vince watched her but said nothing. For once, Vince van Gordon was out of words.

"If you're going to leave, go now," she said without looking up. "Go back to Denver and write your little stories with their lousy endings. Bad endings—that's all you seem to be good for."

Finally, she met his gaze with her tear-filled eyes. Her face contorted like someone was torturing Jess. And someone was. He was.

You just made the biggest mistake of your life, dude.

No. He'd done that while he was in high school, and there was no going back. Not that it would help. Vince simply was who he was, someone who wasn't her first choice and someone not good enough for Jessica Jamison.

For the first time in his life, Vince wished he could die. With underworld thugs looking for him, maybe he would get his wish.

Chapter 27

Before tonight, Jess thought nothing could be worse than the night of the National Honor Society dinner and dance near the end of her junior year in high school. It was the night she knew she had lost Vince, the boy who had been her soulmate for twelve years. Losing him had culminated in Vince leaving after graduation to attend college at Washington State, in Pullman, while she remained in Seattle and went to the University of Washington.

But to have Vince back, headed for a life together, then ripped away again was far worse than when he left for college. This time she had given Vince her heart with nothing held back, no reservations. She had told him that, and he had accepted it. Now, he was throwing it away. Would he also leave her here in danger? Why would Vince do this to her? To them?

Knowing Vince's reason for leaving wouldn't change anything. Just to know Vince would walk away again was enough to know he wasn't the man for her.

But there was a deeper question. What was so wrong with Jessica Jamison that the closest person to her in the entire world, the one who knew her best, didn't want her? That thought started her tears flowing again.

Vince had wandered into the kitchen to get away from her.

Jess stayed in the living room.

Two incompatible people who didn't want the pain of each other's presence were trapped together in this cabin until it became safe to go to the authorities. And what would Vince and Jess do then? Spend agonizing time together testifying to a grand jury? Then they would have to do it all over again in what could be multiple trials required to bring all the perpetrators to justice.

Was the pain of being forced together during the trials even worth it? Maybe they should give Patrick his precious little system and let him make his billions.

No. No matter how heartsick she was, Jess couldn't let Virtuality be used to subject kids to forces beyond their power to control. She couldn't give them what appeared to be heavenly pleasures, pleasures which would take them, ultimately, to hell.

And Scoggins was right. The technology, used the way LACO and their secret partners planned, would destroy every stabilizing structure in American society. It would end civilization after everyone became so addicted and depraved that no one could run the required systems. In the end, the technology would die and people like Walker would become raging demoniacs who would kill to gain access to something millions of times more addictive than the strongest drugs.

Jess couldn't allow that to happen to kids, to families, to America.

What if she walked into the kitchen and begged Vince for another do over? Pretend they were twelve again? He had already agreed to try that once. But it hadn't worked. It never would.

While their relationship ran full-speed ahead, both showing their love and passion for each other, Vince had been able to walk away. There was only one conclusion to draw, what Jess knew all along, she simply was not good enough for Vince. She would always come up short in his estimation.

Jess went into the bedroom and fell across the bed, pouring out her broken heart.

* * *

Jess awoke with her head on a soaked pillow.

How had she fallen asleep? Maybe some pain is so great that the human mind must shut off to survive. But when a person is deserted, unloved, sought by killers, survival isn't a benefit. It's torment.

What time was it? Jess looked out the bedroom window through the gap between the curtain and the valance.

The early light of dawn lit the trees.

Maybe she should check on Vince. Had he left the cabin? Left her here alone?

Jess got up and glanced in the mirror. She was a mess, as if that mattered. She walked out into the living room.

Vince wasn't there.

She turned toward the kitchen doorway.

The front door crashed to the floor.

Jess whirled toward the sound.

Sal leaped into the room, leveling an automatic weapon at her face.

Another crash came from the kitchen, followed by the staccato popping of an automatic rifle.

Vince had been in there earlier. Had they shot him?

She turned toward the kitchen doorway.

A burst of gunfire chewed a hole in the ceiling above her head, showering her with fragments of plasterboard.

"Hands on your head and don't move, you little ..." Sal's vile words meant nothing to Jess. She had to see if Vince was still alive.

Noises continued in the kitchen. Blows, grunts, crashing furniture. Vince was fighting someone. If he hadn't been seriously wounded, Vince would kill that person. He was strong and fierce in a fight.

Jess put her hands near her head but inched toward the kitchen door.

Sal's gun spat fire, filling the room with ear-splitting cracks. A gaping hole appeared in the wooden floor in front of Jess's feet. Wood fragments stung her bare legs.

She stopped.

Vince stumbled through the kitchen door and homed in on Sal.

His gun swung Vince's way.

Jess dove onto Sal's arm. Her body took the barrel of his weapon to the floor.

Sal pulled the barrel loose and jammed the cold, steel barrel against her head. "Stop, now! Or she dies."

Vince pushed his palms at Sal. "Don't shoot! I'm stopping."

Another man ran in the front door, behind Sal.

Louie. He had several zip ties hanging from one wrist.

"Him first." Sal motioned toward Vince.

Louie approached Vince's muscular body slowly, cautiously. "He took out Joe. Almost ripped his head off, Sal."

"Then get the cuffs on him, you idiot."

Louie pushed zip tie cuffs toward Vince. "Hands in here, now."

"Do it, van Gordon," Sal said. "Or I'll think of something really unpleasant to do to your girlfriend."

Vince glared at Sal. "I know a guy who killed a man after they put three bullets in him. You hurt her and you're a dead man, Curly. You can empty your magazine, but I'll kill you before I die."

"Curly? Hey, boss. I think he just insulted you," Louie said.

"Ignore his insults. Put the cuffs on him."

After Vince extended his hands, Louie slipped zip-tie cuffs over them, yanked hard on both ties, then stepped back.

Joe crawled through the kitchen doorway behind Vince and grabbed the arm of a chair. He pulled himself to his feet while Sal watched.

"You okay, Joe?" Sal said, after the man managed to stand.

"Don't know yet, Sal. I'm a little groggy. That guy can punch."

Sal shook his head. "That's why Louie should've cuffed his hands behind him. But, for now, slip another tie around Mohammed Ali's wrists."

Jess lay quiet on the floor with Sal's gun barrel pressed hard against her temple. It would be easy to check out. If she tried something, he would kill her. But for the moment, she had a purpose in this life, prevent these thugs from getting the system that would unleash hell on earth.

But could she?

Sal pulled his gun from her head. "Time to get up, my dark-haired beauty. You have some questions to answer."

Jess rose slowly to her feet, looking for some way to take out Sal without endangering Vince. But Louie had given Joe his gun and Joe waved it in Vince's direction.

Too risky.

Larry approached her with zip-tie cuffs extended. "Don't try kicking me again, or I'll—"

"So that's why we had to straighten your nose. Louie, I'd be ashamed too, to let a skinny broad do that to me. Now, cuff her," Sal said.

After her hands were cuffed, Sal lined up Jess and Vince along the living room wall. Sal paced back and forth in front of them, holding his gun in the ready position.

He nodded toward Joe. "See if they have any weapons."

Joe, approached Vince with caution and patted his pockets. Joe's hands froze after touching Vince's right front pocket. "He's got a gun, boss."

"Well, take it, you dunce."

Joe pulled Jess's .38 from Vince's shorts pocket then stepped in front of Jess.

She stepped back. "You do the wrong thing, Moe, and I'll break your neck before you can kill me."

"Jess, don't move." Vince's voice growled out his command.

Sal pointed the gun at Jess's head and smirked. "Hey, Moe, I mean Joe, I think she just insulted you."

"I'm trying to ignore her. But a babe like her ... that's hard to do." Joe patted Jess's pockets. "They're clean now."

"It's time for those questions." Sal eyes bored into Jess's.

Vince leaned toward her. "I moved the code, Jess. All of it."

He had spoken loud enough to be heard. What was Vince up to?

The answer came like a punch to her stomach. Vince was diverting the thugs' attention to him, trying to take the brunt of whatever these men would do to get their questions answered.

She couldn't let him do that. "He's lying," Jess said. "Only I know where your precious system software is, and you'll never find it."

"That's right," Vince said. "You ask her and you'll never find it, because she doesn't know where it is."

Jess studied Sal's eyes as they narrowed. She gasped when she saw the lights come on. Jess knew where this was going.

"She knows. He knows. Who knows?" Sal's index finger swung back and forth pointing at her then Vince. "Didn't that wise king—what was his name? Oh, yes. Solomon. He had a problem like this with two women and a baby. So I'll tell you what. Since van Gordon insists he knows where the software is, Louie's going to have some fun with our dark-haired beauty until Vince tells us. Got your knife, Louie?"

Jess looked up at Vince. It was one of the few times she saw terror in his eyes. Sal had called his bluff, and it would force Vince to tell them the truth.

Louie pulled a long knife from his pocket, opened it, and pointed the blade at her.

Vince's leg exploded in a kick that hit Louie in the chest and sent him across the room, crashing into the far wall.

"Stop, van Gordon!" Sal pointed his rifle at Vince's midsection. "You okay, Louie?"

Louie didn't move.

"Joe, check him out. And you, van Gordon, down on your knees. You too, Ms. Jamison. Now!"

Jess and Vince complied. But were they being forced to kneel to prevent more kicks or for an execution-style killing?

"He's breathing, boss," Joe said.

A deep, guttural groan came from Louie, who lay face down on the floor.

"Everybody stays where they are while Louie composes himself."

"You mean regains his composure." Vince corrected him.

Jess shot him a sharp glance. "Cut it out, Vince. You're only making this worse."

"I didn't think it could get any worse."

Their gazes locked. What did Vince mean by *couldn't get any worse*?

"Listen to the broad, van Gordon. You might learn something."

Louie crawled across the floor to his knife, scooped it up and rose to his feet, rubbing his chest. "Now, I've got a bone to pick with both of you."

Vince chuckled. "Yeah. It's a wishbone and it looks like you got the short end."

Louie's face contorted to a hideous caricature of itself. He took a step toward Vince, brandishing his knife like he intended to use it.

"Cool it, Louie." Sal said.

Louie stopped.

Sal shook his head. "We've got a little problem here. You see, you two were supposed to be shaking in your boots by now, but you're still playing games. I don't like games, unless I make the rules." He pointed at Vince. "But I don't think he would follow my rules, if you follow me."

Jess leaned toward Vince. "Sal's going to get Patrick."

"To verify the system?" Vince whispered back.

She nodded.

"Shut up, you with the dark hair. Your beauty is fading fast." Sal paused. "Got a job for you, Louie. Take the SUV, drive to the lab, and bring back Patrick Michaels."

"Boss, when we saw him last he was dealing with a mess out there. What if he won't come?"

"Persuade him. With that wuss, it shouldn't be hard. We need him to make sure we got everything these two stole."

"See, Vince. Told you so," Jess whispered.

"Shut up. I don't want to hear any more from either one of you. Besides, we're going to have a private meeting when Louie gets back with Patrick, and you two aren't invited. Joe, check out that shed in back. See if we can lock them up for safekeeping ... with a few more zip ties, of course."

Joe disappeared, headed toward the back door.

Sal stood in front of her and Vince, swinging the barrel of his gun back and forth across their position against the wall.

If Sal followed his plan, she and Vince would be alone for an hour or more. They would be tied up, but alone. It could be their final hour alive.

Tied up with the man who had just shattered her heart—that was no way to die. And the question she'd wanted Vince to answer—why he'd really left seven years ago—did it matter now? And the answer might only bring more pain.

A door closed and Joe entered the room. "That place is built like a fort. No windows and we can bar the door."

"On your feet." Sal prodded Jess with the barrel of his rifle.

Vince glanced at her eyes, then pursed his lips, looked away, and stood. His eyes told her he had the same thought as her. Vince and Jess together, locked in a room, but locked in separate worlds. It was no way to die.

Jess stood beside him.

"So what happened to all your wisecracks?" Sal's gaze went from Jess to Vince. "No wisdom to share right now? You'll share plenty when Louie gets back. Now, out the back door and don't either of you try anything, or I shoot her first."

When they reached the shed door, Sal opened it and shoved them inside.

Joe appeared walking around the corner of the cabin with a half dozen zip ties in his hand.

"Use them all. Make sure they won't get loose," Sal said.

"Sit down on the floor." Joe waited until Jess and Vince sat. "I'm gonna make sure nobody kicks nobody again. It looks like you two have been shacking up out here, so I'm gonna do you a big favor. Give you some more togetherness." He chuckled as he tied their ankles together using two ties. "You're not gonna to get away, but if you do make a run for it, I get to watch a three-legged race."

The rest of the ties went around Jess's and Vince's wrists. Too many to break with the techniques she'd learned in a self-defense class. This was beginning to look hopeless.

"Joe, search the room again." Sal's voice came from outside the shed. "Remove anything that could be used as a weapon."

"There's a shovel here, boss, and the pile of wood. I can't remove that."

"Forget about the wood. Bring me the shovel."

Joe snatched the shovel from the front corner of the shed, walked out and closed the door, leaving Jess, Vince, and a pile of wood inside the shed in the dark.

A loud thunk came from the front door.

"They just barred the door with a shovel handle." Vince's voice wasn't angry, and it wasn't a frightened whimper. It carried no emotion at all.

That wasn't like Vince. He was fiery in a crisis and he never gave up. What was going on with him? Vince wouldn't just give up, would he?

She'd hoped the desperate situation might revive something in Vince, a last memory Jess could take with her to her death. She had to say something to break the foreboding silence. "I don't think we're going to get away this time." Great. Her voice sounded like Vince's, a complete surrender of all hope.

"It's not like we have a lot of choices here. We can try to get away when they come for us. But, if we try too hard, Curly will shoot us. Or, we can wait for them to torture us to find out about the software and whatever else they want to know."

"Torture could mean a lot of things I don't even want to think about." Jess shuddered.

Vince moved. He had felt her response.

Vince lifted her hands, shackled to his, and pulled them to his chest. "Me too, Jess. So we'll fight them until they have to kill us. We don't give them the chance to torture us."

To die fighting alongside Vince—it was better than submitting to a lonely, torture-filled death or the same kind of life. "We need to plan how we'll do that. And we'll have to move in unison."

"Maybe not." Vince spoke softly.

"What do you mean?" Jess managed to cradle one of Vince's hands in hers. She pressed them against Vince's chest.

His heartbeat became a strong drumming. "Joe stopped searching after he found the gun. I still have a small pocket knife tucked away in the change pocket inside my big pocket. Cargo shorts have a lot of hiding places."

"Can you reach it?"

Vince's hands moved, pulling hers with them. "No. The bands are too tight on my wrists. My hand can't slide down far enough."

"Vince, it's just fabric. Slide your shorts up and turn your pocket inside out to so you can reach it, doofus."

"Yeah. I can do that. Sorry, Jess."

"You're sorry about what? Being a doofus?" Something had just changed in Vince. She couldn't see him in the darkness, but his body movements conveyed it. His voice and his words too.

"I am so sorry." Vince's voice broke on the last word.

What was he sorry about? Regardless, she couldn't do this again, and they had no time for sorting through relational baggage.

It was best if she didn't reply.

"I was being completely selfish, Jess."

Whatever Vince's bait, she wasn't going to bite. "Okay. Be selfish. But get out that knife."

"I've got it. Don't move your hands, if you value your fingers."

"I was afraid one of those Mafia guys might cut them off, like in the movies."

"Knife is open. Be still while I work on the wristbands and cuffs."

"Doofus."

"We're back to that again?"

"Vince, it's easy to cut the ones around our ankles. Cut them first, then we can move to a better position to work on our wrists."

"Yeah. I'm a doofus. Lean forward with me. Relax your hands so I can reach our ankles."

Jess leaned with Vince.

Vibrations came through her bands as Vince sawed on the first ankle tie.

The tie broke.

He worked on the second band.

It popped loose.

"We need to stand," Vince said.

Shoulder-to-shoulder, they rose to their feet.

"Over to the wood pile." Vince nudged her ahead. "It's directly opposite that light coming in under the door."

With the Cascades to the east of the cabin, the sun hadn't risen yet, but there was enough light to mark the door and use it to navigate the darkness.

"Ouch." Vince stopped.

"What happened?"

"Cracked my knee on the corner of the stack of wood. Here, put your wrists beside mine and let me press them down on the flat side of this piece of wood. The cuffs are the easiest to get to. I'll cut them first, then the other ties."

She pulled her wrists apart, though they were tangled with Vince's, and pressed them down on a piece of wood.

"Be still, cutting now."

Each push of Vince's hand sliced through plastic.

Her hands came free. "I'm loose."

"I can't reach my cuffs. Jess, would you—"

"Give me the knife."

The warm knife handle touched her fingers. "Got it. Now you hold your hands still."

Jess located the center of the cuff on Vince's hands and sliced it against a chunk of wood. They were free from the zip ties. But now what?

Vince's hands clamped on her shoulders and he pulled her against his chest.

She pushed away from him. "Vince, before this goes any further, you need to answer the question I asked you after the falls."

"Jess, we don't know how much time we have."

"It will take over an hour for Larry to drive to Snoqualmie and bring Patrick back. It's only been twenty minutes. Maybe less."

"We can't count on that. We might not have any more time. We need a plan to surprise them when the door opens."

"You don't want to answer my question, do you? You'd cut off an ear first."

"So we're back to that again."

"You tell me, van Gogh."

"Tell you why I left seven years ago?"

"Yes." She tried to stop her tears but couldn't. And Vince could probably hear her sniffling.

"I'm not sure you can understand. I'm not sure anyone would understand but me."

"Think about it, Vince. Even though you've been away for seven years, there's nobody on this planet that understands you as much as me."

"Maybe. Probably. Okay … Jess, don't get me wrong. I love Paul. But living life five years behind someone like him puts you in a big shadow."

"Someone like him? What does that mean?"

"Paul was impossible to measure up to. Teachers expected me to. People in the community and at church expected it. Even my parents."

"Sounds to me like Vince van Gordon expected it. I don't think anyone else did."

"Everybody loved Paul. He was on his way to making a fortune, developing new technology, and he was a man who practiced his faith, no matter the cost."

"That's all true. Now tell me who Vince van Gordon was."

"He was a guy who always came up short. Could never match what his big brother did. He was also the man who ended up as your only other option after Paul died."

"Only option? You are a fool, Vince. Why would you even say something like that?"

"Jess, you've loved Paul ever since you were thirteen or fourteen. You just had to settle for his little brother."

Jess gasped as Vince's words cut deeply into the quick of a heart already wounded and raw. What hurt most was the words weren't true. But the man she loved obviously believed they were. If that's what he believed, other things, hurtful things, had an explanation that finally made sense. "Do you mean you've thought, since we started high school ... that I wanted Paul more than you?"

"Yeah."

"I can't believe we haven't already had this conversation. We were supposed to share everything, remember? I even admitted to you that I had a crush on Paul."

"But you never said it ended."

"How could you—"

Vince cut her off. "I didn't say anything because I wanted—no, I needed to be with you. But, eventually, I couldn't stand being with you, knowing I was only a friend, not a person you would ever want like I wanted you."

"Is that why you ended our date early after the National Honor Society dinner? Why you let me walk to my door alone, while you just drove away and left me in tears?"

"I hurt you, didn't I?"

"No. You crushed me, Vince. And you nearly killed me a year later, when you left to go away to college and then never came back ... for seven years. You never even called me."

"So losing your dearest friend crushed you?"

"No. Losing the only person I trust, the one who knows me better than anyone, the man I loved—that crushed me."

"But what about Paul?"

"You were evidently so caught up in your sibling rivalry that you didn't even see me. And you didn't know me like I believed you did. I thought there was something wrong with me, Vince. Because there was some reason you couldn't love me like I loved you."

"No, Jess. I loved you so much that I couldn't stand the thought of you marrying my brother. So when Patrick told me that—"

"Patrick? What does he have to do with this?"

"When I forced him to take me into the lab, Patrick let it slip that you and Paul had ... well, you had something going until Paul got sick."

"Let it slip? He's a liar. I'll kill that little twerp! Vince, don't you see what he was doing? He was trying the divide and conquer strategy."

"Keep it down, Jess. They'll hear you and come to check on us."

She didn't feel like keeping it down. She felt like slapping some sense into Vince's thick head. "You believed Patrick, didn't you?"

"I didn't know whether—"

"Don't you lie to me, Vince van Gordon. We could be dead in another hour. This isn't a time for lies."

"What Patrick said ... it seemed to fit with everything I saw, except—"

"Except what? What happened after the waterfall?"

"Yeah."

"Think about it, Vince. I've been hanging all over you since you came back. I even dressed like some hooker just to—"

"Not a hooker. Like a supermodel."

"Whatever. But have you ever seen me do that for anybody? I was still hurt by your leaving, but hopeful about your return. Hopeful for us. I don't make friends easily. You know that. So I invested everything I had in *you*. There was never anyone else except for one, silly, schoolgirl crush on Paul when I was thirteen. It was gone the minute I realized Paul was in high school and had his own friends. He had outgrown you and me. From then on, and even before then, it was *you*, Vince, only *you*."

She rested her head on Vince's chest.

He took his hand under her chin and lifted. "Can you forgive me, Jess. Even if it's too late for us to—"

"Of course, I forgive you." When Jess finished speaking the words, the darkness of the shed seemed awash with light and hope.

Vince pulled her head to his chest. "I'm not going to leave you or lose you again. And I'm not going to let those Three Stooges rob us of what we have."

"And you're sure about what we have?"

"I'm sure. But how can you ever trust me after—"

"After you lied about moving the drive with the software, so they would torture you instead of me? I trust you, Vince. I believe in you. Paul believed in you or he wouldn't have entrusted Virtuality to you. But you need to learn to believe in yourself." Jess paused, wishing she could see Vince's eyes. That would tell her what she needed to know. It always had.

"Jess, I—I ..."

She couldn't see his eyes and Vince was out of words. "We don't have any more time for rehashing our past. Right now, we need a plan, a plan to ambush them when they open that door, or we won't have a future."

Vince kissed her forehead. "When the door opens, we pretend we're still zip-tied together, at least it will look that way to them for a few seconds. That should give us enough time to see their positions and their guns. We need to know that because—"

"Because we've got to take out Curly first."

"Yeah. And I can do that if he's close enough. What I'll have to do is gruesome, but it will take him out of the fight."

Jess leaned her head on his shoulder. "What do I need to do?"

"While I jump Curly, uh, Sal, you watch his gun. If he drops it, grab it. If not, look for somebody to kick. Even if you can only knock them down, or stun them, it will buy us a few seconds."

"Is that it?"

"Yeah. It's all I've got. For anything beyond that, we just wing it."

"And we pray," Jess said.

"Yeah. Harder than we've ever prayed before. I love you, Jess and, after all we've been through to get to this moment, I can't believe that God doesn't want us to spend the rest of our lives together. So I'll ask Him to make that happen."

"What if they kill us? That would answer your prayer. Don't you need to be a little more specific, like asking Him for the rest of our lives to include more than the next few minutes." She paused. "Vince, part of the zip cuffs are still around our wrists. Let's practice putting our wrists together, making it look like we're still cuffed."

"Okay, but let's do it while we're standing, so we're ready to attack."

She pushed her wrists against Vince's. "A dress rehearsal in the dark. But we can't even see if we look cuffed or not."

"It'll have to do."

Footsteps sounded outside.

"They're coming, Jess. Get ready."

Jess focused on the door at the spot where Vince would attack Sal with his pocket knife. She prayed it would be Sal's face there when the door opened.

The rasping noise of the shovel being removed came from the door.

The door swung open.

Chapter 28

Vince held his knife hand over his shoulder, ready to stab whoever appeared.

The door creaked open.

A silhouette appeared.

Vince leaped at the head profiled in the doorway

The face was too low. Patrick?

Vince lowered his knife hand and crashed into Patrick, taking him to the ground.

Jess had slipped out the door behind Vince. She froze beside him.

Vince looked up from the ground.

Five yards ahead, Sal, Joe, and Louie stood with weapons trained on Vince and Jess. Any resemblance of these three men to The Three Stooges had evaporated.

Patrick groaned, then sat up on the ground. "Why did you jump me, Vince?"

"I thought you were Curly, uh, Sal."

Larry poked Sal in the shoulder. "He insulted you again, boss."

Sal ignored Larry and his glaring, wide-set eyes focused on Vince. "Did you really think I would risk opening that door? What do you take me for, van Gordon? One of The Three Stooges? It looks like you're providing the slapstick comedy this morning."

Vince stood and heat rose on his neck. He needed to channel his anger into words. Actions would get him shot. "I'd take you any way you came, Curly. Dumb or dumber."

Sal winced at Vince's words then sneered. "Tough talk for a man on the wrong end of an AK-47. You've caused us way too much trouble, so I'm gonna cut right to the chase. Where is the software you stole?"

"What software?" Vince rose slowly to his feet.

"Funny, van Gordon. So you're a comedian now?" Sal swung his gun toward Jess. "Ms. Jamison doesn't look like a joker. Suppose you tell us where you put the software."

"It's in a place where you can't get it. Only those who are cleared and have a need to know can access it. You know, people like the FBI."

Sal's face turned red. His fingers tightened on his weapon. "Suppose I don't believe you."

"Not everyone can handle the truth, Curly."

How long could Jess keep this up before Sal exploded? Vince studied the big man who had a clenched jaw and a bald head that grew redder by the second.

All he and Jess could do was stall and hope for an opportunity to jump two men at once. He glanced at Jess.

She nodded.

Good. At least they were in sync on their plan of attack.

Sal approached Vince but kept three paces between them. "Down on your knees, van Gordon."

Vince didn't want to leave his feet and lose the advantage of using his legs, but he had no choice. He dropped to a kneeling position.

"No need for a hood. He knows what's coming." Sal took a step forward and aimed his gun at Vince's head. "Say your prayers, it's night-night time."

Vince focused on Sal's eyes and turned his imminent death into a staring contest.

Sal broke eye contact, but his trigger hand tightened. The gun clicked once.

"Don't! Or you'll never get the software." Jess stepped between Vince and the gun barrel.

Her shoulders dropped and she looked at the ground. "The software is all on my laptop."

"Jess?" What was she doing? She had a copy on her laptop, but another on the hidden USB drive. Was she going to risk giving them a copy, hoping the authorities could get it back? If so, Vince and Jess would never be alive to see that happen.

"Where is this laptop?" Sal glared at her.

"In the cabin."

What game was Jess playing? She couldn't be surrendering to them. If these men took the system software, the detailed design, and then hired programmers from Virtuality, the technology would soon be loose in the wild, infecting American society.

"Patrick, get up," Sal pointed a thumb up, then motioned toward the back door. "Check out her laptop and tell us if she gave us what we came for. All of it. And make sure she isn't trying to be funny like the comedian who's about to get shot."

Jess shoved a palm at Patrick as he got up from the ground. "Don't touch the laptop, Patrick. You'll destroy the software ... everything, if you try to access it."

Sal poked his gun barrel at her. "You're lying." He looked at Patrick, who now stood beside him, waiting.

Patrick opened his mouth.

Jess cut him off. "It's like a boot sector virus. If you try to access the encrypted files, everything on my hard drive will be wiped out."

Sal's bald head wrinkled like a Shar Pei. "Boot sector virus?"

"You know, it loads like a root kit, so you can't circumvent it."

"Can she do that, Patrick?"

Patrick looked from Jess to Sal. "It's possible. I don't know how to do it, but if she actually did that, you'll lose everything unless she decrypts it for you."

"Well isn't that a fine howdy-do," Curly said. "But I think our dark-haired beauty is bluffing."

"Maybe we should just shoot van Gordon and then torture the girl until she gives us what we want," Louie said.

"What've you got for a brain, Louie? You kill van Gordon, or hurt her, and she'll wipe out the software just to get even."

Vince rose slowly to his feet. "Sounds like a stalemate to me."

Sal shook his head. "Not quite."

"You still got your knife, Louie?"

"Yes, boss."

"Then we'll start cutting off van Gordon's fingers until she gives us the software, unencrypted. Give me your knife."

So much for his stalemate. "You think I'm just gonna let you do that to me. You'd have to kill me first. In fact, you take one step toward me and I'll force the issue. Now, who wants to get their neck broken first?"

"Hold it, everybody!" Sal emptied his lungs with a sharp blast. "Louie, cover van Gordon. Shoot him if he even wiggles. I've got a phone call to make." Sal went inside the cabin and shut the door.

* * *

Trent had run at least four scenarios through his analytical mind in the past forty-five minutes. Each resulted in a failure, an outcome where either MMI did not get Virtuality's software or did not gain sufficient control over use of the technology.

His conclusion was the same for either case. Trent would have to bail. Leave the country. Get a new identity and live off the money he had squirreled away in various accounts. And, of course, the four million he hadn't used to buy van Gordon's share of Virtuality.

The rhythmical opening to *New York, New York* came from Trent's cell. He snatched it from his desktop, drew a breath, and answered the cell a couple of bars before Old Blue Eyes began singing.

"Del Valle, here. What's up, Sal?"

"We got a little situation here. Thought I should check with you before we start shooting people."

How had it come to this? Before pushing any panic buttons, Trent needed to listen. He might have even considered praying first but, according to the old priest who taught Trent the Catechism, the only person who might grant Trent's request was not reliable. If he existed—what was it the priest had called that person—a liar and the father of lies?

"Are you still there, Mr. Del Valle?"

"I'm here." He needed to listen to Sal's story. Maybe there was a safe way out of their mess. "Tell me about this situation."

"Those two stole Virtuality's software. The software is supposedly on Ms. Jamison's laptop, but it's encrypted and protected by a password. But, if you type it in wrong, the whole hard drive gets wiped out ... that's if she's telling the truth."

"I knew that girl was trouble from the moment I heard she was involved. What options are you considering? That is why you called, isn't it?"

"Yeah. We know there's a thing between the babe and van Gordon, each protecting the other. So we can torture van Gordon in front of her until she breaks down and unlocks the hard drive. But van Gordon says he'll fight us until we have to kill him, and ..."

Not good. "And?"

"We could torture the babe until Vince can't take it and lets us tie him up to torture him."

There were several ways this whole approach could fall apart in seconds. Revenge was a powerful motive, one some would die for. He would bet both the girl and van Gordon would sacrifice themselves.

"Well, Mr. Del Valle, do we have your permission to hurt whoever we need to as much as we need to? You told us to ask before we did anything like this. I'm askin'."

"Do whatever you need to do to get the Jamison girl to unlock the drive. Whatever it takes, Romano."

"You got it. We'll let you know how it turns out in a few minutes."

"Yes. See that you do." Trent ended the call.

He opened his contacts list and selected his private travel agent. Trent would buy a single, one-way ticket to Rio on a flight departing this afternoon. He would specify first class and book the trip under the name Hector Mendoza.

Vince van Gordon and the girl had both demonstrated intelligence and toughness, beating Romano at each previous encounter. Trent would bet money that Sal would not get what he wanted from either of those two before something went terribly wrong.

Trent had already verified that his hidden accounts were in order. He'd cancelled the check for the four million that he had scraped up to buy out Vince van Gordon. He could access that money. Now, Trent needed to brush up on his Spanish and make sure he packed a Portuguese-English dictionary. This might be an extended Rio vacation because, once he left, he could never come back as Trenton Del Valle.

* * *

Vince looked up when Sal came out of the cabin, trying to read his body language. It wasn't comforting.

"Joe," Sal pointed at Jess. "Put your gun on her foot. Shoot it if van Gordon moves."

Jess's gaze locked with Vince's. She had carried her bluff as far as she could. They had run out of options.

Vince began the gut-wrenching process of resigning himself to what was coming.

Sal pointed the knife at Louie. "Zip tie his arms around that big cedar tree. That should keep him still."

Louie, brandishing a zip tie, reached for Vince's arm.

Vince pulled it away, but not with enough violence to get him shot. He looked at Jess.

She wiped her cheek and her tear-filled eyes locked with his. She mouthed the words, "I love you, Vince." Then, Jess's body tensed as her gaze swung to the nearest gunman to her, Sal. She was going to plant a foot on Sal's face.

Vince crouched, ready to spring. He needed to reach Sal first. If so, maybe Jess could get his gun.

"Wait a minute," Patrick said. "There's a better way to get what you want."

"Oh." Sal stared at Patrick, waiting.

"I... I think we—"

A blast of crackling static sounded.

Vince whirled toward the right side of the house, the source of the noise.

"FBI! Put your weapons down and place your hands on your heads, now!"

Vince put his hands on his head and stepped back from Louie. "Move away from them, Jess."

Louie put down his gun.

Sal whirled toward Jess.

Gunshots cracked.

Vince leaped to tackle Sal.

Sal went down. His rifle fell to the ground.

Vince landed on Sal and rolled away from him.

Jess lunged for the gun.

"Stop! Now!"

Everyone in the back yard of the cabin froze.

"Listen closely. All weapons down and put your hands on your heads. Do it now!"

Joe and Louie stood side-by-side with hands on their heads.

Jess stood, put her hands on her head, and sidled up to Vince.

Patrick stood in front of the shed, eyes closed and lips moving.

Was he praying?

Sal lay on the ground, still. Blood drained from his upper torso a foot above where Vince's head had been when he tackled the man. Good thing Vince had tackled Sal at the thighs, like Vince's high school football coach taught him. If he had tried to wrestle Sal to the ground like an NFL defensive lineman, Vince would have gotten a severe headache, his last one.

In a few seconds, crashing sounds came from bushes on Vince's right and his left. Several men wearing FBI SWAT uniforms rounded the house.

"It's over." Jess blew out a sigh.

Vince sidestepped toward her. "If no one does anything stupid, it's over."

Their gazes locked. "But how?" They'd asked the question in unison.

A policeman separated Jess and Vince from the others. "Are you two okay?"

"Yeah," Vince said. "But we wouldn't have been much longer. How in heaven's name did you know about us?"

The man pointed at Patrick, who was being escorted toward them by another member of the SWAT team.

"Patrick contacted you?" Jess's eyebrows rose.

Vince looked at Jess. "I'm also curious about how the goons found us."

Patrick stood in front of them now. "Joe put a GPS tracker on your pickup while you were in the lab, Vince."

"That was my fault, Jess. I should have hidden the truck. But, Jess, did you really booby-trap the source code?"

"What do you think?" Somehow, Jess had gathered enough composure to give him her enigmatic smile.

"You bluffed them?"

"Yes." Jess circled Vince with her arms. "But I was desperate. I tried to stall, making them think they needed us to get Virtuality's code. Thanks for not giving us away, Patrick. But I do have a bone to pick with you."

Patrick's focus darted between Jess and him. "Uh, what's that?"

"You lied to Vince about Paul and me. We weren't having an affair or any kind of relationship. I worked for Paul for a few months, that's all. And you knew it."

"Sorry about that. I ... I was sort of desperate too, trying to keep you from destroying our work. I thought if I could get you two to stop cooperating ... maybe ..."

Jess gave Patrick a look Vince had only seen a few times, right before—"

She whirled and delivered a powerful kick to Patrick's rear that sent him sprawling on his face in the dirt.

"Is everything under control over there?" The leader of the SWAT team looked their way from his position beside the two cuffed thugs.

One of the SWAT members near Jess and Vince smirked. He pointed at Patrick on the ground. "Everything is just as it ought to be, sir."

"See that it stays that way."

The policeman nodded toward the team leader, then turned toward Patrick lying on the ground. "Mr. Michaels, maybe you should stay down in the dirt. After what Ms. Ninja did to you, I don't think you would survive what the big guy would do. But ..." He turned toward Jess. "There will be no more reprisals, however deserved they are. You do understand and will comply, Ms. Jamison?"

She nodded then looked down at Patrick. "Divide and conquer didn't work, did it?" She gave Vince a warm hug. "As you can see, you greedy little geek."

Patrick got up from the ground, wiping the dirt from his hands.

Vince kissed her forehead. "Don't be too hard on him, I'm guessing he called the police, even though the man's got dirt on his hands."

"Louie's not so sharp," Patrick said. "He didn't know that I prepared a text for the police and sent it along with our GPS coordinates when we pulled into the driveway."

"Why the change of heart?" Vince asked.

Jess turned toward Patrick and hooked an arm around Vince. "I'd like to know that too."

"Make it quick," the officer beside Patrick said. "We're about to go for a ride to a place where there'll be a lot more questions for Mr. Michaels to answer. And some for you two."

Patrick wiped his hands on his pants. "By the time Vince left the lab, something I tried to ignore was ... well, I couldn't ignore it any longer. Everything was out of control, the technology, the Army contract, my programming staff. And then, somehow, organized crime got involved."

He shook his head. "I think they got involved through LACO. I had to end it." Patrick paused and shook his head again. "You know, money turns a lot of heads. Billions of dollars turned mine. Now I've got a lot of things to try to make right."

"You're right about that. I've got some things to make right too." Vince looked down into Jess's eyes. "Then I'll call

McCheney and see if there's any hope of getting this project back on track."

Patrick blew out a sigh. "I'll probably not be much help. I didn't exceed the contractual budget, but technically, what I did was misuse of funds. That will probably send me to prison for a while. But I deserve it. You and Jess try to give the Army what they deserve and kill the deep-brain stimulation. After you explain things to McCheney, I think he'll agree. It was a freebie, something we just added on to the contract."

While Sal, AKA Curly, was loaded into an ambulance, Larry and Moe were taken away in the back of police cars.

Vince and Jess had a much nicer ride in a large sedan driven by an FBI agent from the Seattle Field Office.

Their driver stopped before pulling onto the street in front of the cabin. "Before you two get too comfy back there, just a couple of things. Rumor has it that a general is flying in to meet us at the field office. The other thing ... did you play football for Kentridge, van Gordon?"

"Yeah. How did you—"

"I thought I recognized you. I was just a water boy—taped ankles, took care of equipment. But I remember Ms. Jamison too. She broke a lot of hearts."

Jess sat up. "I did not. I never encouraged—"

"No. But you did turn them all down. That was enough. Looks like you did the right thing, though." Two brown eyes looked back at Vince in the rearview mirror. "That's all I had. You two can continue with ... whatever."

Vince did have a question but wasn't sure bringing up the past again was wise to do. He studied Jess's face.

She read his eyes, his face, whatever it was that Jess used to read his mind. Twin frown lines appeared between her dark eyebrows. "Vince, I thought we had settled all of that."

Jess knew. She always knew what he was thinking.

"It's settled. But I'm curious about one thing. Why did you keep—"

"Why all the insults, lop ear?"

"Not again, please."

"You deserved them, Vince. You, my best friend, the person I thought would be much more than a friend, started pulling away from me, started—"

"Started being a jerk. Would only let our relationship go so far."

She nodded. "So somewhere in those high school years, the jerk became Vincent van Gogh."

"And my ears got abused. But I deserved it, Jess. Amputated ears and all the rest. I told you that I spent most my life trying to measure up to Paul and failing. Eventually, I learned to live with that. But when I thought it was Paul you really wanted ... I couldn't live with that. And I couldn't stand to stay here and watch you share with Paul what I could never have. So I left."

Vince had more to say. He needed to say it, because it was time to clear the air, completely. "When Paul died, I thought you might settle for me, your second-choice. But you'd never be happy because you wouldn't have the man you really wanted. I couldn't stand to do that to you. Then we swam the river. We survived the falls. And something happened."

"You big fool. Something did happen. Something like ...." Jess kissed him. But this kiss wasn't like at the falls, where an experiment had ended up releasing their unspent passion from the past. This time, it contained a promise of a future for Jess and Vince, two people with no shadows over them, no serious misconceptions, a deep friendship, and a deep love.

The love brought Vince some deep brain stimulation, but this stimulation came from a person, not a machine.

And Vince would describe it as a virtually perfect love. But this love wasn't virtual ... it was real.

Chapter 29

For the past several hours, things had been going to blazes in a handbasket.

Whatever had happened near Seattle must be over by now. But Trent had heard nothing, and it had been more than two hours since Romano called.

Trent picked up his cell from his office desk. He had packed nearly everything he needed. The fake ID, with a passport, was waiting for him at a small office on Santa Monica Boulevard. He had cash in his wallet.

Now to see if he needed to run or stay.

He dialed Sal's number.

The phone rang until voice mail picked up the call.

Trent ended his call.

Obviously, something had gone wrong. If Sal's phone was in the hands of someone else, like van Gordon or the police—Trent needed to destroy his cell, get his new ID and say goodbye to old MMI.

He jumped when his cell rang. It did not play *New York, New York*. The number displayed looked like it might be a local cell number. Maybe it was the guy who had created his new ID. Trent had given the man his number to use in the event of an emergency.

He should probably answer, then play it by ear.

"Señor Del Valle, how are you today?" A gravelly voice with a Hispanic accent.

"May I ask who's calling?"

"*Si*, but I will answer as I choose."

"Look, I'm extremely busy right now."

"Of course you are. Acquiring dangerous technology is so ... labor intensive, *si*?"

The man's accent and cold, arrogant voice sent a tingling chill up the back of Trent's neck. "I'm not following you. What do you mean about dangerous technology?"

"This technology, Señor Del Valle, it is dangerous to me ... in a very personal way."

"I've got to go now, and I don't have a clue what you're talking about."

"If you go before you and I reach an understanding, you will not leave your building alive." The man paused. "Now, do I have your full attention, *amigo*?"

The nausea came on like gangbusters bringing an urge to run to the men's room. Trent tried to calm his mind and his body. "I—I—" Why had he stuttered? He was Trenton Del Valle, the man always in control ... or in the process of gaining control. Trent took a calming breath. "I'm listening. What do you want, *mi amigo*?"

"This technology, could cut into my business. It might ruin my business. So I let you have it on one condition, señor." The man's voice had hardened, now coming with the sharpness of a tempered-steel blade.

"One condition ... what's that?" Whatever it was, a bluff or not, Trent needed to hear this man's rationale, because he clearly knew far too much about Trent's plans.

"The three billion U.S. dollars you will cost me each year, you must pay me out of your proceeds. Or you must make me your partner. So either we work together and split fifty-fifty, or you may pay me a pittance, annually. You know, compensation. Take your choice, Señor Del Valle."

"That's ludicrous. Who are you to make such demands like—"

"I have a network of informants just as you do, *amigo*. In fact, some of yours are also mine. And who am I? I'm someone who can mail you the heads of your sons. Or, perhaps, mail them yours."

Trent needed to end this call and get out of town. But the threat about leaving the building—Hispanic accent, assassin nearby, heads along roadsides. "Do you work for some organization like ... the Sinaloa Cartel?"

"I work for no one. They work for me. But a Cartel? That has such terrible connotations. No, señor. I am a businessman, just like you."

He was not like Trent. He was the head of some cartel, an international criminal, a murderer. Time to split.

"I hope you are not thinking of leaving, Señor Del Valle. You will not reach your Mercedes."

The knot in Trent's gut tightened. He ran toward the men's room.

If this man made his money trafficking drugs, he didn't need Trent's technology or the uncertainty of a new business venture. He would probably prefer Trent dead and out of the way, so he could continue his current operations.

As Trent reached for the restroom door, a muffled pop sounded. It came with a blow to his back that drove him to the floor.

His world and his dreams faded to gray fuzziness.

Emily had been right to leave, because ...

Thoughts and images faded, until Trenton Del Valle merged with the enveloping darkness.

Chapter 30

Four weeks later, Washington, D.C., Rayburn Office Building

Jess, Vince, Dr. Scoggins and General McCheney sat behind a long, conference-room table with a microphone in front of each seat. Jess said, "I do," to the oath given them by the chair of the House Armed Forces Subcommittee on Readiness, Joseph Wells.

Vince looked her way and put his hand over his mic. "You look nice in a blazer and a skirt. I think it suits you much better than that mini-skirt."

Jess gave him her bug-eyed stare, but she ended it quickly when her eyes focused on the video camera, reminding her that the entire proceedings might end up on YouTube and clips of it could be shown on the evening news.

She didn't reply to Vince's questionable compliment.

Vince scanned her again and covered his mic. "You look more than nice. Too bad those long legs are hidden behind this desk."

Would he ever forget that morning at Starbucks? Jess certainly did not want to hear about it now as she rehearsed her testimony for the committee. "Go cut an ear off or something, Vince. And stop looking at me like that."

"I'm not the only one. See the congressman from Illinois? He can't take his eyes off —"

"Ms. Jamison, do you want to go on the record as recommending Mr. van Gordon cut off his ear?"

Great! She hadn't covered her mic. Her remarks to Vince would probably go viral on the Internet before the day was over.

Her face heated to what was probably hot pink. Jess looked down at her desk waiting for some measure of composure to return.

"I didn't think so," Chairman Wells said.

"General McCheney?" Wells, the committee chair, a distinguished looking white-haired congressman from Missouri, waited for the general's attention. "Please remind us what was so urgent that we had to squeeze this investigative hearing into our packed schedule."

"Thank you, Mr. Chairman, for recognizing the importance of the issue we're here to discuss. Criminal investigations are being conducted by the DOJ regarding the misuse of funds and disclosure of classified information and technology at a facility run by Virtuality Incorporated, a DOD contractor. We requested this hearing because of the disclosure of Top-Secret information and the potentially dangerous—no, the disastrous consequences related to possible commercialization of the technology involved."

"General ..." The chairman flipped a couple of pages in a document on his desk. "Without disclosing any sensitive information, please tell us what you mean by *disastrous consequences*."

McCheney sighed. "The three witnesses here with me can attest to the validity of my conclusion. But, in a nutshell, if members of organized crime and the adult entertainment industry—"

"Excuse me, general. Do you mean the porn industry?" Wells said.

"Yes, Mr. Chairman. If they seize this technology and introduce it into the general population, they would not only make billions, perhaps trillions of dollars, but it would likely end civilized society in the United States of America and could impact the entire world."

"That's quite an assertion. We're anxious to hear the supporting testimony. But first, remind me why the Readiness Subcommittee is hearing this evidence."

McCheney nodded. "Because the system being developed—and this is not classified information—would be used to train combat troops for enhanced readiness. And this work was funded directly by legislation recommended to the house by this subcommittee. Consequently, this seemed to be, not only the logical place to start, but the quickest way to inform the federal government about an issue that needs the government's oversight."

Chairman Wells leaned toward his mic. "I think that we are about to tread on sensitive information. Please cut the video and audio recording and turn off all cell phones. The remainder of this hearing, until I declare otherwise, should be considered classified or highly sensitive. It is not to be discussed or disclosed outside of this room." He looked at a technician in the back of the room. "Mr. Davison, let me know when all recording has been stopped." The chairman waited.

"Recording is stopped, Mr. Chairman."

"Now, let's continue with the testimony of our four witnesses."

General McCheney laid out the basics of the Army contract, the scope of Virtuality's work, and the general nature of the security breach.

As the general neared the conclusion of his explanation, the pounding of Jess's heart grew to a wild percussion solo in her chest. Her testimony would come next.

After Jess introduced herself and her role in developing the algorithms used by Virtuality's products, the chairman allowed the congressman from Illinois to question her.

Vince was right. The congressman had been ogling her, making her uncomfortable. Maybe she would return the favor.

"Ms. Jamison, what do the algorithms you mentioned actually accomplish?"

Evidently, this guy hadn't gotten it the first time around. Maybe the congressman needed a more direct approach. "By efficiently decompressing the nerve-impulse data, we can saturate the human body with so many impulses, in real time, that the subject will experience nearly the same sensations as the person from whom the nerve impulses were recorded. Combine that with the vision from virtual reality goggles and we can put you on a battlefield and let you respond to any combat situation that is recorded or simulated. Without rapid decompression of a large volume of nerve data, this approach wouldn't be feasible. Hence the need for the algorithms I coded."

The representative from Illinois stared down at a notepad on his desk and frowned. "Do you mean you could even give someone the experience of being shot?"

"Yes," Jess said. "But we would be treading onto ethical turf if we did that."

"How so, Ms. Jamison?"

"Can I shoot you, sir, and record the response of your nervous system?"

"Point taken."

"But there's more, congressman. Do you have a son, sir?"

"Yes. He's sixteen. But I'm the one asking the questions here."

She needed to ignore his remark and press on, or her issue might never be heard. "Which would you prefer that your sixteen-year-old son do, play the role of a Special Forces soldier on his Xbox, or virtually experience a visit to a brothel in Southeast Asia?"

The congressman didn't reply.

"If this technology is leaked into the commercial market, companies like LACO and MMI will take your son to any place he wants to—"

"You've made your point, Ms. Jamison," Chairman Wells said.

The room buzzed with conversations between committee members.

"The room will come to order, now!" Wells boomed in his voice of authority as he rapped his gavel.

"Mr. Chairman?" Jess tried to draw his attention while the murmuring subsided in the meeting room.

The chairman's bushy eyebrows pinched until they touched. "As the representative from Illinois said, the committee asks the questions and you provide the answers. Not vice versa."

"But, sir, we haven't even gotten to the worst part of this technology yet, the deep brain stimulation."

"And you weren't asked about it, were you Ms. Jamison?"

The chairman had asked her a question ... "No, sir. I wasn't asked about it, but Vince van Gordon can tell you—"

"And you are out of order, Ms. Jamison. You will cease speaking out until we ask—"

"But you did ask a question. You asked if I was asked."

Wells blew out a blast of frustration. "May I remind you that there were potential criminal activities involved and, therefore, this testimony is being taken much like in a court of law. You will follow—"

Jess threw up her hands in surrender.

Vince leaned her way. "Watch it, Jess. In a court, they consider certain body language as speech."

"Where did you hear that?"

"From my novel research."

VIRTUALITY

"Mr. van Gordon, since you seem so eager to talk ..." Wells motioned to the audience of committee members. "Do you have questions for this witness?"

Four committee members tried to talk at once.

"We will start with the representative from Arizona," the committee chair said.

A nicely preserved, middle-aged woman with dark hair adjusted the microphone in front of her. "This may answer some of the questions several of my colleagues were anxious to ask. Mr. van Gordon, you're the only person here today who has seen the Virtuality lab functioning before it was shut down. Tell us what you saw."

Vince told of his difficulty getting access to the lab. Though he was uncleared, he admitted entering the lab, because he knew things had gone dreadfully wrong.

When Vince told about seeing Walker in the lab, the congresswoman from Arizona wrote furiously for a few seconds. "Mr. van Gordon, what is your understanding of what you saw happening at the back of the lab—the man you said was lying on the floor."

"This dude, uh man—I will withhold his name unless it becomes relevant to the hearing."

"It is not relevant at this time. Go ahead," Chairman Wells said.

"He wore a nerve-activated bodysuit and virtual reality goggles attached to a headset modified for deep brain stimulation. The software he ran—call it a video game if you like—was written to play out his personal fantasies and, while doing so, it stimulated the pleasure center of his brain more effectively than any drug can do."

The congresswoman stopped writing and looked up at Vince. "Is that a medical fact, or your opinion, Mr. Van Gordon?"

"Neither. It is a medical opinion which is currently being validated in a research facility. Shall I give you the name of the facility and the chief scientist conducting the—"

"That won't be necessary at this time," she said. "Please continue."

"What I gave you is the preliminary conclusion from that research. Does that answer your question?"

"Yes, it does." The congresswoman glanced down at a notepad. "But you look like you wanted to say more on this matter. If it will help to clarify the alleged danger of the technology, please enlighten us."

"To provide a clear picture of what was transpiring in the lab, please watch this video clip. May I, Mr. Chairman?" Vince pointed to the big flat screen monitor at the front of the committee meeting room.

"I've already given you permission. Proceed, Mr. van Gordon."

Vince was the hothead, not Jess. But he seemed to be keeping his cool far better than she had.

An official handed Vince his cell, which had been held for him after entry into the meeting room. Vince linked it to the monitor via Bluetooth. In a few seconds, a black-and-white video filled the screen.

"Some of you may remember seeing this video in Psychology 101. It's been around since the '50s. This is the rat with an electrode plugged into the pleasure center of his brain. Once the rat learned that pushing the lever stimulated his brain, he pushed it again and again and again ... if no one interfered, he would push it repeatedly until he died. No cares about eating, drinking, socializing with other rats. Nothing could compete with the ultimate addiction of raw, euphoric pleasure. Can you imagine if a million, two million, perhaps fifty million Americans were so hopelessly addicted?" Vince stopped, and Jess watched as his gaze swept the room. "I see that some of you can.

And, after the point Ms. Jamison made, you can see why this technology must be banned from everything except the practice of medicine and perhaps the military. It must not, under any circumstances, be allowed into anything like video games."

Vince disconnected his phone from the monitor and handed it back to the man who had held it.

There was silence in the room for several seconds.

Jess wanted to hug Vince, but that wouldn't be appropriate during this meeting. Instead, she took his hand when he sat down.

He looked at her and shrugged.

Didn't he know? In his simple explanation and video, Vince had knocked it out of the park.

The silence was broken by a snort of derision.

Evidently, someone thought Vince's home run was a long foul ball.

Jess looked up at the committee members.

The snort had come from the congressman from Illinois. "Lab rats are not human beings. And you can't—"

"Sir, the significance of that experiment, more than fifty years ago, will not be altered by you or anyone in this room. None of us has the credentials to do that, with the possible exception of Dr. Scoggins."

"Well, unless you were the rat, and can tell us what you experienced, I don't think your silver screen classic is relevant testimony. Do you have anything that is relevant?" The congressman gave Vince a blank stare.

Jess leaned his way. "Here's your chance, Vince. This guy is asking for it. Let him have it with both barrels."

Vince's mouth opened, but nothing came out. His face looked like he was watching a horror flick.

"Vince?"

Chapter 31

Jess studied Vince's ashen face when he opened his mouth to speak, but he didn't.

He always had words, a huge vocabulary of them. Wordsmith Vince van Gordon couldn't have run out words to say.

The chairman folded his hands on his desk. "Ms. Jamison is obviously eager to speak. But this question is for you, Mr. van Gordon. Are you going to answer the gentleman from Illinois?"

"Uh, yeah."

When Vince glanced Jess's way, the look he gave her was pitiful, like a puppy, tail between its legs, about to be disciplined for disobedience.

The room remained silent for at least twenty seconds.

"We're waiting." Chairman Wells raised one bushy eyebrow.

"Uh, yeah."

"You've already told us that. Now, do you have an answer to the congressman's question or not?" The chairman waited.

Vince blew out a sigh, but he didn't speak.

"You know, you don't have to incriminate yourself, if that's what you're worried about, Mr. van Gordon."

"I'll be incriminating myself, alright.," Vince muttered as he looked over at Jess.

"The entire committee needs to hear you. Please speak up," the chairman said.

VIRTUALITY

Whatever Vince was about to say, he was certainly trying to avoid it. Heat rose on Jess's neck. Whatever it was, Vince knew she wouldn't like it. "Yes, please speak up, Vince."

"Ms. Jamison, you will wait your turn. Mr. van Gordon, cut the personal conversation and try to stay focused on the question."

Vince's shoulders slumped. "I have more than the video, sir. I knew that if I didn't experience this technology for myself, I could never effectively challenge its commercial use."

"Are you telling us that you experienced this nerve stimulation technology while you were in the lab?" This time both bushy eyebrows rose.

Vince looked at Jess, but quickly broke eye contact when her eyes bored into his. "Yes, I did."

"What?" Jess clamped a hand on his arm. "What happened to *only the truth* and *nothing in between*, Vince?"

A crack sounded when Wells slammed his gavel down on the block. "Ms. Jamison, one more outburst and you will be removed from these proceedings."

Jess nodded and chose not to reply. Vince, however, got her sharpest glare for violation of the vow they'd made as kids. But this might be important testimony. Maybe she should just listen for now and give *lop ear* an earful later.

Jess looked down at her notes.

"Now that we have some semblance of order ..." The chairman gave Jess another disapproving frown. "Please tell us what you saw, Mr. van Gordon."

"Uh, yeah. What I saw."

"You've already told us that. Three times."

Vince cleared his throat. "Chairman Wells, I entered the lab nearly two days prior to—" Vince stopped when Jess's head snapped up.

Something had happened in that lab that Vince believed was shameful. Nothing else could account for his behavior. She needed to listen. But if this went where she thought it was going, Vince might need a kick in the rear like she'd given Patrick.

"Please continue," the chairman said.

"I went alone to Virtuality's office to confront Patrick Michaels about his negligence in submitting Ms. Jamison's and my security clearance applications. When I left, a worker entered the lab. I slipped into the lab behind him. No one saw me."

Jess bit her tongue but clamped a hand on Vince's wrist.

Vince looked at the chairman, obviously trying to ignore her. "I had strong suspicions that certain products under development by Mr. Michaels were not part of Virtuality's deliverables for the Army contract and that taxpayers were paying for products that would be used commercially. The only way to confirm that was for me to experience one of those products."

Jess stood glaring down at him. "So it wasn't the congressman's sixteen-year-old son who visited the Asian brothel. Vince, I ought to—"

The chairman rapped his gavel. "Sit down, Ms. Jamison!"

Jess huffed a sigh. It didn't calm her. Thinking about what Vince might have seen and experienced—she couldn't let her mind go there. Jess took her seat.

"I'm going to be generous and call a fifteen-minute recess in this hearing ..." He gave Jess a laser look from beneath his bushy eyebrows, "... instead of having you escorted out, Ms. Jamison. Please resolve your personal issues. We will continue in fifteen minutes ... with or without you."

Jess curled a hand around Vince's neck and pulled his face in front of hers. "Why am I just hearing about this now, lop ear?"

"Jess, you promised you wouldn't—"

"Whimpering will get you nowhere. Now, tell me what you saw and what you did. Own up to it like a man, not a wimp like Patrick."

Vince described the equipment and what parts of it he had put on. Then he described what he'd seen after pushing the play button.

He described a tropical setting that sounded sensuous and alluring, while Jess rehearsed her kick to Patrick's posterior.

But one thing was obvious. The details Vince had provided so far could only be produced by virtual reality augmented by remote nerve stimulation. Regardless of what he had seen, Vince had gotten the goods on Patrick.

"Jess, there was a woman walking through that pool of water. And when that babe in the swimming suit put her arms around me, I ripped off my goggles—"

"Babe? Don't you mean strange woman?"

"No, Jess. She was a babe ... in a bikini."

Why was she so angry? Jealousy? Yes! And Vince would pay for his transgression. "If she was a babe, what am I, Vince van Gordon?"

Vince put his hands on her shoulders, looked into her eyes, and coaxed her closer to him. "If that had been *you* walking through the water, hands reaching out to me, Jess, I ... I couldn't have taken those goggles off."

All of Jess's anger melted.

Vince, the wordsmith, had defused her with a single sentence.

She studied his face, peered into his eyes and, for the first time, realized that Jess had all three things she wanted from Vince. Or she soon would have—friend, wife, and lover.

It was time to let Vince tell his story to the committee without her boiling over and getting thrown out of the hearing.

But Vince had transgressed, so one question remained. Jess stared at the side of his head beside her. What would it be like to be married to a man with no ears?

As quickly as it had come, Jess evicted that thought from her mind. She had no more use for van Gogh. He was van gone.

After the break, Jess sat beside Vince while he completed his somewhat sensual description of the virtual reality session. "The entire time I experienced this encounter and, even though in real life it would have been wrong, it didn't feel wrong."

Mr. Fighting Illini stood, with an adversarial look. "What do you mean it didn't feel wrong? Are you telling us that—"

"What I'm telling you, sir, is that my brain was being bombarded with ultrasonic pulses stimulating the pleasure center. It's called remote brain stimulation. Everything felt good and right even though, intellectually, I knew it wasn't. But the intellectual part just didn't matter. I was on an endorphin-induced high ... euphoria. And that's only part of what the ultrasonic pulses can do.

"The greatest danger to us is that remote brain stimulation can produce the same high as street drugs without most of the adverse health impacts. No needles. No eroded, bleeding nasal passages. No track marks on a person's body. No tweaker face or rotting teeth. But, when combined with virtual reality, remote brain stimulation creates an addictiveness unmatched by anything we know."

Vince paused. "Knowing what I have told you—an eyewitness account—how can you ever let this technology be commercialized in our society? Combine it with virtual reality and remote nerve stimulation, and you can give a person their own fantasy world that's as real as, and for many people preferable to, reality. Turn this loose on American society and people will drop out in droves. The work force will be decimated. Then, when everyone's hooked, and you no longer have the software developers and engineers to produce the technology, you'll see violence, because people can't have access to what they're addicted to."

Vince stopped and scanned each face in the room. "You, ladies and gentlemen, are the gatekeepers, the sentries on the wall of America's fortress. You are those elected to ensure domestic tranquility and promote the general welfare. So, as you swore to do when you took office ... *do your duty.*"

It grew quiet in the meeting room. Not a word. So quiet that when someone coughed it sounded like an explosion. Even the snarky congressman from Illinois sat, silently. No more ogling.

Once again, Jess wanted to hug Vince. That wouldn't be appropriate, but she did it anyway. It was a quick hug, then she slid back into her chair.

Again, he looked at her and shrugged.

Vince had hit back-to-back home runs. Didn't he realize that?

Jess smiled. Not just any smile. With her lips stretched this tight, it had to be ear-to-ear. And it came because the woven fabric of her life had flipped over in Jess's mind, revealing the front side of the tapestry, an incredible design that only a good God could weave.

Somehow, the design had included their seven years of separation, Paul's death, and more danger in the last few weeks than Jess had ever experienced in her life. Her agony of defeat had become the thrill of victory, not only for Jess, but for American society. And then life-changing love had been woven into the design.

As C. S. Lewis wrote, God wasn't always safe, but He was always good.

Vince looked at her again, a puzzled frown wrinkling his forehead.

He hadn't gotten it yet. Maybe he never would. But Paul had been right all along. He had known why Vince should be the person to take the helm at Virtuality. And Jess had just witnessed part of that reason in action.

A monumental battle would come, as Paul had anticipated, a war to determine if Virtuality's technology should be given license or kept secret, tucked away in the corners of America's technological and medical infrastructure, where it could do no harm. During that battle, the government needed to fulfill its role of protecting the people as it had been commissioned and empowered by the U.S. Constitution.

When people greedy for gain fought those seeking to protect innocent Americans, the battleground would be the halls of government, including congressional hearing rooms like the one Jess and Vince sat in. And the winner of the battle wouldn't be a geeky genius like Paul, or an INTJ woman like Jessica Jamison. The winner would be a strong, good person with passion and words, an orator, a man like Paul's little brother, Vince van Gordon.

The hearing room remained quiet except for a few pens rasping on paper.

Jess leaned her head on Vince's shoulder. "You can keep your ears, Vince."

Her words echoed through the quiet room.

In leaning on Vince's shoulder, Jess had leaned too close to his mic.

"That's very generous of you, Ms. Jamison," Chairman Wells said. "But it's the second time you mentioned—I see ... Vincent van Gordon, Vincent van Gogh."

"Yeah, you see." Vince grunted out the words.

"There will be no ear amputations in any hearing over which I preside." The committee chair paused. "But, should this committee decide to draft legislation to present to Congress, who among our four witnesses will be available to help with that effort and testify, if needed, when we present it to the full Armed Forces Committee?"

"I will," Jess said.

"Of course you will, Ms. Jamison. Thank goodness, I won't have to preside over that meeting."

Vince, Dr. Scoggins and General McCheney all gave their assent.

"Duly noted," the chairman said. "Thank you all for bringing this matter to the attention of this subcommittee ... and for making this a rather memorable meeting." One corner of his mouth turned up when he looked at Jess. "This hearing is adjourned."

The gavel sounded.

It was over. Jess leaned back in her chair and forced out a sigh that sent her lips vibrating.

Vince tapped her shoulder. "Dat's cool. Could ya show me how ya do dat?"

"At Starbucks, you heard?"

"Yeah. It was cute. So were you, Jess. You know, you should wear that mini-skirt more often."

"It was a pair of skorts." Her voice rose in a crescendo. But Vince had taunted her, and Jess was not in a mood to hold anything back. "And I don't want to hear any more about it, Vince."

Epilogue

The hearing was over. They had accomplished their mission. The tension should all be gone, but it wasn't. Not yet. All because of lop ear.

Wasn't he supposed to be van gone?

Yes. But ingrained habits don't die easily.

Jess looked up as a tall figure towered over her and Vince.

"Do you two always fight like this? I can recommend a good counselor." The chairman of the committee gave her his crooked smile. "Or a justice of the peace. Might even be able to convince the Chief Justice to marry you two. Just a thought." He walked, away then stopped. "In about five months, we'll probably be discussing this with the Armed Forces Committee. Maybe I'll get to see how this all turns out." The chairman patted Vince's shoulder and walked away.

"By the way, how is this going to turn out, Vince?"

"If you don't know ..." Vince stood and gave her his arm.

Jess stood and looked at the arm belonging to the most exasperating, manipulative—her gaze followed the arm up to his face—handsome, lovable wordsmith on the planet. She took Vince's arm and they walked out the door of the meeting room.

"van Gordon, Ms. Jamison, do you have a minute before you start looking for that justice of the peace?"

Great! General McCheney had heard the chairman's remarks.

Vince pulled Jess to a stop. "Sure."

She looked up at Vince. "There's still a question that needs to be answered before I hear any more talk about justices of the peace."

"To hear Chairman Wells talk, you'd think you two needed a justice of war." The general grinned.

Jess didn't.

The general's gaze switched back and forth between Jess and Vince. "How's the plan coming to restart work on the project at Virtuality?"

Vince looked down at her.

If the CEO wasn't going to answer the general ... "The lab has been configured with all the software except the games, which I removed. The lab is ready to run the system. I kept two of our programmers, men I know we can trust. They will provide continuity going forward. But we need to hire six more. We have thirty promising resumes, so that should not be a problem."

Vince's eyes appeared to focus on the star-studded epaulettes on the general's shoulders, and then he draped an arm over Jess's shoulders. "The work should be moving ahead in about five weeks. With no more distractions or illegal moonlighting, the original schedule will slide only a couple of months. And Patrick Michaels is cooperating. It looks like there will be a trial at some point, but we've already gotten everything we need from him."

"What's happening with the software engineers you let go?"

"Two of them are completing rehab," Vince said. "The others ... that really depends on whether you pursue charges against them."

"Regardless, they won't be working for Virtuality," Jess said.

General McCheney patted Vince's back. "Keep up the good work. Our country could use some more like you two."

He nodded to Jess. "And good luck in, uh, matters of the heart."

"Speaking of ..." Jess looked up into Vince's dark brown eyes.

"Got a second?" Dr. Scoggins approached them, brief case in hand.

Her conversation with Vince would have to wait ... again.

"You two did great in there. I am so proud of you." The professor shook Vince's and Jess's hands. "Have you decided what comes next for Virtuality, after the Army contract?"

Vince looked at Jess.

She nodded for him to take the professor's question.

"Yeah. We know the military applications will dry up after a while." Vince said.

"There should be some medical applications for the technology, but we haven't talked to anyone about those, yet," Jess said. "Instead of just sending impulses into depressed people's brains, we could entertain them with fun, healthy games while treating their depression. But we would need to bring a psychologist or two onboard during research and development."

Jess looked up at Vince. "Are you going to ask him or not?"

"Dr. Scoggins, would you like to be involved in that development, if the door should open for us?"

"I'd be honored to help any way I can. And I can give you a list of contacts for exploring medical applications. Why don't we talk again in a few weeks, after things settle down and ..." His gaze darted back and forth between her and Vince.

"Yeah. As soon as things settle down," Vince said.

Scoggins strode away, leaving her and Vince alone in the hallway.

Maybe some things were about to settle down, finally.

"It looks like this will make it to the floor of Congress for a vote. You made that happen, Vince." Jess studied Vince's eyes and decided to pop the question, her question. "So what now? You know, I'm not going to let you run away like you did seven years ago."

Vince didn't reply, but he looked like he was sorting through words. Maybe weighing them?

"Tell me this ..." Jess paused. "How did two people who knew each other so well get something so important so wrong?"

"I think you've used up your *so* quota for the day." Vince turned to face her. "But, Jess, the lies we believe about ourselves usually come from our deepest wounds. And we hide those lies and hurts in the deepest part of our hearts. They're buried so deep that we don't even see them for what they are. But I wish we had discovered our lies eight or nine years ago."

He was good, really good. "Did you come up with that just now, or did you read it somewhere?"

"I'm a writer. We're supposed to say things like that. We're wordsmiths." Vince's mouth had uttered profound words, but his eyes were making a profound statement as they scanned her somewhat figure-flattering business suit she'd chosen for today, a navy-blue blazer and matching skirt.

"Don't look at me like that, Vince. That look requires permission."

"Don't look at you like that or you'll what? Do that whirling kick thing and break my nose?"

"I'll—"

"Don't say it, Jess. I'm asking permission."

"No. You're scanning me like one of those old flatbed scanners ... inch by inch."

"Okay. Do I have permission to look at Jesse James however I choose?"

"As long as you're not Robert Ford."

"I'm not, so I guess that means you'll marry me."

"You call yourself a wordsmith? If you meant that as a proposal, Vince van Gordon, I'm going to cut off your ear. No, I'll cut them both off."

"If you'll marry me, Jess, I'll let you cut them off."

Jess gave him her impish grin. "I might as well cut them off now. Men never listen to their wives, anyway."

"That's the most gruesome acceptance of a marriage proposal in the history of the human race. Can we call this discussion closed?"

Jess stuck her thumbs in the waistband of her skirt. "Almost. When are we gettin' hitched, podner?"

"ASAP."

"ASAP? How romantic."

"About as romantic as me marrying Jesse James."

"And how do we seal this deal?"

"Let's rob a bank."

She gave him her best imitation of an icy stare.

"Or maybe a train."

"I had something more like this in mind." Jess pulled Vince into a close embrace and kissed him.

When Vince kissed her back, it was the kiss she had anticipated the night he took her home from the National Honor Society dinner. It was a kiss filled with passion and love, one that told Jessica Jamison that Vince had found what he wanted in her, one that healed deep wounds and buried the lies that inflicted them.

Uh, it had been the kiss Jess dreamed about, until Vince broke it off.

He slapped his side as a drumroll sounded. The beginning of the Washington State fight song? It was not music to the ears of a Washington Husky like Jessica Jamison.

Vince stuck a hand in his pocket.

"You're not going to answer it, are you?"

"I'll just see who it is."

"Vince?"

He looked down at his cell. "It's Jamie, my agent."

"I can see where I stand. Pastor Harding warned me about relationships with writers."

"When did you talk with him about me?"

She didn't reply.

Vince hit a button on the side of his phone, then picked up the call.

A woman's voice came through the speakerphone, loud and clear.

Obviously, Vince had turned it on for Jess's benefit. This ought to be interesting.

"You're a hard man to track down, Vince van Gordon. Rumor has it you've been living an epic adventure in the great Northwest, and then you went back East to tell your story."

"Jamie, your timing stinks."

"You always say that. But did you finish that happily ever after ending?"

"I haven't written a thing since I left Denver."

"No, Vince. The real-life happily ever after. You did see her, didn't you?"

"Look, Jamie—"

"How can I look. This isn't a video conference."

Vince pushed his cell at Jess and mouthed, "She's all yours, Jess."

Jess pushed out her palm and stepped back.

He ignored her retreat and shoved the phone into her hands.

Jamie continued. "Please tell me you didn't blow it, or this story of yours is going down the tube faster than a greased—"

"This is Jess Jamison. He didn't blow anything, Ms. West. I haven't had much experience with happy endings either. But that's about to change. If ... just a second ... Vince, can you write and manage Virtuality too?"

"Sure. I can handle two stories at a time, even if one is reality."

"The bigger question ... can you handle two stories and me?"

Vince's eyebrows rose. "I can handle them *because* of you, Jess. So, yeah. I plan to keep writing."

"I don't know if you heard all that, or not, Ms. West. But Vince and I are getting married."

"Praise the Lord!" Jamie's exclamation, and the laugh that followed, blared from Vince's cell. "And tell that big teddy bear to send me the story when it's finished. Hang on a minute. I've got an announcement to make." Jamie paused. "Hey, HarperCollins!" Her voice had doubled in volume. It echoed down the hallway of the Rayburn House Office Building. "Vince van Gordon's found his happy ending! And you're about to see something that you've never even seen before! So y'all get ready!"

The End

If you enjoyed *Virtuality*, please consider leaving a rating and a brief review on Amazon. Reviews are difficult to get and greatly appreciated by authors and readers. You can find *Virtuality* on H. L. Wegley's Amazon Author Page.

Author's Notes

The inspiration for writing Virtuality came from reading two depressing articles in IT trade journals. One article told of the epidemic of video-game dropouts among young men in America. I wondered what could be so addictive about video games—something I have no personal interest in—that men would drop out of the work force, preferring their game world to the real world.

As social media use proliferates, real human needs for intimacy and meaning are met on such a superficial level that video games and virtual worlds came along at a perfect time, a perfect storm sweeping many people into addictions they would never have if we lived in a healthy society with healthy families.

In a virtual world, people can see that what they do matters. They take an action and see the consequences, immediately. In the real world, they see this less and less. If they work for a large corporation, they often feel that they are only a number, their employee number in a database. What they do doesn't matter, unless they do nothing, which could get them fired.

The second article that influenced me caught me by surprise. In a mainstream trade journal, the use of virtual reality for pornography was treated as normal, something with no stigma attached. This acceptance of the unacceptable arises from the downward moral spiral in our culture. But the downward spiral, itself, speaks to the depravity of the human heart, something that is only explained well by a biblical worldview.

After some research, I learned that the adult entertainment industry—a $100 billion a year industry, accounting for nearly 40% of all Internet traffic—has driven technology for nearly three decades by selectively backing technological advances that would make the industry more money. And future directions, using emerging technology, could increase the addictive power of augmented virtual reality to the level of street drugs, while eliminating some of the physiological damage of those drugs.

Ethicists are already on high alert, and some are calling for a pre-emptive ban on pornographic use of some technologies.

But, as problematic use of technology worsens, and new advances exacerbate the problems, we can't count on government to solve them. The first place we must look is at ourselves, our own hearts and minds. Therefore, rather than worrying about the results of recent technological development, we should worry more about the morality and ethics of the people who control and use the technology.

As I thought about the importance of the morality of those controlling new technology, my plot for *Virtuality* was born.

This story also deals with the question, who is man? I hold to the biblical definition. We are *imago dei*, created in the image of God with a spirit, our real self, that's immaterial and exists even after the body dies.

While I may write about dark subjects, I do not write dark stories. So creating a moral and ethical hero and heroine, who were in a position to risk their lives to control dangerous technology, became my goal for the story.
With that goal in mind, I created Jess and Vince. I hope my readers love them and love the story they entered while still behaving much like the children they were when their deep childhood friendship was torn apart by the lies they believed.

There is a romance in *Virtuality*. The reader won't have to look very hard to find it. It's present even in the thriller-level action scenes. And like all H. L. Wegley novels, the story gets gritty, but it's flinch-free, never graphic, gross, or gratuitous. And heaviness is always lightened with humor.

H. L. Wegley

Don't miss H. L. Wegley's award-winning, political-thriller series, with romance, *Against All Enemies*:

Book 1: Voice in the Wilderness

Book 2: Voice of Freedom

Book 3: Chasing Freedom (The Prequel)

Read all three books in the *Witness Protection Series*—action and romance with thriller-level stakes—clean reads that are never graphic, gratuitous, or gross.

No True Justice

Can witness protection be used as a political weapon? Someone in the DOJ thinks so. And if the political weapon fails, there are other choices.
One way or another, Gemma Saint is
a saint someone thinks should be a martyr.

Witness Protection Series

Book 1: No Safe Place

Book 2: No True Justice

Book 3: No Turning Back

Made in the USA
San Bernardino, CA
31 October 2018